ABOUT THE AUTHOR

AlTonya Washington is a South Carolina native and graduate of Winston Salem State University in North Carolina. She released her first contemporary romance with BET Books in 2003. "*Remember Love*" was nominated as Best First Multicultural Romance by *Romantic Times Magazine*. In 2004 she was named Best New Romance Author by the readers of *Shades of Romance Magazine*. Her 2nd novel "*Guarded Love*" was labeled a "TOP PICK' by Romantic Times Magazine. Her third novel "*Finding Love Again*" won the *Romantic Times Magazine* Reviewer's Choice Award for Best Multicultural Romance of 2004.

2005 marked the release of her first Historical Romance "*Wild Ravens*" released by Genesis Press. In 2006, her fourth novel "*Love Scheme*" was nominated for the annual Romance Slam Jam 'EMMA AWARD' as Favorite Steamy Romance. She released her sixth novel in January 2006 "*A Lover's Dream*" for the Harlequin/Kimani Press label. The sequel, "*A Lover's Pretense*" was released in August 2006. Also in August, she released her eighth novel "*In The Midst of Passion*" with Dafina Books. In March 2007 she released the third title in the Ramsey series "*A Lover's Mask*" which was nominated for the Romance Slam Jam 'EMMA AWARD'. In November 2007, AlTonya released her tenth novel "*Pride and Consequence*" with Harlequin/Kimani. The title was rated a TOP PICK by *Romantic Times Magazine*.

AlTonya currently resides in North Carolina where she and her long time love Derric raise their son. AlTonya works for an academic library as a Senior Library Assistant. In

June 2008 she began teaching the third semester of her course "Writing the Romance Novel" for Central Piedmont Community College in Charlotte, NC. She released the fourth installment in the Ramsey series "*A Lover's Regret*" in Winter 2008 and her second Historical novel "*Passion's Furies*" in August 2008. Also in August, she released "*Rival's Desire*" with Harlequin/Kimani. This marked AlTonya's 13th novel. In February 2009, she released the sixth title in her popular Ramsey series; "*A Lover's Beauty*" followed by "*Hudson's Crossing*" with the Harlequin/Kimani line. AlTonya will round out the year with the release of the final Ramsey installment "*A Lover's Soul*" and her debut audio book title "*Another Love*". Under the pen name T. Onyx, AlTonya shared her premiere erotica title "*Truth In Sensuality*" via her website www.lovealtonya.com .

FIRST PROLOGUE

Seattle, WA- 2 ½ Years Ago….

Michaela Sellars Ramsey hissed a curse and made a quick notation on the pad set next to her on the sofa where she typed away diligently on her laptop. She paused to re-read the paragraph and nodded her satisfaction over the wording.

"Hey woman? We still on for dinner?"

Mick winced. "Shit."

Quaysar Ramsey bristled playfully as a smirk sparked his right dimple. "Should I take that as a 'no'?"

"Sorry," Mick looked up, a weary smile playing around her mouth as she watched her brother-in-law drop down next to her on the sofa. She'd been working all afternoon and had completely forgotten about the weekly dinner date she and her husband held with his twin.

Quay leaned close, pressing a lingering kiss to Mick's cheek before his pitch gaze narrowed toward her laptop. "Working…" he noted. "On?" He probed, the subtle lilt in his bass voice signaling that he already knew.

Mick humored him with a reply anyway. "The book," She grabbed the pad and made another notation.

The book was an apt enough response. Like everyone else in his family, Quay knew Mick's intention to pen a book chronicling the Ramsey history had caused more than a few unsettling moments. "You're gonna invoke my brother's wrath, you know?"

Mick grinned over the tease and shrugged. "I'm shaking."

Quay was quiet for a beat, staring blankly at the words filling the laptop's monitor. "Will you write about my curse?"

At last, Michaela set aside the pen she'd clutched for the better part of the overcast afternoon. "I think I'll save that part of the story until I can include a happier ending."

Quay shook his head while rubbing fingers through the close cut onyx waves of his hair. "I doubt a happy ending is in the cards for me and Tyke. I doubt one ever was."

Mick turned and stroked the back of her hand across his molasses dark cheek. "There's love there," she reminded him softly.

Again, Quay shook his head. "Love and hurt-tons of it," Shamefully long lashes fluttered as his anger set in. "She didn't deserve that. She was an angel Mick. God doesn't look too kindly on people who hurt his angels, you know?"

"You believe you did it for the best reasons- the best intentions." The depth, to which he punished himself, tore at Mick's heart. "I believe God will reward you for that. Why don't you try believing it a little more, hmm?"

Quest Ramsey arrived in time to witness the hug between his wife and brother. "That's too close," he bellowed playfully after clearing his throat very loudly. Dropping keys to the message table just inside the den doorway, he closed the distance between them and knelt before Mick.

Unmindful of his twin's woeful groans, Quest leaned across the laptop resting on Mick's thighs and drew her into a kiss. She whimpered the instant his sweet peck turned heated. Slipping into the sensual abyss he could create with nothing more than a look, she eagerly participated. The laptop shifted on her thighs as she scooted closer, thrusting her tongue more intensely against his.

"Jeez," Quay muttered, flopping back on the sofa and massaging his eyes.

With reluctance; and a slight fear that she and her husband were about to give Quaysar a show he'd not soon forget, Mick pulled out of the kiss. "I um," she brushed away the scant moisture clinging to the curve of her mouth. "I should get dressed if we're gonna make it out for dinner." Hastily, she shut down the laptop, collected her things, scooted from the sofa and speed-walked from the room.

Quest's hazy gaze didn't veer from her until she'd rounded the corner and was out of sight. He took the spot she'd just vacated and slanted his brother a sly wink.

"You guys are killin' me." Quay groaned, still massaging his eyes.

Quest leaned back on the sofa and closed his eyes as well. "You're always welcomed to bring a date along to dinner, you know?" He wasn't surprised to hear Quay snort off the offer.

"No one I'm interested in inviting along to share my time with you guys."

"No one but Ty," Quest didn't bother to open his eyes and glimpse Quay's shaken reaction. "You know you haven't been out with anyone since you saw her at our wedding?"

Quay's fist clenched on his jean clad knee. "I know this."

"Is that what the hugging scene I walked in on was about? Hell, why don't you stop torturing yourself and go after her? You've been keeping tabs on her since the wedding. Might as well make use of it."

"Mick's gonna write that book, you know?" Quay blurted, ready for a subject change.

The easiness in Quest's relaxed position on the sofa began to give way to a visible tension. "She knows how I feel about that." His deep set grays were midnight black then. His words were delivered with a clear measure of effort.

Quay of course was unaffected by the obvious chilling of his brother's mood. "She knows how you feel and *you* know how *she* feels."

"I know my wife." Quest sat up straight on the sofa.

"Do you really?" Quay challenged, pleased he'd succeeded in turning Quest's mood as black as his own had become. "Q, she's not some society princess who was brought up to be demure and submissive to her husband or some sweet young lady out to snag a well to do life-complete with a white fence and a man who brings home the bacon."

Quest left the sofa. "What are you tryin' to say?"

Quay stood as well. Gone was the childish need to piss off his twin. He saw things heading down a disastrous path if his brother didn't ease up on his aversion to Mick's novel on their family.

Quest turned with a look that prompted his brother to offer a reply.

Quay shrugged. "I'm only saying that she was raised different from us-living by her wits, making up her own rules to survive every day of a shitty childhood…Hell Q, we didn't know a damn thing about that as kids."

The muscle flexed along Quest's jaw as visions of what he'd assumed she'd lived through stoked his anger like a poker to fire. "That's not who she is anymore." His voice grated. "She doesn't have to live like that anymore." He gave a flip wave of his hand. "She made her way out of that shit long before she ever knew me."

"And you think that her *making it* really changed who she is at the core?" The laugh Quay uttered then was brief and without humor. "Q, that strength; that toughness that pushed her to play by her own rules…that's what you fell in love with, man."

Quest gnawed his jaw for a few seconds longer and then turned. "Alright. You're right and I agree, so what's your point?"

Quay's laughter that time held more humor. And they called *him* the stubborn one, he mused. "My point is that in spite of how cool she's being your luscious wife intends to write that book and heaven help you if you try to stop her."

SECOND PROLOGUE

Seattle, WA- Present

Quest Ramsey sat parked outside his cousin's seemingly drab, unassuming office building. The key was in the Escalade's ignition but had yet to be turned. He'd sat in silence outside Ramsey Bounty just shy of fifteen minutes. He'd replayed the events of the meeting and words of advice passed on from his three cousins.

None of those words helped. Hell, it was easy for Moses, Taurus and Fernando to offer such advice, Quest thought. He knew they loved his wife as much as he did. But it wasn't the same, of course. Everything inside them wouldn't shatter as they told Michaela she'd been cast aside so that her mother could run off with a monster and raise his child. Everything inside them wouldn't shut down as they watched her-watched her heart shred and her soul be reduced to nothing.

A bit over the top? Quest pondered, studying the rhythm his fingers tapped along the steering wheel. Perhaps it was over the top. Many would think so. After all, Michaela Sellars was a tough as nails beauty. It was one of the million and one things he loved about her. But this…this was different. This was a thing he'd watched her struggle with since he'd known her. All that toughness she'd used to pad her soul diminished like mist when she thought of her mother and the life she'd been forced to live when the woman abandoned her.

Now, he was supposed to give her more ugliness to add to the story. How the hell was he supposed to do that?

She'll hate you if she finds out and discovers you knew and didn't tell her.

Quest's lashes drifted close over his deep-set stare and he nodded.

He knew Mick loved him as insanely as he loved her. But would that even be enough to keep her from hating him if he kept quiet?

Besides himself and four others, no one else knew. While County was the wild card, he believed she'd agree that this would devastate Mick far too much. As for his cousins…they'd never dare cross him on this.

What of his lovely wife? Quest pondered and leaned his head back on the rest. Without a challenge to occupy her time she'd dig into her task of finding out every aspect of the story. That is, unless she had another *something else* to occupy her time. Grimacing, he started the ignition and sped from the parking lot.

CHAPTER ONE

Following the breathtaking beauty of Taurus and Nile's nuptials in Scotland, the marriage bug bit everyone in a big way. Moses and Johari were married in a quietly exquisite ceremony on their special stretch of beach in Marin County, California. A week later, Fernando and Contessa set a date in the following year for their wedding.

Contessa figured she'd done all that was required by setting the date. Therefore, she left the planning and other tiresome details to Michaela-her matron of honor.

"Idiots!" Mick hissed while slamming down the phone on her desk.

Quest was walking in just then and witnessed the outburst. "Problems?" he teased, spotting the bridal magazines covering the office. It didn't take many guesses to figure the wedding of the year was the topic of the ill-fated phone call.

"Stupid flower people," Mick grumbled and stabbed a pad with the ball-point of her pen. "How the hell do I know what flowers compliment the *theme* of the wedding?"

"Ah come on, everyone knows how to figure that out."

Mick didn't bother to spare her husband a glance. "Bite me," she suggested dryly in response to his tease. "I don't know why County chose me for this mess. Why can't she and Fernando have a quiet wedding like everybody else?" she wondered while flopping back against her desk chair.

Quest grinned and offered a flip one-shoulder shrug. "Because she's Contessa Warren?" he tried.

Mick sent him an airy salute in agreement. "And I just *had* to be her best friend. I knew there was a catch. So glad I insisted she pick out her own damn dress."

Quest wouldn't dare celebrate before his wife. Still, County's pre-marital requirements offered Mick much needed time-consuming duties in his opinion. Of course, Quest knew his wife. In spite of all the duties involved with the planning of an elaborate wedding, they wouldn't keep Mick preoccupied enough for his liking. *Especially if she'd doing the bulk of it in Seattle*, he acknowledged silently and studied his wife who now stood in the middle of the magazine cluttered office and listed all the things on her plate besides the wedding.

"…I don't even know when I'll get around to picking up all the things parents are supposed to buy for their child's first Christmas." She groaned.

Thinking of his baby girl then, Quest smiled and crossed the room to Mick. "What if I told you I think there's a way we can do all this together?" he said while drawing her over to the mocha suede sofa in the corner.

Mick watched him suspiciously as she straddled his lap. "You're gonna help me plan a wedding?" she asked, the skepticism evident in her voice. Her brows rose when Quest began to laugh.

"Not exactly," he sighed trailing a finger along the scoop neck of her candy pink Henley sweater. "I'm talking about helping you with shopping for Quinn. Maybe we could go away for it." He explained hoping she'd take the bait. Though Christmas was over two months away, shopping for their only child would offer a perfect excuse to get away for a while.

Mick was shaking her head. "Boy, she really does have you wrapped around all ten of her little fingers." She teased and fiddled with his silver belt buckle. "Don't you think that's a bit much? You know she's not even a year old-it's not like we're gonna have to fight the crowds for the latest Cabbage Patch Doll."

Quest threw back his head and laughed. "Thank God," he bellowed and appeared to shudder at the thought. "Ms. Bobbie had to do some serious hustling when Ty said she just *had* to have one." He reminisced, referring to his sister-in-law and her mother.

"Well then," Mick sighed, coming down off her own bout of laughter. "I don't think this merits an elaborate trip, do you?"

Quest shrugged focusing his hazy gray stare on his thumb where it caressed the outline of her breast. "Shopping's the best reason for going but it's not the *only* reason," he admitted with a slight wince.

"Ah ha," Mick breathed linking her arms about her husband's neck. "Out with it Mr. Ramsey."

"Nothin' much...some meetings I should take in person. I've put 'em off for a while-with everything going on..."

Mick frowned a little then. Tilting her head, she took in Quest's dark features. Beyond the beautiful chocolate-dipped exterior she could see the hint of weariness. His incredible deep-set gray stare mirrored it clearly and Mick was stunned she hadn't noticed it before.

"You know, you might have a point," she said them and snuggled deeper into his lap, "I guess we could both use some time off."

Quest's expression seemed to lighten. "So you'll come away with me?"

"On one condition."

"Name it."

"Don't leave all the shopping to me while you have fun with all your power meetings."

Quest chuckled. God, he loved her. How many women would prefer a boring conference to shopping? "Come on, I know I'd never get away with that," he said his words taking on a serious tone. "I want you with me every minute-for everything."

Mick tilted her head again. "Baby are you okay? I'll admit you're looking drained, but is that all?"

Quest tapped one hand against Mick's bottom while the other continued to cup her breast. "I miss you is all," he admitted.

Mick's concerned frown cleared and understanding eased in place. "Well I'm sure we can take care of that too while we're away," she promised softly.

Quest's sleek brows drew close and he focused then on undoing the tiny buttons along her sweater. "I'd rather take care of that now." He murmured and handled the remaining buttons with little effort.

The moment was steamy and sweet. Quest ground Mick upon the ever-stiffening ridge of his sex while inhaling the fragrance of perfume clinging to her skin. The scene stopped just short of becoming torrid when the sound of a waking Quinn through the monitor, interrupted the couple.

"Surprise, surprise…" Mick whispered against Quest's temple as he groaned.

"I'll get her." He decided before Mick could move. Squeezing her hips he kissed her jaw. "Thanks for agreeing to this," he spoke against her skin.

Mick felt her heart thud with anticipation of time alone with him and realized how much she needed an escape as well.

Quest gave her one last kiss before he set her aside and left the office.

***

Near Invernesshire, Scotland

"Are you sure you don't want to stay? We can always visit Montenegro another time." Taurus told his wife while resting his head on her chest.

Nile smiled, raking her fingers through his gorgeous hair. They were sprawled across the tangled bed trying to catch their breath following yet another delicious honeymoon romp.

"That's where it all started for us," she sighed and snuggled into him. "I think it's only right we christen it properly."

Taurus began to drop kisses along Nile's body working his way up her lovely dark frame until they were face to face. "Why does everything you say make me want to kiss you?" he asked and proceeded to ply her with another kiss.

Nile whimpered when he freed her lips. "It's the accent," she explained with a wink.

"Must be," Taurus agreed and leaned down to help himself to another taste of her.

Nile eagerly participated thrusting her tongue as languidly as she moved against him. "Nooo," she moaned when he pulled back.

Taurus wouldn't oblige. "Now that we've got our travel plans in place, why don't you tell me what's wrong? Is it your parents? The truth," He added quickly spotting the uncertainty in her dark eyes.

Nile's gaze had indeed clouded over. The unease surging through her was an emotion she'd not felt since before she told Taurus the truth about her father.

"I'd like to know," he whispered, his long brows drawing close as he grew more concerned by her silence. "What is it? Now," he insisted cupping her cheek to keep her from looking away.

"I…um…my mother wanted to leave when she found out what my father was really into." She blurted when he gave her chin a warning squeeze. "Cufi Muhammad was a master manipulator though. He-he could think up the best stories, the best…*reasons* to explain how what he was doing was…okay-not harmful."

Taurus closed his eyes regretting then that he made her speak of it. "Baby shhh…" he soothed, kissing her forehead. "You don't have to-"

"No-no you see um…his talent for reasoning was how he got all those girls to come with him." Nile went on, holding onto the sheet as she scooted up in bed. "That's how he got most of them to become part of his disgusting lifestyle. He pacified himself with the thought that those girls were there because they wanted to be-because they'd been rescued from horrible lives, taken from people who didn't understand them."

Taurus couldn't help but think of Jahzara Frazier.

Nile read his thoughts without having to ask for confirmation.

"She'd been through a lot before she was…taken. When Zara killed herself, I couldn't help but wonder."

Nile reached out to stroke his cheek. "About what?"

Taurus rested back on the pillows. "If her being rescued and coming back here was worth it or if she regretted the day we found her."

"What my father was…the things he'd done…I never believed my mother was fully on board with any of it." Nile confessed and turned over in bed to stare at the flames licking the hearth.

Taurus stifled his grimace. The last thing he wanted was his wife pitying a woman who did more than help a monster peddle and destroy young girls. Yvonne Wilson had destroyed her eight year old daughter's life with no help from Cufi Muhammad. Tugging on the sheet, he pulled Nile against him.

"Why are you doing this to yourself, hmm?" He asked, trailing his fingers along her brow.

Nile bit her lip and debated only a second. "I know you won't approve…"

"What?" He prompted when she quieted.

"I want to help her. I want to help my mother-provide counsel, something…it may sound strange to you but I owe her." Nile kept her eyes on the embroidery lining the edge of the top sheet. "She's saved my life three times already-at six when she came to be my new mother, at eighteen when she sent me to California and then just weeks ago when my father tried to kill me."

Taurus nodded. How could he fault her for that? If anything, he loved her even more for wanting to offer her support. "We'll get her the best." He promised and pulled his wife into a hug.

***

The phone rang just as Contessa was heading into the shower to join her fiancé. Recognizing the name on the faceplate, County glanced across her shoulder before answering. "Alan," she almost whispered greeting Alan Claude head of Contessa House's shipping department.

"Hey Contessa, hope this isn't a bad time to call?"

"No uh, no Alan," County glanced across her shoulder once again. "It's not a bad time at all."

"Well you wanted to be contacted when the books arrived from the printer."

"You've got them?"

"Yep. *'Royal Ramsey'* hot off the presses and ready to go."

County clenched her hand in a triumphant fist but managed to keep too much glee out of her voice when she addressed her shipping manager.

"I want you to contact Jenean Rays in the fact-checking department. She'll know where to go from there."

"Alright," Alan said while jotting down Jenean's name, "and will she call Spivey or should I-"

"Listen Alan, Spivey Freeman is not to be notified on this do you understand?"

"Well yes, but-"

"Alan if I find out Spivey was contacted-that he's got any idea those books are there-the next thing delivered to the shipping department will be your pink slip."

Alan cleared his throat in recognition of the threat. "It'll be handled just like you asked." He promised, stifling any and all interest in why the publisher was cutting her senior editor out of the loop.

"Good. Thanks Alan, I'll be in touch." County said and set the cordless back to its set. She'd delved into a few moments of deep thought when she was tugged back against a massive frame.

"Thought we were gonna shower together?" Fernando growled deep into her shoulder.

County hooked an arm about his neck. "Well if that's all, then no," she purred.

Fernando chuckled. Effortlessly, he lifted her across his shoulder and carried her into the waiting shower.

***

"Now, I want you to tell me right now if this will be a problem?" Mick was saying to the young woman who sat on the other side of the coffee table.

"It won't be any problem at all Mrs. Ramsey. I always look forward to working for you and Mr. Ramsey."

Mick smiled and focused a soft yet stern look upon Sonja Worliss the sitter who'd take care of Quincee while she and Quest were away. "You're sweet to keep your schedule open for us but we'll be gone a while longer this time," she cautioned.

"I promise it won't be a problem." Sonja insisted, smoothing her hands across the suede fabric of the loveseat she occupied. "I love sitting for Quinn. I never consider it a chore." She confessed unable to hide the dreamy tinge from her eyes as she gazed around the elaborately designed home office.

"Well we really appreciate it," Mick said while leaning over to top off Sonja's coffee. "I just want you to be aware that this won't be the same as the other times-your time with Quincee will be quite lengthier and involved than an overnight stay."

"Quincee's a dream." Sonja declared.

"Give her a night or two." Mick grumbled.

Sonja had to laugh. "I promise we'll be fine."

Mick leaned back on the sofa. "I apologize for sounding like a stressed out mom here, but this is the first time we've left Quinn for so long-she's still very young." She cautioned once more, wanting the young woman to understand the importance of the job.

Sonja nodded and came down a bit off her high. "Your daughter is secure with me Mrs. Ramsey. The same care and attention I give Quinn for one night will be the same care and attention I'd give her for one hundred."

Mick laughed then feeling a few more shreds of her angst drift away. "Well it won't be *that* long regardless of how much fun we're having." She swore and added a bit more cream to her coffee. "Besides, Quinn's grandparents will probably come by more than once a week over the next few weeks to take Quinn off your hands for a night or two. That could be true for any of the other ten people on that list." She noted while tapping a finger to the list of family members lying on the edge of the coffee table.

Sonja leaned forward to take the sheet and nodded.

Mick enjoyed a few sips of coffee and gave Sonja time to read over the page. Afterwards, the two delved into discussions on what else Sonja would need to know during her time with the baby.

Michaela was waving Sonja goodbye just as the phone rang. Checking the name plate, she laughed and greeted her publisher.

"What'sup?"

"What'sup is you sound too happy to be planning a wedding." County snapped. "I thought it was supposed to be stressful-precisely why I didn't want to do it."

"Well trust me, it *is* stressful." Mick confirmed on her way back to the office where she'd been meeting with Sonja. "But if I sound happy, it's because I'm doing more than planning a wedding. Quest is taking me away," she announced and gave her friend a quick run through of the trip.

"Damn," County uttered in an adoring fashion. "I hope Fernando will be so romantic when we're an old married couple."

"I take offense to that." Mick said in spite of her laughter. "Anyway…I'm glad he suggested it. He's seemed so drained lately. I don't know if it's business or family mess…all I know is he looks like he's got the weight of the world on his shoulders."

County sighed and silently agreed with her friend's summation. *Weight of the world* was a perfect description. "Well sweetie, maybe you could both use the time away."

"I won't argue there," Mick said, fixing the phone in the crook of her neck and then drawing up the sleeves of her black cotton sweater. "I've been edgy as hell since Houston and Daphne died."

"Well it was a very upsetting time inside that courtroom."

Mick agreed, stooping to load the mugs and silverware to the coffee tray. Silently however, Mick acknowledged that she was thinking about what happened *outside* the courtroom and the woman she'd seen speaking with…Suddenly, her expression cleared. "Johnelle and Josephine," she whispered.

"What?" County called, having misunderstood. "Mick?"

"Um County listen, I'll have to call you back alright?" Mick was saying and blew a kiss through the phone seconds before she ended the connection.

"Mick? Mick? Dammit…" County hissed when the dial tone rose in her ear. She hadn't even gotten around to why she'd called but decided news about the book could definitely wait till after Mick returned from her trip.

CHAPTER TWO

Quest and Quaysar were shaking hands with members of their construction crew at the conclusion of their meeting. The soft soothing rumble of male laughter filtered along the corridor from the first floor conference room where the meeting had been held. In spite of having the 'weight of the world' on his shoulders, Quest felt surprisingly at ease during the meeting. Quay had pretty much commanded the agenda with a patience Quest never knew his twin possessed. As a result, Quest spent majority of the meeting an observer which provided a few stolen moments of mental relaxation.

Jasmine Hughes watched her bosses say goodbye to the last of the meeting attendants before she attempted to grab a moment of their time. She waved a stack of envelopes in their direction and smiled when she caught Quest's eye.

"Got your mail. You guys wanna take it now or should I put it up in the office?" She asked.

Quay sat on the corner of Jasmine's organized desk and shuffled the envelopes she'd handed him. "Office is fine for me Jazz. I'll probably get around to opening all this sometime this week." He teased.

Jasmine only shook her head. "Quest?" She inquired of Quay's mirror image.

"I'll take it with me," he said focused on checking the missed calls on his cell. "Leave it on your desk and I'll grab it all on my way out the door."

"Sounds good," Jazz sighed and set the small box and stack of envelopes bearing Quest's name to the edge of her desk. "I'm gonna grab another cup of tea," she decided reaching for her mug and then flashing Quest an adoring smile. "You and Mick have a good, safe trip alright?" she urged.

"Thanks J," Quest said easing the phone into his trouser pocket while brushing a kiss across Jasmine's cheek.

"I'm proud of you man," Quay said slapping a hand to his brother's back once they were alone in the lobby of the gorgeous high-rise office building. "Never thought I'd see the day when you'd up and take a spontaneous minute to play with your luscious wife."

Quest grinned. "Thanks. I'm guessing there was a compliment in their somewhere."

Quay shrugged. "Of course."

"Mmm," Quest murmured, the drawn look returning to his striking dark face. "Anyway, this isn't all *play*. You sure you're gonna be alright runnin' things on your own?"

"Please Q, this is me remember?"

"Mmm hmm. Let's try this again. Are you sure you're gonna be able to handle this on your own?"

"Funny. *Very* sure. Besides, I need something to keep my mind off that funeral."

"That's right," Quest sighed, recalling that his brother and sister-in-law had just returned from Lena Robinson's funeral. The woman had lost her battle with cancer. "How was that?" He asked.

"Sad."

"How's Wake?"

"Devastated. You know how close he was to his mom. But I think the fact that she didn't suffer long with it made it easier for him to deal…"

"Did he see the guys?"

Quay thought of his adopted twin sons Dakari and Dinari. "Yeah."

"He having any regrets about letting you and Ty have them?"

"Doesn't seem to be. Told me losing Ms. Lena would've killed him had he not known his sons were being given a good life with a real family."

"He's a good guy."

"One of the best."

Quest slanted his twin a meaningful look then. "As for this trip, there's also business to be handled out in Vegas." He shared while taking a seat in Jasmine's chair.

"Ah Vegas," Quay noted folding his arms across the front of his tan shirt.

Quest massaged the bridge of his nose. "Vegas…and I'm not looking forward to even one day with Aunt George and Michaela in the same room."

Quay laughed. "I don't envy you brotha. Still," he sighed, "I think whatever's goin' on out there with Sabra deserves to be checked out."

"Anytime I hear the name Tesano it deserves to be checked out." Quest said, leaning back in the chair and crossing his legs at the ankles.

Quay's charcoal stare narrowed suddenly. "I gotta tell you I'm impressed Q. I wasn't sure you'd feel that way considering it might put you on the outs with your frat *bruh*," he drawled.

"When are you gonna get over being jealous of the guy?" Quest teased.

Quay shrugged. "When you stop being my brother."

"Uh, uh, don't put me in this. Remember it was *your* temper that kept you from pledging."

"And I thank God everyday for that."

Quest shook his head at Quay even as he thought of Isak 'Pike' Tesano. "Sabra's family," he said in response to Quay's probing stare. "*Female* family. The fact that Smoak Tesano might be involved makes it worth checking out."

Quay turned on Jasmine's desk and faced Quest more freely. "You think any of what Nile told Taurus might be connected?"

"I hope not," Quest groaned and began to massage his eyes again. "I'm praying we're due for some positive press right about now."

"You're forgetting we *had* positive press for quite a while before all our uncles' dirty secrets hit the fan." Quay smirked. "Maybe we're in line for more scandal."

"Hell man, in line for how much?" Quest inquired with a laugh. Silently however, he accepted the fact that all the ugly new pieces that had drifted in as of late could very well be connected. If they were, what would that do to his family, to his female cousins who had all loved and lost men in the Tesano family?

Quay took note of the emotion drifting across his brother's face and leaned over to nudge his arm. "Didn't mean to bring you down," He apologized softly.

Quest propped his chin to his fist. "That's not it. I'm just ready to get the hell out of town."

"You sure you're up to handling that feisty wife of yours?" Quay began to tease though a ripple of concern lay just below the surface of his words. "I never seen you looking quite this run down Q," he noted when Quest glanced up at him.

"You and your imagination," Quest offered a half-hearted tease.

"I'm serious Q. Is everything alright-really?"

Quest shook his head finally, knowing it was pointless to hide it any longer. Especially from Quay. "Cufi Muhammad's wife- Yvonne Wilson. Her name is really Evette Sellars and she's my wife's mother."

For the first time in his life, Quaysar Ramsey was truly speechless.

***

Mick sat drumming her fingers to the desk while the dial tones buzzed in her ear. She'd tried to reach Josephine first and had been told that the woman spent little time at home unless Crane Cannon was with her.

Good for her, Michaela thought knowing the woman deserved happiness after the life she'd lived with Marcus Ramsey. Still, it didn't stop Mick from feeling agitated over not being able to speak with her. Next, she was dialing Johnelle Black's line with fast and furious fingers. The lines connected after four rings and Johnelle answered sounding thrilled to hear from her friend.

"That man of yours sure knows how to take a vacation." Johnelle marveled once Mick told her about the upcoming trip. "Sure you're gonna want to come back after three weeks?" She jibed.

'I'd better be." Mick groaned. "Packing for three weeks is no joke. I don't think I can muster strength to pack for longer." She admitted, joining in when Johnelle laughed.

"Well I'm glad you took time out to call and let me know what was going on with you two."

Slowly, Mick's easiness turned a bit more serious. "Actually um, I wanted to talk about what happened the day Houston and Daphne Ramsey died."

Silence.

"At the courthouse, you remember?"

"Yes. Yes, yes Michaela-who could forget that? But…why are you thinking about that and now of all times?"

The change in Johnelle's voice was quite noticeable but Mick made nothing of it. After all, it had been quite a while back.

"Just that something about it all has been nagging at me and-"

"Well can't you put it out of your mind?"

"No. No Johnelle I can't. I keep wondering about it and until I have some answers…"

"Well did you call to ask if I think you should look into it? Because I'll tell you now that I think you should let it go."

Mick smiled and began to pull at one of her curls while pacing her home office. "I called to ask about the woman I saw you and Josephine talking to."

"A woman?"

"Mmm hmm-after the two of you argued…I came to check on you and saw you and Johnelle down the hall. There was a woman talking to you and-"

"Michaela my goodness, it was a crazy day, you know? How would I remember all those people?"

"Only one person," Mick said, growing intrigued by the sharp tone in Johnelle's voice then. "Aside from you and Josephine, there was only *one* other person. Who was she?"

"For heaven's sake, Mick…all I remember was some court clerk who stopped to ask about Marc's disappearance." Johnelle blurted the first lie she could compose. How could she explain that she and Josephine Ramsey had worked with Cufi Muhammad's wife to arrange a little…vacation for that bastard Marcus?

"A clerk?" Mick breathed, rapping her knuckles against her chin while her quick brain did the calculations. "I don't see how she could've been a clerk. Why would a court clerk ask civilians about such a matter?

"I don't know Mick, maybe it's because Josephine's his wife. Anyway, that's who she said she was."

Mick paid no heed to Johnelle's obvious unease then. Instead, she was thinking perhaps Johnelle and Josephine had unknowingly spoken with someone involved with Marc's disappearance.

"Mick? Are you there?"

Realizing she'd zoned out, Mick laughed and cleared her throat. "Yes, yeah Johnelle I-"

"Listen if there's nothing else, I really do need to get going now."

"Sure. Sure yes and I'm sorry I sprung this on you. I've been so turned around lately- I'm sorry…"

"It's fine sweetie." Johnelle soothed, her voice taking on a mothering tone. "You take advantage of this time away with your husband. Get some rest and stop thinking of such gruesome things."

"Right," Mick's tone was absent while she brushed her thumbnail across the mole situated above her mouth.

"We'll talk when you get back, alright? Goodbye honey."

The phone buzzing in Mick's ear barely registered. Johnelle's supposed *court clerk* could've easily been an accomplice in Marc's disappearance, she thought. Unfortunately, accepting that as fact only made her more unsettled for the woman speaking to Johnelle and Josephine bore a striking resemblance to her mother.

***

Far Rockaway, NY

Brogue Tesano smiled, his handsome face was a picture of pure delight as he savored a long drag from the cigar he held. In spite of the delicious flavor of his specially blended vice, agitation rumbled in the pit of Brogue's stomach while he sat in the office of his right hand man, Frank Deeks. Brogue disliked having to track down his own employees especially an employee who was to be by his side at a moment's notice.

Taking another drag, Brogue expelled the smoke slowly and studied the elaborate swirling pattern it cast upon leaving his mouth. Again, his potent blue stare studied the closed office door. There had better be an excellent explanation for his being kept waiting.

Unfortunately, Frank Deeks hadn't returned from the job he'd been sent to handle in Seattle. Having to learn of Cufi Muhammad's death via news link, put a bad taste in Brogue's mouth. Still, the news reported nothing of Cufi's dearly beloved. Heaven help Frank if Yvonne Wilson was in police custody, Brogue raged silently and allowed ashes from the cigar to sprinkle across the papers littering the desk.

The cherry wood office door opened then and Frank Deeks entered looking rushed and weary.

"Forgive me B; I've been putting out one fire after another since I got back here." He huffed.

"They must be pretty destructive fires for me not to have already received a report on the Seattle trip." Brogue noted in that quiet cool way of his that unnerved far more than it settled. "Don't bother mentioning Cufi," he said just as Frank opened his mouth. "I know he's out of the picture." He moved out of the chair to perch on the edge of the desk. "I don't appreciate having to run down my own people Frank. Makes a man nervous, you know?"

Frank nodded and clenched a fist to keep from rubbing a clammy hand across the front of his wrinkled beige shirt. He knew from firsthand knowledge that when Brogue Tesano got 'nervous' people got dead.

"Everything happened so fast B," Frank shuffled into the office as he spoke carefully. "After the fiasco at the hotel, I continued my tail on Nile Becquois-hoping to run up on another time when I could catch her alone. The Ramseys had her covered and with a shit load of protection." Frank smoothed a hand across the stubble darkening his pale face. "I think they were more interested in snaggin' Muhammad than me and then Yvonne showed up, pulled that gun…"

"Tell me about Yvonne," Brogue requested, unbuttoning the caramel suit coat that flattered his lean frame. "I'm guessing it's safe to say she didn't meet the same fate as her husband."

"She um, she's in police custody." Frank confirmed and went cold all over. The look that flashed in Brogue's gaze stifled further explanation.

"This is not good news for you Frank." Brogue promised, following several moments of silence. "Not good news for you…or me." He stood and used Frank's desk to douse the rest of the cigar. "If you want somethin' done right…" he murmured.

Brogue checked his trouser pockets for keys and had almost cleared the room door when he looked back at Frank. "Don't go far and don't think for a second that I won't find you if you do. Although running will make it much harder on you than it already is."

***

Quest and Quay had taken their conversation to the parking deck outside Ramsey. Quay had regained the bulk of his speaking abilities but still had trouble fully participating in the conversation. Once Quest finished the story and included how their cousin Taurus's new wife and Mick were at the center of it, Quay remained silent for at least five additional minutes to absorb it all.

Quest stood leaning against the driver's side of his Escalade, arms folded across the crisp ice blue shirt he wore. Patiently, he enjoyed the chill setting into the September afternoon and waited for his brother to ask the question he knew was on the tip of his tongue.

Quay was indeed turning to ask the very question his twin had anticipated. Unfortunately, he couldn't seem to get the words out of his mouth.

"I'm not telling her." Quest answered anyway.

Quay's sleek brows drew close. "What?" He whispered blinking at his brother's set expression. "Man that's crazy!" He raged, and closed the distance between them. "You can't keep this from her."

"Can't I?"

'Q, this is her mother."

"Correction-the bitch gave birth to her but she was never a mother to her." Quest seemed to hiss the words as he pushed out of his leaning stance against the truck. "She saved her mothering skills for Nile, remember?"

Again, Quay blinked, a healthy dose of realization surging through him. He knew his brother's temper was at that dangerous point that made his moods so unsettling.

"Alright look I…I agree with your perspective on this," Quay began trying to choose his words carefully, "but Q, Mick's wanted answers about her mother for a long time. You're crazy if you think she'll let Moses or anybody else stall her."

"Nobody's going to go against me on this." Quest stated simply and with an unending supply of confidence. His eyes narrowed and he cupped his brother's cheek. "I expect that group to include you." He warned.

"I won't step into this." Quay promised, feeling his own temper simmer at his twin's pigheadedness. "But you best remember Mick wasn't an investigative journalist for nothin'. She'll start with the minutest piece of information and she'll pound at it until it gives her more to go on." He sighed when Quest stepped back and appeared thoughtful. "Either way Q, she's gonna get to the bottom of this. Now it's up to you to decide if she'll be alone when she takes the blow this'll deal her or if she'll have her husband there to lean on."

Quest struggled not to allow it, but he couldn't ignore the valid points in Quay's argument. Hell, he'd gone over those points a million and one times in his head before accepting the decision that it was best not to tell her.

Quay studied the emotions playing across Quest's face and gave him room to think. He'd noticed Quest massaging his left arm-the frat brand that only ached when he was frustrated. Quay knew it wouldn't be long…

As expected, Quest's temper erupted seconds later. He kicked the tires and side paneling of the SUV with such explosive blows that Quay was surprised one of the tires didn't go flat beneath the pressure. He kept waiting for his brother's boot print to show in the driver's side door and noted that the step rail would definitely need replacing for it now hung on for dear life after the pounding it took from Quest's size fifteens.

Once he'd deemed it safe, Quay moved close to pat Quest's shoulder. It was then Quay realized his brother was shuddering. Unaccustomed to the sight of Quest in such a state, Quay only stood squeezing his shoulder for several moments. When the gesture appeared to be doing little good, Quay pulled his twin into a tight hug.

Tears were added to the shuddering as Quest dropped all pretenses of being strong and unwavering for his sibling. On the deserted parking deck, the two stood embracing for a long while. Quay didn't bother uttering words to soothe. Quest needed to vent the emotion that was weighing down his ability to do what needed to be done.

"This will kill her," Quest breathed into Quay's shoulder.

"Yes it will. Even more reason for you to tell her and be there for her, right?"

"I got no idea how to do that." Quest admitted even as he nodded. "I know it's as easy as opening my mouth and letting the words come out but…"

"I know, I know but I think you'll come up with the right way. You're the suave one, remember?"

Grinning at the tease, Quest pulled out of the embrace and wiped the back of his hand across his eyes.

"Use this time, man," Quay squeezed his brother's shoulder again. "Tell her slowly, but tell her."

"What if she hates me for it?"

"You think she will?"

"She's come to grips with it Quay," Quest massaged his arm and began to weigh the pros and cons once more. "She's finally accepted that Yvonne Wilson can't tell her anything that'd make a difference now." Leaning back against the abused Escalade, he sent his twin a bewildered look. "What if she hates me for opening up all that again?"

Quay wouldn't comment, knowing the situation was destroying his brother inside as surely as it would destroy Michaela once she was told. Quest was grasping at the flimsiest straws to reason himself out of doing what was right. Quay knew that until the man had exhausted all excuses he wouldn't say a thing. Quay could only hope Quest would tell Mick before it was too late. Otherwise, he feared the couple he loved would never be the same.

CHAPTER THREE

Michaela took advantage of a rare quiet moment in her 'mommy world'. She could've kissed Sonja who arrived several hours earlier than expected. With the added bonus of a sitter for the evening, Mick hoped she and Quest could indulge in an uninterrupted night of sleep before several nonstop hours of travel the next day.

Quest however was already getting a start on his rest time. He'd come home a few hours before Sonja arrived and collapsed right on the bed. Mick wouldn't allow herself to read more into his exhaustion. *He was just worn out from all the prep work from the trip and meetings he'll have to handle*, she told herself.

Not quite ready for bed yet, Mick uncorked a bottle of Riesling, grabbed a glass and carried the treat to the portion of the heated pool outside she and Quest's split level bedroom. The climate controlled area was shielded for privacy and a seductive oasis Michaela and her husband could enjoy any time of the year.

Living dangerously, Mick savored two glasses of the wine. She let the drink course through her body in a relaxing swirl that made her eyelids deliciously heavy. The sun was setting on the chilly September evening, John Legend was crooning and she was relaxing on the cushioned padding surrounding the pool. She was in heaven.

Correction: She was on her way to heaven and arrived there when she felt Quest's hands and mouth on her body.

Mick continued to lie on her stomach. "Thought you were sleeping," she sighed.

"I'm up." He covered her with his weight.

Mick giggled and nudged her bottom against him. "You're right." She confirmed suggestively before succumbing to the burp that had built in her throat. "I've been drinking." She confessed.

"One?" Quest had already spied the wine bottle and glass set a few inches away.

"Two."

He chuckled. "You mind if I take advantage of you?" His deep voice had grown muffled within her glossy curls.

Mick could scarcely find her own voice for Quest was already 'taking advantage'. "Please," she managed and shamelessly whimpered as he plied her with a double caress. He manipulated a firming nipple while his fingers disappeared beneath her navy bikini bottom. "Please do," she finished, arching against him when his middle and index fingers slipped inside her to rotate amidst the heavy moisture which had settled there. She shuddered, overcome with the desire to turn on her back.

Quest wouldn't allow it just then. He alternated between thrusting his fingers inside her and fondling the hypersensitive bud of flesh above her womanhood.

"Mmm...Quest please," She nudged his arousal more persistently and opened her mouth to beg again but no words came. He was suckling her earlobe and nibbling her into oblivion while she expected to faint any minute from the pleasure of it all.

Mick gasped her delight into the foamy cushion she lay upon. Her nails created half moon impressions as she clutched the fabric-she was desperate to feel him against her palms. When Quest finally turned her on her back, he simply trapped her wrists in one hand and raised them above her head. His free hand smoothed across her trembling frame, paying special attention to her breasts. He made quick work of the front ties securing her bikini top and kept his hazy gray stare focused on her face when he brushed the back of his hand across her breasts.

"Mmm no," she ordered when he would have released her wrists.

Quest's left dimple appeared when he grinned and leaned close. "Kinky wench," he whispered against her ear.

"You like it," she gasped when he nibbled along her jaw. The gasp merged into a moan when his thumb outlined a bare nipple.

"Jesus Michaela," He groaned and had to fill his mouth with her then.

Quest Ramsey did everything well and pleasuring his wife was no exception. For countless moments he feasted on her full bosom, the valley between and the silken undersides. His nose explored every dip and curve inhaling her scent. He paid homage to her bellybutton, tonguing it as she quivered beneath him.

Mick felt him cupping her bare bottom and realized he'd removed what remained of her bikini without her ever being aware. Seconds later, she felt his mouth on her gliding across the satin triangle above the part of her body that he'd taken complete possession of.

Maintaining control, he kept hold of her wrists taking one in each hand and keeping them at her sides. Again, he returned to the hypersensitive mound of flesh above her sex. He'd subjected it to slow affecting nibbles that forced the most erotic shrieks past her lips. Quest alternated between driving his tongue deep inside her and suckling that sensitive patch of tissue. His expert skill had her crying his name in another octave.

Quest squeezed his eyes shut and tried to ward off the need to take her then. Unfortunately, the demands of his sex overruled any intentions to carry out the interlude a bit longer. He released Mick's wrists and let her tug the cotton boxers past his taut ass.

Using her toes, she just managed to drag the garment down past his ankles when he imprisoned her thighs and sank deep inside her. Mick thought she'd melt as every part of her weakened in a manner that had nothing to do with the wine she'd consumed.

Again, Quest trapped her wrists and buried his gorgeous dark face in the dip of her shoulder. "I love you," he whispered as though he were both tortured and elated.

Michaela would've reciprocated the sentiment but he began to kiss her. His tongue mimicked the lunges of his rigid length which carved a new place inside her. Quest broke the kiss, bowing his head while adding more heat to his thrusts as if that were possible. Clenching a fist he pounded lightly against the cushion and prayed for just a few additional moments before filling her with his seed.

"Everything I do is for you," he groaned into her shoulder. "Everything…"

Michaela was lost in the exquisite pleasure he brought her. "Yes," was all she could say.

"I'd never hurt you, you know that…"

Even through the haze of lovemaking and one glass of wine too many, Mick felt her concern mount over the phrase. Her concern however drifted onward when he grew impossibly stiff inside her and they climaxed in unison.

Later, they lounged beneath the starry skies visible through the enclosure's glass ceiling. Quest rested between Mick's thighs with his head on her tummy.

"I didn't doze off," She boasted in a lazy, delighted tone.

Quest frowned. "Should I be flattered?" He asked, sounding hurt.

"My tolerance is building."

"For *me*?"

Mick arched her hip playfully, causing him to raise his head. "For alcohol, idiot."

Quest sent her a wink. "Congratulations."

"Speaking of dozing off," she noted, smoothing her fingers across his brow before he could lower his head, "you dropped into bed earlier like you were dead to the world."

Quest allowed her to see the unease darken his gaze. "There's a lot going on." He admitted finally.

"Well I know there's a lot of planning involved with the trip." Mick tilted her head. "Are you sure you want me tagging along? I know you've got business to handle and-"

"Hey?" Quest interrupted and gave one of her curls a tug. "I don't want you anywhere but with me, understand?"

"'Kay," she whispered and bit her bottom lip while her lashes batted madly around her stunning amber eyes.

Quest could no longer resist and moved up to capture her mouth in a lusty kiss. Mick smoothed the back of her hand across his cheek and kissed him with the same possessiveness he used. She moaned his name out of sheer disappointment when he pulled away and pressed his forehead against hers.

"Can I ask you something?"

But for the sound of her trying to catch her breath, Mick was silent. Patiently, she waited bracing her weight on her elbows as she leaned away.

"What dammit?" She snapped when she saw Quest trying to form his question and then seeming to change his mind.

"It's about the talk you had with Taurus during Houston and Aunt Daphne's will reading."

Mick rolled her eyes. "Curse that Georgia Ramsey," she hissed and sat up with fire in her eyes. "Quest I'm tellin' you now, that aunt of yours is just itching for me to tell her where she can take all that nosy bullshit. Taurus was in a bad way and I wasn't about to let him act like he wasn't affected by it." She shook her head, recalling the man's dreadful state just after his parent's death.

Quest began to laugh but paid for it when his wife rained down fisted blows across his back. "I'm sorry, I'm sorry!" he gasped, still laughing. "I swear I wasn't talking about that!" Still laughing, he raised his hands defensively to ward off more blows. Tentatively, he leaned close to press a quick kiss to her jaw. "I heard what George said to you. I would've stepped in but you handled it just fine."

Mick blinked. "Oh." She muttered and grimaced while trying to dismiss her loss of temper.

Quest had sobered a bit as well. "I was concerned too. I talked to T later before we left. He told me about what you said…about him not dwelling on Houston or what *evil* he may've passed on." He cleared his throat and studied the tune his fingers strummed along her thigh. "He said you told him that you've wondered the same…about your mother." He waited then, watching closely for her expression.

Mick swallowed with noticeable effort and averted her gaze. She said nothing.

Quest looked away as well. "Taurus said you told him you didn't need her to validate or predict the kind of mother you'd be because you knew you loved Quinn more than your life and what meant more than wondering about a woman who was pretty much dead to you…"

"Jeez, he told you a mouthful," Mick breathed, dragging a hand through her hair. She recalled the rest of the conversation with her husband's cousin in stunning clarity. "Where are you going with this?"

"Do you still feel that way? Would you really be content with never knowing why your mother…"

The buzz and afterglow of lovemaking was effectively doused. Mick pushed Quest away. "Why do you want to know? Where's all this coming from?"

"Just that you hardly talk about her anymore-your mother," He shrugged. "I wanted to ask about it for a while but I didn't want to upset you." He winked a bit then. "Your talk with T opened a door, I guess."

Michaela watched Quest closely and eventually decided she believed him. After all, how could he know she was searching for information on her mother? A voice inside her head said *Moses*, but she'd been checking and he appeared to be having as much difficulty getting the goods on Charlton Browning as she'd had.

You do realize that could be a lie? Michaela ignored the voice that time and focused on her husband. God, he was so worried for her. If that worry triggered his protective streak again, she'd never uncover a thing.

She kneeled next to him then on the cushioned area surrounding the pool. Cupping his face, she looked into his eyes and lied. "I meant everything I said to Taurus."

Nodding once, Quest lowered his gaze and pulled his wife into a hug. Partly relieved and partly unnerved, he took her response as his answer. If she had finally found peace with this who was he to shatter it? A nagging part of his soul whispered that she was lying-pacifying him so that he wouldn't worry.

But the part of him that was pleased as punch over not telling her, overruled all the nags and doubts. Standing then, he swung her against his chest.

"Let's go to bed," he spoke against her hair.

***

Chicago, Illinois~

"Jenean, Spivey says they really need you in there."

Jenean Rays grimaced as her assistant's voice came through the line. It was the third time the woman had voiced the announcement, Jenean realized. "Tell him to keep his boxers on, I just want to scan this email I got from Alan down in shipping."

"Okay…" Pauletta Orey sounded skeptical and she hesitated a few seconds. "Just so you know-Alisa Breems decided to come up from South Carolina to take the meeting in person."

Jenean's fingers paused over the mouse. "She's here?" She fiddled with the cuff of her burgundy blouse while pondering the presence of one of their top mystery authors. "Jeez, this *must* be serious."

"Yeah, she and Janet were about to come to blows before breakfast arrived." Pauletta shared referring to their senior editor Janet Harvey.

Jenean waved her hand and turned back to her monitor. "Just give me two minutes." She urged. Contessa had personally requested that she handle anything having to do with the rather covert publication of "Royal Ramsey". Following Alan's voice message that the first shipment had arrived and that he'd emailed the necessary paperwork; Jenean didn't want to waste time devoting her full attention to whatever matters might surface. This time, a senior editor and top author would have to play second string to the publisher.

"Finally," Jenean murmured, spotting Alan's email in the usual morning slew of correspondences. She scanned the attachments to confirm everything had come through properly. She'd go over them more thoroughly later that day. "Coming Pauletta…" she sang to herself while browsing the attachments, "just a quick check to make sure I've got it all and-" She sat a bit straighter in her desk chair. "Review copies?" She clicked on the link. She couldn't recall having spoken to Contessa about review copies.

Of course such copies were standard procedure. With the situation being what it was however, shipping preview copies was probably not in the plan. Jenean decided to give the list a quick read through, hoping the reviewers would be those Contessa House could depend on to work with them on timing the publication of their respective reviews.

"Oh my God…" Jenean blinked as though that would make the name Quest Ramsey disappear from the screen. "How the hell did he get on this list?"

Jenean's hands went weak over the mouse but the phone bussed again before they could commence to shaking.

"You need to get in that meeting ASAP." Pauletta's firm advisement loomed through the phone's speakers.

Flipping a few stray micro thin braids from her face, Jenean ignored her assistant and scoured her rolodex for Contessa's cell number. Clipping off Pauletta mid-sentence, she dialed the number once it was located.

"Shit," she hissed when County's voice mail kicked in after the first ring. Jenean didn't waste time with a message but printed a copy of the email and attachment. She scribbled down the fax number. County had provided the information when she informed the executive staff that she'd be conducting business from Seattle for several months.

Jenean scurried across her sunny, cluttered office to snatch the email from the printer. She circled Quest Ramsey's name and raced out the office.

Pauletta's round vanilla toned face was a picture of relief. "Thank God, Spivey's screamin' bloody murder for you to-"

"I'm on it!" Jenean pulled Pauletta from her seat and turned the woman towards the fax machine. "I need you to send this to Contessa before you do another thing." She ordered, pushing papers at Pauletta before she raced off toward the meeting.

***

"Enjoy the infant years, because when they start walkin' that's all she wrote."

Mick laughed despite the words of warning. She was engaged in an enthusiastic conversation with Everett Shepard- the topic: kids.

"But Quinn seems rather laid back Ev," Mick told her husband's co-pilot. "I think she's gonna be a lot like Quest."

Everett was already waving his hand. "Don't buy it. It's an act, it's all an act. She's already got a list of things she plans to check out the minute you put her little butt in a walker, trust me."

Michaela slapped Everett's jacket sleeve as her laughter resumed. Quest strolled up just then and linked his arms about his wife's waist.

"I frown on any negative talk regarding my perfect lady," Quest warned the duo.

Mick rolled her eyes toward Everett. "She's got him completely wrapped around her finger and he's happy about it."

Everett nodded. "I was the same clueless fool once," his light brown eyes harboring a playful far-away gleam. "Don't say I didn't warn you."

"Mmm..." Quest murmured though he was moments away from laughter himself. "Steve's looking for you," he said instead, referring to the jet's captain Steven Twols.

"Yeah, we need to run through the check-list." Everett explained leaning in to squeeze Michaela's arm. "I'll pray for you darlin'." He said and winked when her laughter lilted forth once again.

"Hmm...clueless fool, that describes you to a tee," Mick sighed when Everett walked off.

"Shush," Quest ordered, turning Mick and keeping her trapped against her Infinity SUV they'd driven to the jetport that morning.

Mick smiled anticipating a delightful kiss before Quest's mouth met hers. It didn't take long however, for the *delightful* kiss to go from nice to naughty. Quest's fingers were already venturing beneath the hem of Mick's zip front thunder blue hoody. Mick was standing on her toes to take more of his kiss and caress when she heard a throat clearing nearby.

"Sorry Mr. and Mrs. Ramsey. Sorry for interrupting. Just wanted you to know I'm about to load your bags."

"No problem Paul," Quest greeted the young baggage attendant. "How've you been?"

Paul Yaeger nodded. "Good. Good Sir."

"How's school?" Quest asked, keeping Mick close as he conversed with the young man.

Paul's pale face beamed as it usually did whenever the chance to speak with one of the Ramseys presented itself. "Good Sir. My last year. I hope Captain Twols will have a place for me when I'm done with the flight program."

"You keep us informed on your progress and we'll set up a time to talk, alright?"

Paul nodded frantically. "Yes Sir!"

Quest chuckled as the boy delved enthusiastically into his task of taking bags from the SUV. He looked down at Mick and pinched her cheek. "You ready?"

Taking a deep breath, Mick forced herself not to feel guilty for leaving Quincee. It was only for a few weeks, she reasoned. A few weeks of jet-setting, wearing something besides ratty jeans and oversized sweatshirts and dining to the sound of exquisitely erotic music instead of one of the many sleepy time tunes for the baby…Smiling brilliantly then, she tugged on the lapel of Quest's black fleece jacket.

"I'll race you to the cabin," she challenged.

They were just setting off when Quest snapped his fingers and headed back to the SUV. He collected the stack of mail he'd taken from the office the day before-mail that contained his very own copy of "Royal Ramsey" by Michaela Sellars.

CHAPTER FOUR

Once they were airborne, Mick put her worries to rest and decided to savor the time away with her husband. She hadn't realized how much she needed a getaway until Quest suggested it. Motherhood was a demanding job for those who cared about doing it right, she thought. Those who held demanding jobs deserved luxurious vacations every now and then.

With that thought in mind, Mick left Quest talking with the pilots in the cockpit. Eager to reacquaint herself with the posh surroundings, she took a stroll around the cabin with its rich wood grain paneling and large cushioned seating. Mick indulged in a few moments of enjoying the view of the full clouds beyond the windows. Afterwards, she went to freshen up in the private wash area at the rear of the cabin.

Wash area of course was a poor description of the plushy designed space with its crafted cabinets and mirrored walls. Beyond the washroom's slide doors was a rest area complete with a maple encased double bed. With the press of a button an overhead screen retracted for a breathtaking view of passing skies.

Michaela didn't take time to enjoy the view just then. She'd brought along her cell, but shut down the phone shortly before she and Quest arrived at the jetport. The only person she needed or wanted to be on call for was Quincee. Quest had his phone should Sonja need to contact them for any reason. Therefore, Mick happily decided hers was unnecessary. She was placing the device at the bottom of a lingerie stuffed case when her husband found her.

Immediately, his brows drew close in pretend suspicion. "What are you up to?" he demanded playfully.

Mick shrugged. "Would you believe I'm hiding my cell phone?"

"Ha! Not in a million!" Quest's rich laughter filled the confines of the washroom.

Again, Mick shrugged. "See for yourself." She moved away from the tanned leather overnight bag.

Quest set out to do just that. Less than a minute passed though before he became sidetracked by all the enticing garments he touched.

"Jesus," he breathed pulling out a frilly piece of nothing that he'd never seen. "I want you in this the second we get off this plane," he ordered his gray stare never leaving the garment he held.

"Well that's a thought…" Mick sighed and set her most serious expression in place. "But don't you think we'd get too many weird looks if I step off the jet wearing nothing but a Baby doll top and a pair of crotch less panties?"

Again, Quest's haunting gaze drifted back to the garments. "Crotchless? Good God," he groaned and began to venture through the bag with renewed intensity.

Mick folded her arms across her chest. She had the best time watching her husband rifle through the scandalous pieces. His devastating profile held the awe-filled look of a little boy opening the biggest present under the tree on Christmas morning. Lithely, she perched atop the wood grain counter next to her overnight bag.

"So now that you've got me here and have gone through all my underwear, why don't you tell me what else this *kidnapping* is supposed to involve?" She tugged her bottom lip between her teeth and fixed him with a look that was innocence and naughtiness combined.

Quest dropped a black satin teddy with its pink lace trim. He moved to tower over her on the counter space. "This kidnapping involves *you*- out of your clothes. Often." All teasing was removed from the moment following his words.

"I see." Mick's tone was still saucy, though her heart skipped more than one beat beneath the unwavering intensity of his stare. "So I guess if I'm very good, you'll let me go then?" She breathed, feeling a shiver race her spine when his hand encircled her neck.

"Never," He promised using his thumb to lift her chin. A second later, he'd captured her mouth in a sultry kiss. His tongue thrust lazily past her parted lips, traced the ridge of her teeth and the roof of her mouth.

Michaela whimpered. Her core tensed out of sweet pleasure. The warm ooze of sudden need surfaced then and she was returning his kiss with a sultriness of her own.

Quest uttered a vicious curse as need tornadoed through him. The experience weakened his legs in such a manner that he gripped the edge of the counter with both hands. The sheer force of his kiss kept Michaela pressed against the mirrored wall behind the counterpace.

Regaining his strength, Quest released the counter top and captured both Mick's thighs- parting them to accommodate his frame. Mick uttered something incomprehensible when his thumbs worked the middle of her jeans. The thrusts of his tongue inside her mouth gained intensity and permitted nothing but her equal participation in the kiss.

She convulsed between the pleasure of his clever fingers and desperation to be rid of her confining attire. Quest was just as agitated by her clothing and didn't mind voicing his frustration with muffled curses and grunts of discouragement.

"Damn jeans," he muttered while suckling her earlobe and fiddling with the button fly. "Why the hell did you wear these things?"

"You- you said dress comfortable." She almost sobbed while eagerly brushing rigid nipples against the slabs of his carved chest. The fact that he was still garbed in the dark fleece jacket did nothing to diminish the power beneath it. "You said dress comfortable," she repeated when he growled another agitated curse against her ear.

"Comfortable meant accessible."

"Oh." A high pitched gasp followed when his lips found a nipple only partially covered beneath her violet lace bra- she hadn't even felt him unzip her top. Mick bit her lip while looking down at him-his sleek brows drawn close in concentration as he tongued the nipple past its confines. "Sorry," she moaned when he cursed against over the button fly.

"Hush." He ordered and to ensure she obeyed, he abandoned her nipples to thrust his tongue deep inside her mouth again.

After a while, Mick's jeans and Quest's; for that matter, were a non-issue. Michaela's hoody was discarded and she wore only the lacy violet bra. The front clasp had been unhooked and the garment dangled open at her chest. Quest only had to undo the fly of his own sagging jeans and they; along with his boxers, pooled around the hunter green Lugs he sported.

"Hush up, will you?" He commanded once again. Resting his forehead in the crook of her neck, he secured her leg beneath his arm and took her with a savage beauty. "They'll think I'm killing you in here," he muttered into her skin while filling her with his slow lengthy thrusts. "Damn," he grunted overwrought by the feel of his sex growing stiffer with desire for her.

Mick wanted to laugh in the midst of pleasure, but that only heightened the shrieking quality of her cries. "Mmm…" she pressed her lips together to silence herself.

The scent of her was like a drug and Quest was practically drunk with lust for the curvy chocolate beauty in his arms. She gasped his name in the most incredible, ego-stroking fashion. When he bent his head to alternate suckling one breast and then the other, Mick had to bit her lip then in order to obey his orders that she stifle her orgasmic outbursts. Unfortunately, the trembling moans carried almost the same volume and affected Quest just as strongly.

"God Mick," he grunted and filled his hands with her derriere. The movement deepened his penetration. Mick rolled her head back and forth against the mirror while arching fiercely to capture every inch of his satisfying length…

***

"This is not fair." County grumbled and kicked a bridal magazine across Fernando's usually pristine study.

Tykira Ramsey; who was seated on a sofa that teemed with even more magazines, didn't bother to raise her head. "I don't think those are for kicking but for browsing." She appeared to be quite interested in the bridal mag she was browsing just then.

County simply rolled her eyes towards the publications covering the floor. "Damn that Mick, leavin' me here to handle this mess."

Ty looked up at last. "Cut her some slack, huh? I mean what woman wouldn't drop everything to run off with Quest Ramsey?"

"Let's see…" County pretended to be in deep concentration. "Ah! The woman married to his twin." She sighed, waving a hand towards the woman in question.

Ty acknowledge the remark with a dazzling smile. "So cut her some slack, why don't you?"

County considered that and shrugged. "Lucky wenches," she muttered and joined in when Ty laughed.

"Now don't tell me there's tension between the soon-to-be newlyweds?" Tykira settled back against the sofa as she voiced the tease.

"Oh Ramsey," County groaned while referring to her fiancé. She clicked her teeth. "Everyday he's bitching about how bad his office looks. Everyday I'm thinking of new places to tell him where he can shove his office."

"Lord County can you blame him?" Ty breathed, taking time to glance around the unkempt room. "After all, choosing a gown shouldn't be cause for this much…disarray."

"Easy for you to say," County grumbled, pulling away a magazine she'd stabbed with the heel of her navy blue boot. "*You've* been in love with Quay since you were five. Probably had your dress picked out by age ten."

Tykira took no offense. "Try seven." She clarified and again the office was filled with laughter. "Alright, enough of this," Ty slapped her hands to her jean clad thighs. "I think a change of scenery will do you good."

"Scenery?"

Ty pushed herself off the deep sofa. "Try seeing the gown with your own eyes instead of through the pages of a magazine or computer screen."

County leaned against Fernando's desk. "What have you got in mind?" She crossed her arms over the gray scoop neck sweater she sported.

"Shopping, of course," she folded her arms across the cream V-neck she wore. "And if we're lucky, maybe we'll pick up a wedding dress while we're at it."

County was already grabbing her purse. "My credit cards are ready to beg for mercy and I'm ready to get the hell out of here."

The two headed out of the office soon after. Their conversation and laughter drowned the sound of the fax machine beeping to signal the arrival of Jenean Rays' transmission. The document slid onto the tray just as a gust of air from a heating vent sent it swirling to the floor amidst the slew of magazines.

***

"Have they extradited her yet?" Brogue Tesano questioned Katie Mavins, one of his many contacts inside the county courthouse. He nodded when the woman confirmed that Yvone was still in their custody.

"It'll be tricky for you Brogue," Katie warned glancing across her shoulder to ensure no one was passing her cubicle just then. "They're about to assign counsel since she doesn't seem to be opening up to anyone-they don't want to risk losing her on some technicality because she's not represented."

"You mean she hasn't requested anyone? Not screaming for a lawyer to shield her?" Brogue inquired straightening a bit in the large leather chair he occupied behind his desk.

"No counsel's been requested." Katie whispered. "It's like she's a mute. A few of us are speculating whether she'll try for some insanity plea."

"So she's not talking."

"Not a peep. What are you thinking?" Katie asked when Brogue was silent for more than a few seconds.

"Just speculating…same as the rest of you."

Katie knew the man far too well to believe that.

"Maybe she's considering the danger in telling what she thinks she knows." He continued after a while sounding as though he were weighing the argument to himself. "Maybe she's wondering what she can *get* by telling them everything she *thinks* she knows."

Katie tapped her fingers to her cheek. "Which speculation are you leaning toward?" She asked hearing the man grumble a low sound across the line.

"Not sure yet. The fact that she won't talk- hasn't even asked for counsel yet, could be a good sign. There's no one to *advise* her that it'd be in her best interest to talk about things that could get her pretty throat slit."

Katie swallowed tugging at the neckline of her blouse. She felt the chill in the man's words as he spoke so casually about something so lurid. Clearing her throat, she cast aside her unease.

"What do you want me to do?"

"Wait, watch and keep me posted."

***

Los Angeles, California~

Taurus drew Nile back against him. Setting his arms neatly about her waist, he rested his cheek next to hers.

"Kids missed you. I could tell."

Nile cuddled back into her husband's solid frame and smiled. "I think the boys missed me. The girls…let's just say they were so busy drooling over my husband, I can't be sure."

Taurus' low chuckle rumbled. "Can't fault them for having good taste."

"Or eyes that work."

Taurus was poised to utter another tease when he noted the humor leaving her face. "What?" he turned her to face him more fully. "What?" he insisted, giving her a little nudge.

"Just the damndest thing," she sighed and focused on the subtle design of the emblem on Taurus' sweatshirt. "I think I really need to be there for my mother. I need to see her."

Understanding, Taurus only drew his wife closer.

"I know you don't approve of me having anything to do with her." Nile spoke into his shoulder. "I don't blame you."

Taurus stifled his response and let her continue.

"I was all set to cast her off too- to let her rot for what she stood by and let my father do to those girls…I wasn't even thinking about helping her and then the craziest thing happened."

Drawing back then, Taurus waited. His light eyes were narrowed in curiosity over the strangely awed look she wore.

"During the wedding…everyone I met…they were so wonderful." Nile spoke in an almost absent manner while she fidgeted with the tassels on her olive green jacket. "They all welcomed me and acted like they didn't give a damn that I was Cufi Muhammad's daughter."

"That's because they *don't* give a damn." Taurus leaned in to kiss her nose. "They love you because *I* love you."

"And I felt it too," Nile's eyes were wide with happiness. "I'd never laid eyes on some of them until the wedding and they welcomed me just like that." She snapped her fingers.

Beyond the sweetness of her words, Taurus could sense that there was something else fueling them. "Where're you goin' with his love?" His champagne gaze narrowed while he rubbed a lock of her hair between his fingers.

Nile bowed her head and braced herself. An utterly insane thought had camped out in the back of her mind since her wedding day. "I could've sworn I was looking at my mother when I met your cousin's wife Michaela."

The statement, delivered so briskly and laced with such subtle terror, brought a rush of realization to Taurus' face. Nile noticed before he could mask it and the awed look on her face glossed over with regret.

"I'm sorry," she whispered smoothing both hands across his solid chest. "I'm sorry." Her hands inched up to cup his face loosely. "I know it's crazy-just a weird reaction to someone I'd never seen before." She smiled easily then and shrugged. "I guess it's just my own consciousness urging me to…no?" She probed watching as he shook his head.

Taurus pulled her hands from his face, pressing double kisses to her palms before clutching her hands to his chest. "No love, I'm afraid this is about a little more than your conscience."

***

Nendaz, Switzerland~

Michaela was prepared to be bowled over by the beauty of Switzerland and bowled over she was. Nendaz was accessible by direct trains from France, Germany and Italy. Mick felt the place had to be where the wealthy played for who could resist (or afford) the luxuries nestled amidst the stunning snow capped mountains? The glorious peaks were visible from every angle, it seemed. Not surprising, the ski slopes boasted challenges that beckoned the world's best.

Of course, Mick planned to content herself with the indoors and leave the skiing to…well…everyone else. Spending time indoors wouldn't be a chore at all she realized once they'd reached their final destination. The car that shuttled them from the airport arrived at the chalet that would be home to her and Quest for the next week and a half.

Elaborate, exquisite, elegant…Mick just couldn't seem to lock onto a word appropriate enough to describe the dynamic scene before her eyes. The magnificent construction sat amidst a sea of white with the mountains in the distance. The view was like the backdrop of some artist's rendering. The chalet itself looked to be a two or three story construction of brick and stone. Its finely crafted windows offered opportunities to enjoy the wintry views from any indoor location.

If Michaela thought a pristine five bedroom five and a half bath chalet was a bit much for a ten day stay, she said nothing. Such *over the top* luxury had become a rare treat for the new mom and she planned to enjoy every minute. Mick took time to observe the spacious kitchen with its richly polished hardwoods and cabinets. The cozy dining area sat far in the back as if on its own enclosed balcony. Mick could imagine taking a candlelit meal there and enjoying the twinkling lights from the ski lifts in the distance.

Still, for all the beauty at her fingertips, nothing proved to be more stunning than watching her husband and the attention he commanded without saying a word. Never had she seen such bowing and scraping except in movies or books about kings and queens.

Strolling the rear staircase leading up from the kitchen, Mick recalled the driver who met them at the jetport. The man also wore the hat of bartender for he'd provided her with a deliciously sinful mug of authentic Swiss chocolate cocoa the moment she settled into the limo.

While Quest had demanded no fuss, it was clear he approved of a fuss being lavished upon his wife. Mick couldn't decide if she'd wanted to doze off in coziness or take in the brilliance of the atmosphere.

"Too much," she uttered when her steps carried her into the master bedroom. The shameless allure of the suite had her shaking her head in wonder.

She was sure the bed had to be a *double* king built into a gorgeous wood grain headboard. Soft lighting radiated from the mounted lamps and spotlights along the board. There were cabinets to house books for nighttime reading with matching dressers, armchairs and desks on either side of the room. Mick was just peeking into the lovely bath-complete with sauna and Jacuzzi when she heard Quest's voice.

"Just where I want you," he called when he strolled into the room. "Bags are on the way up but I can stall if you want a few minutes alone with me." For emphasis, he kicked the wood grain paneling surrounding the base of the bed.

Mick's laughter was full but brief. "Please tell me you don't own this place?"

Quest's teasing expression turned serious. He looked around the room while closing the distance between them. "Why? Would you like me to?" He asked once he towered over her.

"I don't think so. Seeing as how it's been almost three years and this is the first I've seen of it."

Quest was concerned and dipped his head to more closely survey her expression. "Don't you like it?"

"Are you crazy? I love it!" She whirled around towards the view.

A lazy smile in place, Quest drew Mick back against him. "If it makes you feel better, I plan for us to make use of all the rooms."

Mick couldn't help but bow her head and laugh.

Quest toyed with the zipper of her hoody. "Also, I don't own the place-not completely." He explained, propping his chin atop her curly head of hair. "The company keeps it for extended trips any of the executives might make out here."

That made Mick feel better and she snuggled a bit more deeply into her husband's embrace. "Are you the only exec out here now?"

"No there was a guy out here for about two weeks before I announced my trip."

Horrified, Mick turned to glare up at Quest. "So he has to wait til *you're* done before he can settle in and get his bearings while *we* could've just gotten a hotel room?"

Quest shrugged yet winced playfully as her point hit home. "Are you losing respect for me?"

The natural arch of Mick's brows rose in playful skepticism. "I'll tell you in the morning." She purred and tugged on the collar of his jacket.

Quest was about to accept her kiss when a bustle sounded in the room that announced the arrival of the baggage. Chuckling softly, the couple held onto one another and enjoyed the view while their things were put in place.

CHAPTER FIVE

After a restful night's sleep, Michaela woke the next morning feeling refreshed and content. Desiring her husband's touch, she stretched across the bed. Cool sheets were her only reward.

"Damn double king," she grumbled and stretched a bit further. Still, no Quest.

Opening an eye, Mick scanned his side of the bed and found that he was no where in sight. Frowning, she braced her weight on an elbow and pushed a slew of curls from her face.

Quest entered the room then, drawing to a halt when he noticed her awake. Grimacing, he dragged his gaze back to the task of tugging the cuff of his shirt from the dark tailored suit coat he wore over it. "I really don't want to go to this meeting," he muttered, his body reacting instantly to the sight of Mick naked and tousled in the middle of the mammoth bed.

"You have to," Mick braced herself on both elbows now and fixed him with a narrowed amber glare. "Besides," she paused to yawn. "I thought I was going with you?"

Without a care for his clothes, Quest returned to the bed. Crawling to the middle, he forced Mick back down into the coverings. A tiny whimper left her throat mere seconds before his mouth was on hers. The kiss was thorough and slow. Smoothing her hands across his collarless shirt, Mick linked her fingers behind his neck. Instantly needy, she rubbed her bosom across the crisp midnight blue fabric and moaned at the delightful friction of the material against her nipples.

Quest deepened the kiss and wanted out of his dark suit then and there. He was already shrugging out of the charcoal coat with one hand and undoing the buttons of his shirt with the other.

"Quest no…" Mick urged only to have her resistance smothered when the kiss grew deeper. "Wait- you can't."

"I can. I am." He grumbled still shrugging out of his clothes.

"Uh-uh." She pressed on his shoulders and broke the kiss. "Stop."

His eyes darkened then and he simply stared down at her.

Mick was undeterred. "You're going to that meeting and I'm going with you. Now let me up so I can get dressed."

"I promise you'll hate yourself for agreeing to go." He warned but decided it'd be pointless to remove his clothes. "You'll be bored stiff." He added, his sleek brows rising in the hope that she might possibly change her mind.

No such luck as Michaela was already shaking her head against the bed. "You told me you didn't want me anywhere but by your side."

Quest tugged down the sheet baring more of her to his gaze. "You always listen to everything I say?" He asked while nibbling the satiny underside of one breast.

Mick's lashes fluttered. "Only the good stuff." She gasped ready to surrender to his persuasive touch. When he gnawed at her collarbone, she giggled and managed to push him off. A screech followed as she just barely evaded his grasp.

With effort, Quest managed to pull his eyes away from her bare bottom when she left the bed. *Down Quest*, he ordered himself. "You've got one hour!" He called out to his wife.

***

"Word is, with Quest taking those meetings in person some heads are gonna roll."

"Q doesn't operate like that." Quaysar championed his twin while watching his own twin sons playing on the sofa in his study. "We're taking over for the Elders not cleaning house." He saw fit to add.

From his office in Phoenix, Arizona, Smoak Tesano sat perched on the edge of an uncluttered desk and studied his view of downtown. "Cleaning house may just happen if these folks argue with the changes he's threatening."

"Watch it man," Quay's dark gaze remained soft though his voice held an all too familiar edge. "You sound like you've crossed over to the other side of your family."

Smoak grimaced in the direction of the speaker phone. "Never," he vowed.

"Stranger things have happened," Quay sighed reaching down to grab the ball one of the twins had tossed near his chair. "Never in a million did I think I'd see Q runnin' it all." He shared tossing the fuzzy green ball back to Dakari.

"You think he can handle it?"

"Hell man, he should've been handling it all along. He's the one who *handles* everything else for this family."

"You think he'll make the tough changes?"

Quay shrugged. "If he thinks they're necessary." He stroked the Seahawks emblem covering his sweatshirt and pondered the statement.

Smoak had gone to stand before the windows in his lab office. "You think he'll make those changes even if it means dissolving certain branches of Ramsey?"

"Oh especially if it means that. You know Q don't give a damn about turning his back on money if it's for the good of the family." The stony edge that began to darken Quay's face diminished when Tykira peeked into the room. She crooked a finger at the boys urging them to follow her. To her husband, she blew a kiss and left with the twins to give him privacy.

Alone then, Quay focused all his attention to the call. "Let's cut the shit, alright? Now I know you didn't call me at ten p.m. just to check on my family's welfare. I know you've got my wife workin' on some kind of research facility and; though no location is specified, the fact that my cousin's callin' and sayin' she's got Tesanos *inquiring* about her property makes it all pretty easy to figure some kind of bull is in the wind. Now why don't you get to the point and stop wasting my time?"

"Sabra…" Smoak had been preoccupied by the mere reference to the woman. "You're talkin' about Sabra? Is she-"

"She's just fine. Get to the point Smoak."

"Quest taking over has a lot of people nervous and before you ask, no one's gonna touch him or any Ramsey." He confirmed massaging his chest as thoughts of Sabra Ramsey began to affect his breathing.

Quay was chuckling and switched his phone to the other ear. "You'll forgive me if I don't take your word over the past actions of your family."

"Quay-"

"And before *you* ask, the keys are gone. We thought we'd save ourselves a shitload of time trying to figure out how to handle this and just turn the damn things over to the cops."

The smile came through in Smoak's clear deep voice when he spoke. "Certain folks on the *other* side of my family already figured on that. You're mistaken Quay if you think the authorities'll prosecute any of the big wigs on those cards. Besides, with Houston dead and Marc gone-so to speak- that corrupt element is pretty much out of the picture on your end. Everyone knows bribery and strong arm tactics with the younger Ramseys is futile."

"So why the hell are we talkin' then, Smoak?"

"Because all this is about a lot more than pictures on pieces of plastic. And it's about a damn bit more than taking ovaries with the hope of making mothers out of barren women."

"Jesus." Quay went cold.

"Mmm…forget what you *think* you know." Smoak advised in a hushed tone. "Cufi Muhammad, your uncles and most of the men on those cards were tools to obtain what was needed. They were told what was necessary in order to um…encourage cooperation."

"What the hell is goin' on?" Quay breathed standing in the middle of the study and riveted on the conversation.

"Those organs and many more elements were part of studies ranging on everything from reproductive therapies to biological weapons. Now while there is certain government involvement, those actually responsible for acquiring said organs are…let's just say, on the flip side of government."

Quay appreciated the heavy silence following Smoak's monologue. He took a seat on the arm of the sofa and tried to process the details. "Go on," he said after a while knowing there was more to come.

"Quest taking over is very important to a great many people."

Quay tried to massage the furrow from his brow. "I hope you're gonna clarify that."

"He's got a rep for no bullshit. He'd shut down the whole operation without a wince. That, combined with the clout and Ramsey connects would ring a death bell and leave the *other side* of the Tesano family looking for a new backer."

"Don't screw with me Smoak."

"I wouldn't do that." Smoak tread carefully not wanting to rile Quay's easy temper in spite of the fact that they were hundreds of miles apart. "Ramsey made money hand over fist with that weapons division especially after your uncles hooked up with Muhammad and my family."

Quay's dark eyes narrowed in realization. "Why'd you call me tonight?" He needed to hear Smoak say it.

"We need Quest to shut down that branch of Ramsey. If he's smart and I know he is, he's already read the weapons division's files and he's figured you manufacture more than guns for our military and he knows our military aren't the only customers."

It was crystal clear to Quay then. "God…Smoak are you tryin' to take down your family."

Smoak's voice was void of emotion. "I've been tryin' to take down those racist jackasses since the day I understood why they hated me so. We were hoping to persuade you guys to pass over those keys but…well…"

"Who's we?"

Smoak chuckled. "Let's just say it's not the *other side* of my fam."

Quay relaxed back on the sofa then. "What about Sabra? Why does she have Tesanos on her phone?"

Smoak was quiet for a while once again his thoughts were riveted on Sabra. "It's me they want- or rather, they want info on what I'm up to."

"Why?"

"If Quest dissolves weapons, they'll need a new facility. Weapons research and engineering is my field." Smoak grinned at his reflection in the windows lining the lab. "I never dreamed my lowly job as a scientist would set my feet on the path I'd need to take to destroy my family."

"What can you tell me about it?" Quay asked.

"Just that I'm in the process of constructing transportation around a new facility. My folks contacted Ty because her name is everywhere and they decided to see if she's as good as all the hype." He shrugged. "I went along with it figuring in some round about way it'd be extra insurance- that word of my expertise would get back to my family. I'm figuring they heard I was expanding. They know my…history with Sabra and were probably just covering their bases by calling her. They'll do most anything to get me to come back into the foal and lend my weapons knowledge. That includes going after the woman they think I love."

"You're thinking about going back to Vegas." Quay guessed, and then smiled in spite of his agitation. "Don't you think that'll prove it to 'em?" *To yourself*, he added silently.

"I know where you're coming from Quay, but I'd have to go out there anyway." He massaged his eyes. "I couldn't rest wondering…" he sounded as if he were making the admission to himself.

"We can protect our cousins, you know?"

"I have to be there Quay."

"We don't want her hurt again. You know seeing you again is going to do exactly that."

Smoak grimaced and smoothed the back of his hand across his square jaw. "She'll be too angry to feel hurt."

"What's your plan?"

"To have her not only hating me for being out there trying to take over but letting everyone know how much she hates me for it."

"And if you both fail."

Smoak pushed off the edge of his desk and moved closer to the windows. He thought of all the ugliness between him and Sabra Ramsey…all the hate. "We won't fail."

"I don't like it." Quay's voice resembled a growl.

Smoak lost his temper then as well. "When the hell will y'all stop oversteppin' into your cousins' lives?"

"When Tesanos stop tryin' to *overstep* into their beds."

Smoak was angry enough to slam down the phone. He slammed down his fist instead and resisted the urge to end the call on a low. "Your point's made and taken." He managed the cool response.

"How's all this suppose to go down?" Quay couldn't help but probe a little deeper.

"You'll forgive me man if I can't say. I already told you more than I should have. I only wanted you to know your family's safe."

"There'll be hell to pay if they're not."

Smoak acknowledged the threat. "Believe me Quay, the Tesanos have a lot on their plate right now. It'll all start to close in and very soon. I'll let you get back to your family now. Good night."

***

As Smoak Tesano hoped and predicted, Quest was indeed contemplating the idea of disbanding one of Ramseys largest money makers. While his brother was in Seattle and preparing to settle in for the night, Quest's day in Switzerland was just beginning. The meeting he'd thought of shrugging off that morning was bound to turn ugly. His only concern was whether Mick could handle what she was about to witness.

Moreover, Quest hoped he could focus on his job with his wife in the same room. As usual, her presence was murder on his concentration. Not to mention her perfume. It filled the car with an intoxicating fragrance that was a cross between coconut and mango. The dress she wore gloved her curves in a walnut color that accentuated her dark chocolate complexion. Clearing his throat, Quest opened a file and did his best not to think of what lay beneath the soft wool frock.

Michaela was too absorbed by the exquisite sights passing before her eyes to pay much attention to her husband's distress. While Quest was busy praying statements and numbers would help him to focus, she was leaning across him to peek out the window at the passing view from his side of the limo. Innocently, she braced her hand on his thigh to steady herself.

"Mick please," Quest whispered then as though she were torturing him. In truth, her hand inching up his trousers and her breasts nudging his arm had every part of him as tense as a bow.

"Sorry," Mick took notice at last and offered a sheepish smile as she moved away.

***

Ramsey World was a seductively stark high-rise located just outside Sion, Switzerland. The organization was established when Ramsey Group transformed from a simple family owned business of real estate, law and construction to vast land development, corporate architecture and scientific research.

Mick held onto Quest's hand as her head turned this way and that trying to view as much as she could of the dark elegance encamping her. They were greeted like royalty, signed in and escorted to the elevators which would have been standard enough. The elevators however, were like mini lounges complete with cushioned deep burgundy panels and matching benches of the same padding.

"Wow." Mick's eyes were wide as amber moons when she saw the glass ceiling.

"Don't let 'em see you drool," Quest advised coolly and grunted when she elbowed his side.

The double glass doors opened with barely a swoosh. Before them stood a tall, impossibly lovely blonde gentleman with striking teal eyes and even more striking white grin. He offered up a surprisingly hearty laugh and clapped as Quest stepped off the elevator car. They shook hands and hugged.

"Good to see you D," Quest greeted Drake Reinard squeezing the man's shoulder when they separated.

"Good to have you here Quest I…uh…" Drake's bright eyes sparkled with unmasked appeal. "Very nice," he murmured losing interest in his old friend while taking note of the woman at his side.

Quest allowed Drake a few seconds to stare before stepping forward to burst the man's bubble. "Drake Reinard, I'd like you to meet my wife Michaela."

Noticeably embarrassed and unnerved, Drake blinked and retreated a step. Clearing his throat, he prepared to apologize for damn near propositioning his boss's wife.

"Forget it," Quest interjected, "I do the same thing every time I see her."

"Very nice to meet you Michaela," Drake recovered from his uncertainty and stepped forward again.

"Mostly everyone calls me Mick," she shook the hand Drake extended.

"Mick it is. Please," he urged drawing her hand through the crook of his arm and escorting her into the corner conference room with its regal view of the snowy landscape.

Quest leaned against a wall folding his arms across his chest while waiting. He watched Drake getting Mick settled in one of the deep claw foot chairs at the rear of the room. The smile curving his mouth simply deepened when he heard his wife request a mug of the delicious Swiss cocoa she had when she first arrived in town.

Michaela whispered a hushed 'thank you' when her request was granted. Warming her hands around an oversized gray porcelain mug, she caught her husband's eye and blew him a kiss when he granted her a wink.

"Christ Q, had I known she was that stunning, I'd have flown through that blizzard to get to the wedding." Drake was full of compliments when he crossed the room.

"She would've married me anyway."

"Yes, but at least I would've had the chance to kiss the bride."

Male laughter rumbled between the two business associates turned friends. Once the laughter simmered however a more solemn aura slipped in.

"Meeting her now makes what I'm about to say even more important." Drake lowered his voice a bit more when he noticed a few meeting attendants making their way into the conference room.

Quest slanted a look toward Mick. Satisfied that she was content with her cocoa, he nodded toward Drake directing him to continue.

Drake took Quest's arm urging him to veer off to a small alcove. "If you're here to do what you alluded to when talk of your taking over was just…*talk*, then this meeting could get quite ugly-quite fast."

Easing both hands into his trouser pockets, Quest took a quick scan of the room. "What are you saying?"

"Perhaps the things about to be said are things Michaela shouldn't hear."

"Ah," Quest bowed his head and smiled. "Understood." He nodded once more and took a step closer to Drake. "You should know that if we try to usher her out and keep it from her, it'll only make her more determined to find out what's up."

While Drake considered his input, Quest stroked his jaw and turned the words over in his head. With great effort, he managed to dismiss them in light of what he was currently *keeping* from his wife.

"Let's get on with it then," Drake gave a quick nod and clapped Quest's back.

The next half hour was set aside for a meet and greet with the executive committee of Ramsey's European offices. Of course Michaela's charm capacity was in full gear that morning. No one could resist her refreshing allure. Quest and Drake scarcely spoke a word during the socializing session. Drake was a charmed as anyone while Quest found himself hoping for a swift conclusion to the meeting. His thoughts were almost completely centered on finishing what he and Mick started in bed that morning.

The good vibes radiating throughout the understated elegance of the conference room diminished once everyone took their places at the long table. As Quest had no use for small talk, he began with the announcement the group both dreaded and anticipated.

"Within the next twelve to eighteen months Ramsey World's weapons division will be thoroughly dismantled. A task force has been selected to oversee the process. They're set to arrive in four days."

Not surprising, the committee was silent following the statement. The silence however gave way eventually to raised voices and fists pounding upon the glossy oak table. Arguments were thrown at Quest from virtually everyone at the meeting. Mick had long since moved to the edge of her chair to observe the scene. She wasn't alarmed by the raised voices. Instead, it was the unnerving intensity shown by her husband. Quest remained focused on the notes in his portfolio. He seemed unaffected- unmindful of the anger directed his way. Gradually, the raised voices lost some volume as others tuned into Quest's mood.

"As I said, the task force will arrive in four days. Attached to the agenda before you is an itinerary of the visit. This is subject to change depending on what aspects of the division disseverment the group feels they'll need to cover with you all."

"Dammit Quest you can't do this!"

Quest made a notation on his agenda. "It's done," he replied quietly without giving the angry speaker the benefit of eye contact.

"Do you have any idea what sort of money is involved here?!"

"Course I do."

"Fucking millions!"

"That's enough Jacques." Drake warned the V.P. of the weapons division.

Jacques Cuary left his chair to move closer to the head of the table. "Think before you do this Quest. Think hard. This is about more than simply *shutting down* a part of the company you no longer have an interest in. Think how this decision will devastate the people who'll lose their jobs." Jacques whispered hiss was as furious as the look in his pale blue stare.

"That's what the task force is for." Quest reminded the man but seemed unmoved by Jacques argument. "They're charged with finding spots for everyone in the division."

"And you really believe this will happen?" Jacques refused to take heed of the soft dangerous undertone in Quest's words. "That's pretty naïve thinking young man.

Perhaps you're not as ready to take over for your uncles as you think."

"Jacques!" Someone in the room called out in a warning tone.

"Let me remind you Quest of all that's transpired within this division." Jacques refused to be silenced by the well-meaning words of caution from the other meeting attendants. "Your uncles took Ramsey to heights no one could've predicted." He stepped closer to the head of the table then. A knowing look enhanced the sharp features of his salon-tanned face. "Take heed son. Things are a lot less realistic from your big real estate mogul's chair in Seattle."

Drake stood when Quest finally gave Jacque the benefit of his gaze. Michaela gripped the cushioned arms of her chair in an effort to remain seated. Slowly, Drake closed the distance between the two adversaries.

Of course everyone knew Quest Ramsey had excellent control over his temper- the physical aspect that is. It was however, the dangerous aura that loomed over him like a shroud that made him a man one did one's best not to rile. Jacques Cuary realized his mistake too late once he'd taken heed of the waiting rage in Quest's now onyx stare.

"Point taken," Quest closed his portfolio and let the eerily polite tone of his words hang in the air. "But now that I've traded my real estate mogul's chair for this one, if you're craving Marc and Houston's return and the corrupt old days they brought into Ramsey, then you can feel free to either follow Houston to hell or crawl down the same shit hole Marc's disappeared into. Don't for a moment think you're about to convince me to reverse my decision by making me feel like a child trying to squeeze in at the adult table. You're welcome to leave now if you like. Don't bother stopping by your office, I'll have everything in there packed so fast it'll be waiting at security by the time you step off the elevator."

Jacques blinked and took note of the expectant gazes from everyone around the table. He reclaimed his seat and studied the meeting agenda as though nothing had happened.

"May we proceed?" Quest scanned the faces of the executive committee.

The meeting continued without further upset. Michaela; who had been riveted on the morning's events and full of questions, felt as subdued by Quest as everyone else when he came to collect her once the conference adjourned.

CHAPTER SIX

Michaela had hoped she and Quest might find time to shop and have lunch once his business was done, but decided not to mention the suggestion. She was happy to return to the chalet knowing her husband needed the solitude. She wanted to go to him but it was one of those rare occasions when she had no idea how to approach him. As food was always an effective icebreaker, she decided to try that.

Quest had headed upstairs to shower once they'd returned. Mick found the heavy drapes drawn close in their room when she went to look for him. The fire blazing in the hearth offered the only illumination. She heard running water and went to investigate. The spacious bath was steam-filled when she peeked inside. Mick opened the glass shower door just a crack and watched her husband for a while.

Quest simply stood there soaking his head beneath the heavy spray of water. The muscles in his arms were powerfully defined as he braced one fist on the burgundy tiled wall before him and the other on the wall next to him. The stance came across as both strong and defeated. Mick felt her heart ache with concern for him.

Quest shook the water from his head and turned to Michaela as if he knew she were there.

"Hey," he cocked his head and slanted a glance across his shoulder. "There's room," he offered smiling when she laughed.

"That's the best offer I've had all day, but I'd rather feed you."

"With what?" He asked in the boyishly innocent way he'd mastered.

Mick slapped at his wet shoulder. "Food, idiot."

"Food…you sure?"

"Yes. Hey?" She called when he shrugged. "You need to eat. Tell you what, I'll bring it up and we can eat together."

Quest leaned out of the shower and silently requested a kiss. Mick complied, unmindful of the water soaking her wool dress. His arm linked around her waist and he would've pulled her into the shower dress and all.

Mick enjoyed the kiss for a while longer, but was soon pressing against his shoulders. "Wait, wait you need to eat."

"I will," he growled into her mouth one hand cupping her breast to work the nipple into a rigid peak.

"Quest wait!" She shrieked when he would have picked her up and set her inside the shower. "Food first."

He muttered a curse into her neck. "You're really sure?"

"Positive." Mick pushed him into the shower and closed the door before he made another grab for her. Before heading back downstairs she exchanged her soaked dress for a warm cotton robe.

***

"I know it sounds like an unbelievable story."

Claire Boyer smiled. "Thanks for saying so. If it's true it'll be next to impossible clearing your mother. With your father dead, the outcry for justice will call for someone's head on a platter if…you'll pardon my phrasing."

"I understand." Nile perched on the corner of Taurus' desk. He'd arranged for her to take the meeting with the well known defense attorney in his home office.

"I don't expect Yvonne to get away with this. Even if what I told you of these ovarian surgeries is false, there are far too many atrocities my mother still has to answer for. Still…" Nile left the desk to pace the room. "She's my mother-raised me like I was her own after…she protected me Ms. Boyer and I have to do…something."

"I understand." Claire stood and crossed the room.

"Does this mean you'll take the case?" Nile asked when she and Claire shook hands.

"I'll take the file," Claire glanced toward the sofa at the stack of paperwork, "spend tomorrow familiarizing myself with the facts and then I'll go visit your mother day after."

"Merci, thank you. Thank you for coming by so late Ms. Boyer."

"Claire please."

Nile nodded. "Claire." She watched the woman take the file from the sofa.

Satisfied that she had everything she needed, Clair straightened and fixed Nile with a probing stare.

"Is there anything else I need to know? Anything you can think of?"

Nile toyed with the capped sleeve of her top and winced. "I'm pretty sure everything's in the file. Taurus has a very thorough staff."

Claire's lovely plump face softened. "This I know," she agreed. "What I'm asking for is anything personal. Anything that may help to convince your mother that full cooperation would be in her best interest." Claire hooked the strap of her leather tote across her shoulder. "Anything I could use to give her that extra push to confide in me."

Nile tapped her nail to her bottom lip and debated. Her thoughts turned immediately to Michaela Ramsey and the fact that her existence and proximity might prompt Yvonne in some way. *Stupid!* A voice hissed inside her head. It would be beyond cruel to give her mother such hope. Moreover it would be thoroughly insensitive to assume Michaela would want any sort of attachment to a woman who abandoned her.

"Nile? You alright?" Claire tilted her head to ask.

"I'm sorry. Yes." Nile reclaimed her perch on the corner of the desk. "There is something um- keys. Card keys."

"Yes, yes Taurus mentioned those. They're in police custody."

"Right," Nile smoothed suddenly damp palms across jean-clad thighs. "But there are dangerous people who want them. People my mother had frequent contact with. She may know things they'll want to silence her for."

The thought riddled Nile's arms with gooseflesh. "She may resist talking in hopes of assuring them she's not a threat."

"She should know that won't help her." Claire pondered as well, tapping her fingers to her chin as she strolled the office. "The fact that she's in police custody is enough to have her killed." Claire's pensive expression vanished when she heard Nile's shuddery in take of breath. Instant regret flashed in Clair's brown eyes. "I'm sorry- I shouldn't have…that was insensitive."

"It's true." Nile smiled when Claire stepped close to rub her shoulder.

Claire gave one last reassuring pat. "Try not to worry. I'll call after speaking with your mother."

Nile squeezed the woman's hand. "Thank you so much."

Claire gave a quick efficient tug on her olive suit coat. "I'll be in touch."

Nile waited until the door closed behind Claire. Then, she covered her face with both hands.

***

"I pride myself on keeping a neat office Contessa."

Faking a yawn, County studied her nails as she reclined in the massive desk chair behind Fernando's desk. She batted her lashes adoringly when he kicked aside one of the bridal magazines littering the floor.

"I'm serious County," he warned spying the smile curving her mouth.

County was now toying with the fringe around the scoop neckline of her sweater. "So I assume your pride keeps you from picking up the damn things?"

Chuckling softly, Fernando pulled his hands from his jean pockets and moved behind the desk. Curving his hands over either arm of his chair he trapped her efficiently.

"You'll never be properly housetrained if I do it for you."

"I see," County breathed, tingling from the mere sensation of his nose brushing her jaw.

Fernando took a moment to suckle her earlobe. "If my verbal warnings won't work then I'll have to get physical and turn you over my knee."

The tingling turned to a scandalous throb then,

"If I pick them up will you turn me over your knee anyway?" She bargained.

Fernando chuckled at the devilish intent he saw in her eyes. "I'll think about it. I love you." He said, turning serious then.

"I love you." She arched close to take his mouth with her kiss.

"Clean up my office and come to bed." He ordered, breaking the kiss. "I'll be waiting with my belt."

Contessa giggled. "Promises, promises…" she sighed watching as he strolled out the door. The content on her face turned to agitation when she studied the room.

"To hell with it," she pushed herself out of the chair and decided to just jump into the cleaning job. Quickly she grabbed and stacked magazines on the corner of the glass coffee and end tables. She was about to shove a loose sheet inside one of the periodicals but took a closer look at the page when she saw Quest's name circled.

On first glance, she assumed it was something for Fernando. After a cursory second glance she noticed her house logo and fax number at the top of the paper.

"What the hell…" The page slowly grew familiar. It was page two of two so Contessa set off to find page one.

She wouldn't acknowledge the eerie feeling that she knew what the fax involved.

In the carrier tray she located the cover sheet and her heart dropped when she saw Jenean Rays' name.

"God," she choked and made a mad dash for the nearest phone.

***

When Michaela returned to the bedroom suite, she carried a silver tray filled with sandwiches, fruits, veggies, dip, juice and hot tea. Quest was done with his shower and sat in one of the armchair facing the raging fire.

He looked relaxed enough in the ankle length navy cotton robe, but Mick knew differently. She could see the agitation still etched on his profile thanks to the firelight dancing against his incredible features.

"No, no that's okay I'm fine." She said when he saw her and stood to help with the tray. "There," she set the burden to the cushioned bench at the foot of the bed. "I've got it all here. What do you want first?" She propped her hands to her hips and surveyed the spread.

Finally, she tuned in to the silence and turned to find his pitch stare focused on her. Leaving the food, she joined him on the chair and straddled his lap when he caught her hips. For a time, he simply held onto her. Words weren't needed; Mick rocked him slow, brushing soothing kisses along his temple.

The sweetness of the moment began a slow simmer into something spicier. Quest untied the belt securing her robe and; in seconds, she was bare in his arms. He cupped her

breasts and nurtured himself. Mick whimpered and bit her lip in response to the heated mastery of his mad suckling upon her nipples. He abandoned one breast to curve his hand around her body and massage her hips and the small of her back.

Mick was drawn deeper into the embrace and her fingers trembled as they traced the powerful chords of muscle in his chest and shoulders. There was urgency in the way he touched her and she sensed it was fueled more by anger than arousal. She wasn't frightened and allowed herself to be the tool for the venting of his frustration.

Quest muttered something incomprehensible between her breasts. Seconds later, Mick felt her wrists in one of his hands and imprisoned at the base of her spine. With his free hand, Quest loosened the belt of his robe and parted it. Mick gasped at the sheer strength he exerted when he lifted her easily and settled her beautifully upon his stiff length. With her arms trapped as they were, her breasts were thrust more prominently before his mouth. The frantic pace of her breathing kept her nipples just out of reach of his mouth.

An animalistic grunt rose in his throat and he pressed her arms closer to her back. A helpless shriek lilted from her mouth when he captured a nipple. His teeth and tongue began a dual assault on the sensitized peak.

Michaela watched his sleek brows draw close in concentration as he filled his mouth with more of her body. At the same time, the depth of his thrusts increased and Mick cried his name until she was hoarse. The emotion in the room heightened to a powerfully intense state. Even the pop and crackle of the burning embers seemed to gain volume. Quest ravaged her neck scraping his perfect teeth along the flawless brown column of her neck while her head was thrown back in response to the pleasure he subjected her to.

"Mmm…" she moaned feeling the hot rush of his release filling her then.

Quest weakened, his head sloping forward to rest on her shoulder. His shaft throbbed relentlessly against the walls of her sex as remnants of his desire continued to ooze inside her. A frown fleeted across his face and he gave Mick's wrists a warning squeeze urging her to still her movements.

She obeyed when all she wanted was to contract and release sex around his rigid length. Her tortured breathing was mingled with the hint of a groan.

Quest's breathing seemed to calm and shortly he released her arms and circled his own about her curvaceous frame. Mick raked her nails across the silky close cut waves of his hair. Slowly, she began to rock him again.

"Remind me to never come to work for you." Mick teased later but bit her lip and waited to see if her husband was in a teasing mood.

The dangerous black of his stare had softened to gray and there was definitely laughter there. "It depends on what you'd come to do for me." He said, allowing her to see the hint of intensity that crept back into his eyes.

"Ah," She wiggled a bit on his lap, straddling him while she fed him fruit from the tray they'd taken to the massive bed. "You can be a scary guy to work for," she wasn't teasing so much then.

Quest didn't seem to take offense. He accepted the slice of cantaloupe she held before his mouth and leaned his head back. "I'm not so hard to work for."

"Ha!" Mick disagreed and earned a smack to her bare bottom as a result.

Quest shrugged. "I only expect my people to do what I ask- no questions."

"But isn't that what good business is about? You know…questions, disagreement, discussion?"

"In some cases- others no so much," Quest grimaced as he considered his reply.

Michaela spent more time than necessary dipping another cantaloupe slice into a bowl of whipped cream. "Would you have fired Jacques Cuary today?" She asked.

"I'd have accepted his resignation." He rephrased softly. "Once my decision's made, that's it." His deep voice hardened noticeably then. "Person doesn't abide by that, they're out and wishing they'd done as I'd asked."

Mick shook her head and held a creamy cantaloupe slice before his mouth. "Like I said, you're a scary guy."

"Damn straight," he teased and savored the fruit. He caught her wrist to stop her reaching for more. "That's who I've been since forever Mick."

She blinked. All teasing had evaporated from the room then.

"Quest Ramsey," he said looking off across the room with clear regret in his gaze. "The man who cleans up the mess. 'Go to Q, he'll take care of it. He'll know what to do'."

"That wasn't fair to you. They had no right to expect that of you." Mick felt a sudden rush of dislike for her husband's family then. "They had no right," she repeated, smoothing the back of her hand across his brow.

"Don't be upset with them. They didn't expect it as much as I volunteered." He took her hand and pressed a kiss to her palm. "It's who I am Mick- part of my soul. I think if they hadn't needed me so much I'd have found someone who did."

Michaela couldn't fault him. After all, wasn't she as much a slave to whom she was- who her soul demanded she be? Turning back to the food tray then, she selected a slice of kiwi and fed it to her husband.

"Spill it," he commanded gently having noticed Mick biting her lip.

"I just um…I'm not gonna butt in on your business again," she blurted and popped a tiny strawberry into her mouth. "I'll just stay here or go shopping like a good little wife."

The left dimple flashed in Quest's cheek as he smiled over her decision. He nudged her chin with his fist until she met his gaze.

"I really don't mind." Mick went on using her fingertips to thrum a little tune across his collarbone. "I won't even nag at you to tell me what's happening. When you get here, I'll take your mind off it all."

No doubt, Quest thought resisting the urge to fondle her bare body as she straddled his. "You know, at first I wasn't sure about asking you to come along. I didn't think I'd be able to focus on a damn thing with you hanging around."

"See?" Mick nodded her agreement. "Now this way you won't have to worry about that."

Quest grinned and let her finish her say. "Have you ever noticed the thing I do when I'm frustrated?"

Mick's amber eyes narrowed in instant awareness. "You mean when you rub that grizzly brand on your arm?"

Quest managed a nod amidst his chuckles. "Do you know I didn't touch the thing once during that meeting? I didn't even think about it? I think it's because you were there."

"Oh Quest I-"

"Hold on, let me say this. I could've been a lot colder to Jacques had you not been around."

Michaela stifled a shudder as she imagined it.

"Besides, I promised we'd shop together, didn't I?"

Mick nodded but still seemed unconvinced. "Please tell me the truth. Are you really sure you want me travelling around with you?"

"Positive. No where but by my side, remember?"

Laughing then, Mick let go of her uncertainties. Quest tugged her into a kiss and they settled down for another lengthy love session.

***

"We need Yvonne Wilson before she makes bail." Brogue Tesano blew across the surface of the coffee in his mug.

The two men seated across the table at the 24 hour café, exchanged looks.

"You sure she'll make bail?" One of them asked.

"She's got counsel now. Claire Boyer has a very recognizable name in the legal community." Brogue smiled and savored the strength of the regular brew. "Yvonne's new son-in-law selected one of his very powerful friends to protect her interests. If Boyer gets Yvonne bail, the Ramseys'll ship her off to parts unknown until her trial."

"But you're sure she doesn't know any of what's really going on?"

"What she *thinks* she knows is no good for us either," Brogue told his other dining partner. "Hell, if she mentions Marc Ramsey or me; for that matter, it'll bring stress we don't need."

"You think anybody'll take her seriously?"

"Whether they do or not, there would be no choice but to check it out." Brogue allowed a passing waitress to top off his coffee. "Don't for a minute believe she wouldn't jump on the chance to spill everything she knows if there's a chance to deal her way out of a cell."

"So what's the plan once she surfaces?"

Brogue grimaced. He'd stressed over that particular detail in spite of the fact that he'd always known what had to be done.

"B?" The man who'd asked the question uneasily inquired again and straightened on the booth when Brogue looked his way.

"She's dead." He said in a matter of fact tone, finished his coffee and left his associates at the table.

***

"Until I met her, I couldn't believe you'd actually taken the vows," Drake Reinard mused when Michaela had left the table to take a call on Quest's cell.

Drake joined Quest and Mick for dinner out that evening. Not surprising, Drake spent the heaviest portion of the night commending his friend's choice.

"Finally coming round to appreciating holy matrimony?" Quest grinned over the tease.

Drake chuckled even as he shivered beneath the finely crafted almond brown suit coat he wore. "Appreciative only if I were taking vows with a lovely like your Michaela."

Again, Quest grinned and leaned close to clink glasses with Drake. "You should consider yourself lucky that we're such good friends with all these compliments of my wife."

Drake's resulting apology was playful and delivered with a wealth of laughter surrounding it. Within moments however, somberness was overshadowing the ease. "I suppose Jacques Cuary wouldn't have minded being a closer friend the other day, hmm?"

"I knew that wouldn't go well." Quest grimaced and trailed a finger around the mouth of his glass. "We both know it couldn't be avoided." He slid a glance toward Drake.

"Well I-" Drake stifled his remark, his striking ice blue stare warming as he spotted Mick making her way back toward them across the candlelit dining room. "You know, despite my reservations about having her there to witness all that nasty business, I can understand your need to have her close."

"Oh yeah?" Quest propped his fist to his jaw as he too observed his wife's approach. "Because she's so lovely, right?"

"Of course," Drake purred and accentuated the confirmation with a playful shrug. "Seriously though, a woman like that makes a man feel invincible."

The friends were clinking glasses again just as Mick arrived. They both stood to greet her. Drake helped her into the vacant chair.

"Everything okay?" Quest reached over to brush his thumb across the back of her hand.

Mick whispered a hushed 'thank you' to Drake and then smiled for her husband. "Damon and Catrina decided to take Quinn for three nights instead of one and Sonja wanted to know if it'd be alright to go into the city with friends." She explained, referring to their sitter Sonja Worliss. "I feel like I just interrupted something serious." Her vibrant amber stare shifted between both men.

Drake offered a careless wave. "I'm always serious when discussing a beautiful woman."

Michaela accepted the obvious compliment with a gracious dip of her head. "Still, I'm guessing you'd also want to discuss that meeting a couple of days ago?"

Drake's ease didn't wane. However he couldn't resist slanting Quest a look.

Quest raised his glass to swirl gin and tonic water around the ice inside. "Told you we wouldn't be able to keep her occupied with talk of all the winter festivals about to take place around here."

Drake's laughter was as full bodied as his Belgian accented voice. "You're right Mick, that meeting is very prevalent in my thoughts, intense as it was."

Mick seized the opening she'd been waiting on. "I take it the weapons division is near and dear to everyone's hearts."

"Near and dear to their pockets is more accurate." Drake leaned back to finish off the rest of his bourbon.

Mick gave a quick toss of the onyx curls framing her dark face and sighed. "Guess it's understandable people would be upset by the big money maker being taken off the table by the new kid on the block." She studied Quest beneath the fridge of her lashes.

"Weapons have been the biggest source of pride for Ramsey since it was first put in place." Quest shifted in the cushioned chair he occupied. "A black owned company acquiring defense contracts from private *and* government entities- not the norm by any means. Ramsey was one of the front runners in the game." His lashes fluttered on the wake of rising disgust. The emotion marred his devastating features as he massaged his hands one over the other. "Somewhere along the way it all got out of control- corrupt. Money poured in like water while we created terrifying products and sold them at top dollar to any who'd meet our price. *Anyone* Mick."

She blinked, in perfect understanding of what he was telling her. She got why it all had to be shut down and the important statement he'd made by being the one to come and do it in person. Subtly, she drifted out of the conversation preferring to watch as Quest and Drake carried the discussion deeper.

Mick's attention though, was more focused on her husband's mannerisms. The glint in his striking stare and tone of his voice seemed changed somehow given the topic of talk. She had never felt more riveted or subdued.

"You okay?" Quest was asking Michaela once they were done with dessert.

Drake had said his goodnights about twenty minutes earlier yet Mick hadn't felt much like conversing once she and Quest were alone. Clearing her throat softly, she did manage a nod in response to his question.

"Dance with me?" He offered his hand and stood when she put her fingers on his palm.

The soulfully erotic crooning of Les Nubians in the air relaxed Mick almost as much as the feel of Quest holding her snug and possessive against his lean athletic frame.

It wasn't everyday a woman realized the true extent of her husband's power. In the span of a week, Michaela's perception of Quest had gone from knowing him as a smart, instinctive businessman to acknowledging his immense command and importance.

Whether or not he completely understood her mood, Quest was intent on soothing whatever had her unsettled. His beautifully sculpted mouth feathered a barely there kiss from her temple to jawbone. One hand cupped her upper arm, his thumb stroking along the dip at her elbow.

"Quest…" she breathed, lashes batting at the onset of the seductive tingles that threatened to buckle her knees. For support, her fingers curved about the lapel of his black suit coat. Helpless to resist the urge, she rubbed against him in a subtle fashion desperate not to let on to the other dancers how very aroused she was.

It was useless of course. To salvage just a bit of her dignity, she forced herself to still. "Don't," she moaned when he began to nip a diamond-adorned earlobe.

He obeyed but only in order to cup her neck, tilt up her chin and slide his tongue past her parted lips. Mick's resulting gasp merged into a groan and seconds later she was eagerly and wickedly kissing him back. Her slight tug on his jacket lapel had grown tight as she gripped them both. She was moments from pulling him down to her so she wouldn't have to stand on the toes of her chic black cherry pumps in order to meet him.

What sounded like a tiny shriek flew past her lips when; without warning, Quest ended the kiss. He caught her wrist covered by the clinging sleeve of her dress and led her from the restaurant.

Cane Sanai was already starting the car when he saw the Ramsey couple returning. His heart flew to his throat when Quest Ramsey knocked once on the driver's side window. Rarely did Cane's passengers bother to spare him a glance, only rushed orders regarding their next destination. For one to rap on the windows, clearly meant something was wrong and that he was to blame. Rolling down the window, he cleared his throat.

"Mr. Ramsey?" Cane greeted. Nothing prepared him to see the man press a $50 bill to his palm.

"Have a drink on me." Quest urged.

"Sir?" Cane knew he must've mistaken what he thought he heard.

"Nothin' alcoholic Cane," Quest grinned. "Just give me about thirty minutes out here, alright?"

Cane cast a glimpse at the curvy beauty standing behind the man and smiled. "Yes sir, Mr. Ramsey." He moved from the driver's side of the car and tipped a non-existent cap toward Michaela. "Mrs. Ramsey." He greeted and nodded when she waved.

Quest followed Mick to the rear of the car; watching her ease inside, sit on her knees and begin to unbutton her dress.

"Cane?" He called before the driver had ventured too far. "Make that an hour."

Inside the spacious, elegantly crafted vehicle, Quest pushed away Mick's hands and finished the unbuttoning job himself. When she wore only a seductive yet simple cream bra and panty set, he smothered her into the long back seat.

A shaky whimper lilted past Mick's throat when he covered her with kisses from neck to abdomen. Next were the throaty cries that filled the car when his nose nudged against the middle of her underwear. She reached down to tug away the lacy obstruction and was thwarted when he grasped her wrists, holding them to her sides. With his perfect teeth, Quest tugged aside the desire moistened material and thrust his tongue inside the fragrant canal that existed beneath.

Mick arched, moaned his name and flexed her fingers against the hold he kept on her wrists. His name tripped from her mouth on a sob when he stopped making love to her with his tongue and started nipping at the silken petals of her sex with his teeth. Infrequently, he treated her to a few more lunges of his devilish tongue.

She could hear him chuckling arrogantly when she tried to ride on the plundering organ to find release in the act. He prevented that. Maintaining the grip on her wrists, he brought them over her head while rising above her. A deep shiver coasted through her when he treated her mouth to the same oral skill he'd used below her waist.

As though starved, Mick kissed the proof of her desire from his tongue all the while rubbing against his fully clothed form like a mad woman.

"Quest please… I need something…"

"Such as?" He tongued her ear while making the inquiry.

"You inside me."

He grinned. "But I have been."

"Please," she almost sobbed. "Yes…" she laughed in the next moment feeling his fist nudging her as he undid his belt and trousers.

With her freed hand, she struggled to unbutton the black shirt he'd worn with no tie. Lathering his neck with soft grazes of her tongue, she stilled at the feel of him entering her. Her body began to tremble as though it were the first time again.

In response, Quest dropped his head to her shoulder as memories of that time revisited him as well. He groaned her name as if it were a litany and spoke it in sync with the moves of his hips while he took her.

"Mine," he swore, bathing her neck and shoulders with soft open-mouthed kisses. "Mine, no matter what," his nose outlined the mole at the corner of her lips.

Mick could only mouth the word 'yes' while staring into his passion darkened eyes.

The hour spent in the darkened confines of the car was all too blissful and passed all too soon…

CHAPTER SEVEN

Mick never dreamed she'd enjoy being bored out of her mind nearly as much as she'd been over the course of the last week. Three to four hours of seemingly endless dry conversations about production ratios, stock projections, profit and loss…Still, it was all a pleasant change from the ugliness that had clouded the first meeting.

Thankfully, there were elaborate mid morning breaks and lunches that offered the most delicious cuisine. Additionally, Mick considered it a bonus that every now and again while the executives bowed their heads to read through yet another lengthy report, she could look up to find Quest watching her. The intensity of his gaze would almost stop her heart. Life was good.

They took advantage of the quaintly designed villages. The structures somehow managed to maintain their old world appeal in spite of the state of the art products they sold. Michaela was grateful they were travelling in the Ramsey jet. That in itself was a thing she had yet to become accustomed to. After all a good old fashioned seat in coach had always served her well. However, seeing as how they'd practically bought out most every store they'd visited it'd take no less than a private jet to cart all their wares back to Seattle.

Now, they were approaching the end of their stay. Quest wanted to fly up to Zurich and spend the last two nights there. But, as they had several more stops before the trip was completely finished, Mick had a better idea. She asked if they couldn't enjoy the last night cuddled in that splendid *double* king bed and make love as the fire roared. Quest wasn't hard to convince. Unfortunately, since Mick's provocative suggestion only covered the last night of their stay, they were still in need of an activity to fill the evening prior to it.

"Why not?" Mick whined and stomped her boot in the snow as she scowled at her husband.

Quest gave his gloves one last tug. "Because you didn't suggest it."

"I suggested the restaurant."

"And a lovely suggestion it was. Pity you didn't think about how we'd get there."

Mick's scowl darkened and she folded her arms across the front of her blue ski jacket. "I assumed we'd be traveling in one of those over the top limos we've been zooming around in since we got here."

"Tsk, tsk, tsk," Quest shook his head regretfully. "When you assume…"

"Well…you were already an ass." Mick said in her most polite tone.

Quest laughed, sparking his left dimple. "Don't be that way."

"Then let me in the driver's seat."

Quest's full laughter had simmered down to a chuckle. Instead of obeying his wife's order, he reached for one of the helmets and passed it her way. That evening they were heading out to dinner. Mick asked if they could dine at a small café they'd discovered during one of their shopping trips. She was thrilled when Quest said they could eat there that evening. She was less than thrilled when he showed up on a gorgeous two passenger snow mobile and informed her that she'd be riding shotgun.

"Do you even know the way, babe?" Quest asked still waiting for her to take the helmet.

Mick's amber stare narrowed as she leaned close. "It's got GPS, *babe*."

Quest conceded her point with a shrug.

"Are you afraid to let me navigate this thing?"

"Not a bit."

Mick stopped him before he could put on his helmet. Her expression turned sultry as she linked her arms about his neck. "I'm in the driver's seat on the way back or forget my promise to grant sexual favors on demand for the duration of our trip."

The helmet went weak in his hands. Quest closed his eyes to acknowledge she had the advantage. "You're a cold lady Mick Ramsey," he grumbled.

"Mmm," she agreed happily and then kissed his cheek and hopped in behind him.

***

Melina Ramsey was delighted to have her friends arrive in her office at Charm Galleries for brunch that day. The gathering was organized by Contessa and it promised to be an enjoyable event. Johari had recently returned from her honeymoon and everyone wanted to talk about it. Tykira was there and she, Johari and Melina were laughing hysterically by the time County arrived. They laughed even harder at the morbid look on County's face.

"Girl cheer up," Melina urged, "planning a wedding is *not* that bad. I swear."

"Oh please, all she had to do was pick out a dress." Ty gave a flip wave. "Unfortunately, *that* still remains to be handled but Mick's taking care of all the rest."

"Y'all get off County's back." Jo moved to the edge of her seat and added more sugar to her tea. "*Any* aspect of planning a wedding can be a pain in the ass. That's why Moses and me did it quick and quiet."

"Spare us Jo," Mel rolled her eyes. "We ain't here to talk about your sex life."

Another swell of laughter filled the room.

Ty noticed that County had barely moved a few feet from the door. "Girl stop looking so grim. It's not as bad as it seems."

"I'm not here to talk about the wedding." County pulled a page from her portfolio and tossed the leather case to a shelf. "This won't be a *fun* conversation."

Sobering a bit, the women exchanged glances and then fixed County with three pairs of expectant stares.

County presented the fax she'd spent the last few days dying over. "See anyone you know on that list?"

Johari pointed to Quest's circled name.

Again, the expectant looks resumed.

"That's a manifest my publishing house produces." County gave a nervous tug on the hem of her wine colored cardigan. "We use 'em to keep track of where our product goes. It's usually quite a hefty stack but this sheet," she nodded toward the paper now being held onto by Tykira, Johari and Mel, "it notates preview copies for reviewers and other interested parties."

"County what-"

"Wait a minute Ty," County massaged the dull ache in her temple. "This sheet documents those who've received advanced copies of *Royal Ramsey*."

Silence covered the room for quite some time.

"Boy Count, I hope that's the title of a cookbook." Mel sighed.

County seemed to wilt and took refuge in the nearest chair. "I wish it was."

"County please tell us this isn't the book Quest and Fern put a padlock on?"

"One and the same Ty."

While everyone groaned and settled back in their seats, County moved to pour a cup of tea. She tilted the mug toward Melina who hitched a thumb across her shoulder in the direction of the bar.

"Lord County what were you thinking?" Johari's eyes bulged from her face like fixed silver moons. "Fernando's gonna have a fit when he finds out you did this."

"It was Mick's decision, dammit." County splashed a healthy dose of rum into her tea. "Y'all know how persuasive she can be when her mind's made."

Ty fidgeted with the collar of her blouse. "Why would Mick do this?"

"She's been edgy lately- a lot more so after Quest and Fernando put the smack down on the book." The flavored of the spiked tea caused County to give a little shimmy of delight. "She lost it. Said she was sick of Quest always taking over and running things. She said this was her life, her work and she'd be damned if she'd let him take that away from her."

Ty let her head fall back to the chair. "Hell I can understand that as well as anyone, but what's gonna happen when that book hits the shelves?"

"It's Mick's best." County came to quick defense of her friend and raised the mug in a mock toast. "Tasteful, passionate, thorough and a damn sight more truthful than any of the other versions on this family that you can bet are waiting to be published." She downed half the tea "You can best believe none of what *we* put out would've meant a hill of beans after a scathing version by my competition was released."

Melina puffed out her cheeks and stood. "I'm less concerned about what'll happen when that book hits the stands than I am over what'll happen when Quest sees it."

"Have you told Mick yet?" Jo asked.

"Been trying for the past few days," County groaned and set her mug to the coffee table. "Her phone goes right to voicemail, which probably means she's got the damn thing off."

"I wouldn't think so." A thoughtful look brightened Mel's dark face. "She and Quest would need to be reached about Quincee."

County was already shaking her head. "I talked to the girl keeping Quinn. She's been instructed to call Quest if she needs them. I can't risk talking to Mick about this on his line while he's around."

"So what are you gonna do?"

County went to sit on the arm of Johari's chair. "I've left several *urgent* messages on her phone. I can only hope she'll call me back when she's got a minute to herself."

"Jeez, what's gonna happen when all this comes out?"

"Ty, I think it's safe to say all hell will break loose." County's prediction was made lightly enough. Inside, her stomach was twisted into knots.

"Dammit! I should've known she was gonna do something outrageous!"

"Mel?" Jo watched her cousin bolt across the room.

"I talked to Mick about this a while back. We were going over stills of Nile's paintings." Mel stared out the window but absently took in the view of downtown Seattle. "She was agitated just like County said. Quest was…taking over and she didn't know how to tell him about it." Mel fiddled with a loose threat on her jacket sleeve. "I told her sometimes the way was in the *doing* and not the telling. Guess she took it to heart."

Johari, Tykira and Mel continued the discussion. County was silent and walked over to observe the view Mel had abandoned. Two people she loved a lot were keeping two explosive secrets from one another. There was no doubt all hell was about to break loose. What frightened County most was not knowing whether that hell would engulf her best friend's marriage.

***

Louie's was a cozy, comfortable bistro in a small village just outside Nendaz. The chic yet understated style appealed to the vast ski clientele of the area. Still, the establishment was spacious enough to keep its patrons from feeling crowded.

Quest and Mick shared an intimate U-shaped booth which faced a lovely picture window that offered a captivating view of the slopes. Quest felt Mick shudder in his arms while she leaned back against him.

Squeezing her close, he buried his face in her blue black curls. "You okay?" he murmured.

Mick nodded. "I was just thinking about the night you proposed. The stars reminded me- the sparkling."

"We were in Driggers' room." Quest recalled and squeezed his wife closer.

"Just after he passed," Michaela's voice was strong but she relished the feel of Quest rubbing her shoulders. "I was asking him if you were the one. I looked down and your ring was sparkling on my finger. It was like he was saying yes."

Quest kissed her temple and they were silent until after the server topped off their coffees and told them their entrees would be out in five minutes.

"Quest I want to put the house in Chicago up for sale." Mick blurted almost immediately after the server left them.

Quest made her face him on the booth. "You sure?"

"I've been thinking about it for a while." She nodded. "I'm sure."

"Baby why?" Quest could see the struggle in her light eyes.

"So many memories… Good memories and memories of when he…left. But it's the good memories I'll live off of." She took a deep refreshing breath. "Those are the ones I'll want to keep always. I don't- I can't live there anymore."

Pulling her close, Quest pressed a lingering kiss to her temple.

"Besides…we have the cabin up there. It makes sense. I do think the house would be the perfect place for Fernando and County's wedding though. After that, I'll put it on the market."

Quest cupped her face, searching her eyes intently with his soft grays. Convinced, he gave a slow nod. "You want me to take care of it?"

"No. It's something I need to handle myself, okay?"

Quest smiled, wondering silently why everything couldn't be so simple. If only what he knew about Yvonne Wilson could be so easy for him to let her handle. *God all I have to do is tell her*. He berated himself silently feeling disgusted by the weakness that prevented him from speaking.

"Quest? Are you alright?" Mick clutched his hand and gave it a tiny shake.

"Mmm hmm. I'm very alright," he said, seeming to snap out of the mood as quickly as he'd snapped into it. Gracing her with his left dimpled smile, he turned her to lie back against him once more. "Just thinking about my own memories of the house."

"When you came to find me after I left Seattle," she guessed.

"Hmph, not quite. It was seeing you wearing next to nothing and bouncing around in your yard."

Mick's laughter bubbled forth as she recalled the dance rehearsal he'd been lucky enough to catch- thanks to Driggers.

"Good 'ole Driggers," Quest said then as if reading her mind. "I'll always feel indebted to him for that. For you," he rested his cheek against hers.

Silently, they studied the sparkles in the sky.

CHAPTER EIGHT

Because France was accessible by direct train from Nendaz, Quest and Mick opted for that mode of travel when they embarked upon the second leg of their trip. There was much to be said about the view of the French countryside but Mick found that she was utterly speechless as the images passed in a wondrous blur before her eyes.

"Tell me about this trip," she asked Quest but kept her gaze focused past the windows. "Is it more business about the weapons division?"

"Partly," Quest sighed, resting his head back against the seat and closing his eyes. "It's complicated." He remembered the call he'd made to his brother the previous afternoon. The discussion revolved around Quay's conversation with Smoak Tesano.

Michaela had turned away from the passing view. When Quest looked at her face he knew *its complicated* had only stoked her inquisitive juices. A deeper explanation would most certainly be required.

"We're going to see Pike Tesano."

The curiosity in her eyes mixed with intrigue. "Is he as gorgeous as his name?" She emphasized her question with a saucy wink.

Quest propped his feet to the booth opposite the one he occupied. "Isak's his first name. Pike- his nickname and don't get excited. He belongs to Belle."

Now, thoroughly intrigued, Mick folded her legs beneath her on the bar car booth. "Details, man! Quick!" She leaned across the table and slapped his arm. Her husband's cousin Sabella Ramsey had never mentioned a thing about Pike Tesano in all the time they'd known each other.

"They were married." Quest shared, earning another incredulous stare from Mick. "It fizzled. One day she just told him they'd never work."

"Why?"

Quest smiled having anticipated the question. "No idea."

Mick leaned against her side of the booth and chewed her thumbnail.

"Quay always blamed Pike for what happened and told me I was just blind because he was my frat brother." Quest shook his head finally opening his eyes to stare out at the passing scenery. "That wasn't it. Pike was a fool for that girl. Loved her to obsession. He would've never screwed that up."

"I wouldn't be so quick to say that." Mick smoothed her hands across the long sleeves of her clover polo top. "People aren't always the same as the image they portray for the public."

"True. But I know my cousin." Quest shrugged. "I know back then she was always on edge…worried she'd never be able to keep him."

"I remember Belle telling me once that she'd struggled with her weight- was that a reason?"

Quest was nodding before Mick asked the question. "She went through a lot because of it."

Mick raised her hand for emphasis. "Maybe Pike got disillusioned with her."

"You'll never convince me of that." Quest's smile was a mix between humor and pity. "The man asks about her every time I see him- which hasn't been for quite a while. I know he was going to every play he discovered she was working on and I know *that* because he told me." He folded his arms across his pine BOSS sweatshirt. "I think the reason he told me was because everyone else would've thought he was a fool to still be caught up over a woman who up and left without giving him a reason."

Mick propped her chin to her fist and watched him thoughtfully. "So in addition to business, you're going to have to soothe a broken heart? Sorry." She added when her husband didn't appear to appreciate the jibe.

"Nah, you're fine." Quest winced. "Like I said, I haven't seen him in a while. Who knows where his head is at over Belle."

"Then what is it?"

"You know I spoke to Quay last night." He waited for her nod. "He got a call from Smoak Tesano. Pike's brother. Smoak and Sabra had a highly…dramatic relationship that ended just as dramatically."

Mick nodded, recognizing the name of Quest's other cousin Sabra Ramsey.

Quest was massaging his brow as he recalled the fireworks of the ill-fated match. "People contacted her, said they were looking for Smoak. My concern is why they'd contact her and mention Smoak to her when they haven't been in touch in years."

"And you're sure of that?" Mick dragged a hand through her curls. "Sabra's out in Vegas. She doesn't keep the family informed of all her escapades, you know?"

"It was bad with Smoak." Quest massaged his jaw as he thought it over. "I think she'd let somebody know if it was back on between them. The fact still remains that the jackasses called her."

"Hmm…perhaps trying to draw him out, put their minds on one another?" Mick's brainstorming juices were in full gear. "Contacting Sabra…it'd get back to Smoak that they did this. His reaction to that could tell them if-"

"She still means something to him." Quest sounded as if he'd come to the conclusion long ago.

"You think they'll try to use her to force him out?"

Quest shook his head. "I can't say."

Mick laid her hand palm up on the table and fixed her husband with a cool look. "Couldn't you be over reacting here?" She stifled herself from saying *overprotective*. "I mean these people were probably just covering ground, I don't think there's anything to worry about. If there's one thing I've realized watching you handle business over the last week is that these people take their work very seriously. *Theatrically* serious-if Jacques Cuary's scene is any example. But I don't think it'd go any farther than that."

A muscle danced a wicked jig along Quest's jaw and he debated only a second before leaning across the table to take both Mick's hands in his. "Daphne didn't kill

Houston or herself. My aunt and uncle were killed to *persuade* the return of the card keys." He shared the information and ignored the horror filtering his wife's brilliant stare. "Those keys held finger print and photo information on various…high-powered figures- many with political and government connections. The keys were to the house Cufi Muhammad kept in Nice."

Mick gasped, trying desperately then to tug her hands free of Quest's. He prevented it.

"Those keys were in Nile's possession. That's right," he confirmed the question in her eyes. "That's right. Taurus' new wife. She gave them to us. We gave them to the authorities."

"But Quest what- when they find out, they-"

"Shh…shh…Smoak assures Quay they aren't looking to tangle with us."

"But Houston and Daphne-"

"Smoak says the whole family wasn't in agreement on it."

"And you believe that?"

"No choice, but I think it's safe to believe it…for now."

"Hmph. I'm so sorry that I can't share your sense of contentment."

"Hey," Quest came around to share the seat with Mick. He pulled her close and squeezed until her tremors subsided. "I honestly believe we're alright, but that doesn't mean we haven't taken every precaution. We're safe, trust me."

Mick kept her fingers curled into the neckline of his sweatshirt. "That takes care of us in Seattle. But what about the rest of your family? Sabella, Sabra…"

"The main reason we're heading into France now." Quest wound his fingers in Mick's curls when her head fell to his chest. "My good friend's family is about to go to war with itself and I don't want my cousins in the middle of it."

***

Seattle's chilled air and bleak skies matched Nile's mood to perfection. *God what a mess*, she thought recalling all that was happening with her mother not to mention the explosive news her husband shared with her over a week ago. Learning the truth about Michaela, Nile was close to asking Taurus to forget bringing counsel in to help Yvonne- better known as Evette Sellars.

How could she do such a thing? Nile pondered. Regardless of what Yvonne had been part of with Cufi, Mick was her own child- a part of her. How could she leave her own little girl to fend for herself against God knew what evil?

Still, this was the same woman who had taken care of *her*. Nile thought tugging restlessly on the pin-striped lavender cuffs of her blouse. Yvonne Wilson had come to *her* rescue, loved her and protected her against countless evils. What madness was it that would drive a woman to leave her own child to raise another?

Contentment showered her suddenly and Nile knew that Taurus was there long before he smoothed his hands down her arms. She relished the feel of his lean, powerful frame. She absorbed his strength-revitalizing herself with it.

He gave her time and simply held onto her for a while. "Claire's here," he said finally and waited until his wife was strong enough to turn from the towering windows in their penthouse apartment. "You up for a talk?"

She nodded. "I'm fine." She said, knowing he wouldn't believe it unless she spoke the words.

Taurus' bright deep-set gaze scanned her face for any sign to prove otherwise. Finding nothing that gave him cause for real concern, he brushed his thumb across her mouth and helped himself to the taste of her kiss.

Nile moaned instantly and eagerly matched the firm thrusts of his tongue. Taurus had to force himself back knowing he was seconds from disappearing upstairs with his wife.

"We'll make this fast." He spoke into her neck and chuckled when Nile smacked the back of his head.

She pushed him to the door and only waited a few moments before Claire Boyer was stepping into the living room.

They all took their seats and exchanged pleasantries before Claire got right to the point.

"I've seen your mother. I did most of the talking but she didn't ask me to leave. She seemed calmed by the fact that you sent me." Claire's brown eyes softened as she recalled the hope on Yvonne Wilson's face. "She seemed to be actively listening. Before I left…she told me she'd cooperate on one condition. She wants to see you."

Nile instinctively reached for Taurus's hand and held on for dear life.

Claire bowed her head, momentarily shielding her plump face by the clipped locks of her bobbed hairstyle. "I know things ended ugly between the two of you- perhaps she wants to apologize."

"Did she say that?" Nile asked.

Claire focused on the tent she made with her fingers. "She said there were things she had to say to you- things she could say to no one else."

"May I think about it and let you know?"

"Of course," Claire scooted forward on the sofa to pat Nile's hand. "Just call once you've decided."

Taurus showed Claire to the door once the meeting had ended. When he returned, Nile was once again standing before the windows in the living room.

"I want to see her."

Taurus closed the distance between them. "You positive?"

"There are things I want to say to her as well."

It didn't take Taurus long to figure the meaning of that. "Be careful," he urged. "You know Yvonne doesn't know about Mick- last thing we need is to have her pop up with Mick unaware- unprepared."

"It won't be like that." Nile vowed, reaching out to toy with the zip front of the gray fleece hoody Taurus wore. "I don't need to accuse her of anything. These are just idle questions."

"About Mick?"

"Most definitely, but within reason," Nile promised. "I have no intention of leading my mother to the child she abandoned, but I do have questions." She looked blindly at the zipper she toyed with.

"About why she came to be my mother," Nile frowned once the words left her tongue. "Why did she stay when she knew what my father was?" Nile let her hand drop from Taurus' chest. "Why didn't she just take me with her and run before…"

"Shh…" Taurus could sense tears on the horizon and pulled Nile close. He rocked her slow reaching beneath the silky black of her hair to massage her neck.

Speaking no words, he simply offered her the nourishment of his embrace and she wholly accepted it.

***

Carcassonne, France~

"Please tell me you don't own this." Mick said to Quest as she gazed upon the walled city that housed one of Europe's oldest citadels.

The almost perfectly preserved medieval structure was as magnificent there in the twenty first century as it must have been centuries earlier during the time of knights and maidens.

"Well I don't own it." Quest assured his wife and chuckled when he noticed the relief on her face. "Do you have a problem being rich?" He asked, tilting his head as he fixed her with a playful probing look.

Michaela kept her eyes on the structure. "Being rich is one thing. Buying things for the sake of boasting you own them is another."

Laughing heartily, Quest planted a hard kiss to the top of Mick's curls. "God, I love you." He gave her a quick squeeze and urged her forward.

While her husband not owning the intimidating beautiful piece of architecture made her feel loads better, Mick knew no one earning less than a six figure salary could afford a night in the hotel nestled inside the citadel. She could only imagine how incredible the place must look from a distance at night- a glowing oasis in the midst of the darkened expanse of land surrounding it.

By day the loveliness was almost staggering. *Hotel de E'spirit* was accessible by car, train or ferry. Those with more romantic notions in mind opted for horse and carriage rides. Michaela was stunned her husband hadn't thought of that and gave him an elbow to the ribs when he informed her of how expensive they were.

Checking in was done with such ease it might have been imagined. No time was wasted on such petty things as trips to the front desk or the swiping of credit cards. Payments were handled well in advance of a guest's arrival. The only hotel employees a guest had to see first off were the baggage clerks and greeters who escorted them to their suites.

Mick studied the invigorating beauty while Quest spoke with the gentleman who was to lead them to their room. Though there was a definite chill in the air, the sun beamed down wonderfully upon the green of the countryside.

"You wanna head on up?" Quest asked having noticed Mick shiver. "It's fine, Henri'll show you." He smoothed a hand at the small of her back while nodding toward their greeter.

Mick graced Henri with her loveliest smile. "What about you?" She asked Quest.

"I need to talk to Pike first. Besides, his parents are here but set to leave tonight and I need to see them too."

Amber eyes bright with curiosity, Mick clutched his wrist. "I'd like to meet them. Do you mind if I tag along?"

Quest shrugged. "You heard her Henri." He took the pad from Henri's hand and signed off on a generous tip for the greeter and baggage clerk.

"So how often do you stay here?" Mick was asking once Quest pulled her hand through the crook of his arm and led her deeper into the hotel.

Quest was smug. "What makes you think I've stayed here before?"

"Oh please, judging from the way you're leading me around, you know the place well."

"Good eye," Quest commended though he expected nothing less of her. "I got back from a trip here just before I met you."

"Ah…pleasure?"

"Of course," his reply was cool, "it's always a pleasure staying here but the reason I came was for business." He qualified, grinning when her elbow nudged him again. "Ask Quay if you don't believe me. He was here."

"Forget I asked." Mick groaned knowing 'pleasure' was synonymous with the name Quaysar Ramsey.

"Just as well, we didn't spend much time together anyway. I wasn't as interested in sampling the French cuisine as he was. I think that was around the time he started referring to me as a stick in the mud. You probably heard him call me that a time or two?"

Mick ordered herself not to laugh. "A time or two," She admitted quietly.

Quest led them to an express elevator that opened up right in the middle of paradise. A terrace lounge encompassed the entire southwest corner of the rooftop and offered yet another provocative view of the unending landscape. Michaela would've thought the place closed for business had it not been for the three people occupying a round table at the edge of the terrace.

Actually, a man and woman occupied the table while a second man observed the view from his leaning stance against the terrace rail. He turned to laugh at something the woman said- it was then that he noticed the couple approaching from the elevator. After a moment, he threw back his head and laughed.

Mick hung back a bit as Quest walked on to meet the man who headed toward them. She noted that he was as tall as her husband and when he came into view, she noted that God must have been having a very good day when he created the two men she stood practically staring holes into.

Isak 'Pike' Tesano extended a hand and caught Quest's as the two fell into a hearty hug.

"What the hell is this?" Quest whispered in exaggerated surprise and slapped a hand playfully against the light beard his friend sported.

Pike shrugged. "It happens when one becomes a man," he cocked his head in a teasing fashion. "I see you still know nothing about that brotha." He reciprocated with a slap against Quest's flawless cheek.

More boisterous laughter and pleasantries were exchanged; yet once Pike glanced past Quest, his tone grew hushed.

"This is Michaela?" He asked, though there was no need for confirmation. "Jesus," he breathed and brushed past Quest en route to greet Mick. "Isak Tesano. Your husband and I go way back."

"I heard." Mick's light eyes shifted between her husband and his friend in unmasked awe. *Gorgeous as gods* was a truly inadequate description but it was the best she could manage just then.

Pike's grin sparked double dimples just visible beneath the shadow of a beard darkening the lower half of his bronzed complexion. His eyes were deep set and dark as crude oil. They matched the heavy brows and black waves of hair that almost brushed the broad shoulders beneath the cinnamon brown shirt that hung outside the cream trousers he wore.

"Have you eaten?"

Mick spared a scowl in Quest's direction before responding to Pike. "He wouldn't let me- said the food here was to die for. I hope that's true since I'm about starved to death."

Pike and Quest's laughter filled the air with sounds that were full-bodied and honest.

"I like her Q!" Pike said even as a hint of melancholy sobered his expression. "How's Bella?" He asked when Quest was near.

Exchanging a knowing look with his wife, Quest clapped Pike's shoulder. "She's good- handling wardrobe for a new play."

A small furrow signaled the beginnings of a curious frown. "Which one?" Pike asked.

Cab Crew. Playin' to sell out crowds every night in Harlem right now from what I hear."

Though he nodded coolly, it was clear Pike was avidly assessing the new info that he'd as yet been made unaware of. "I'll have to check it out."

"Hey! You two stop towering over that poor girl!" The order came from the man seated at the table.

Jumping to, Quest and Pike each offered Michaela an arm and escorted her forward.

"She's lovely Quest- absolutely. I've heard that all you young Ramseys had finally been captured by a team of beauties who have brains as well." Imani Kamande Tesano stopped her wheelchair to cast another pensive stare at the table where her husband and son sat talking with Michaela. "I can see the rumors were true."

Quest leaned down to brush a kiss across the back of Imani's hand. "Thank you." He knew the woman was ever-prayerful that her own children might find such happiness. So far, it had eluded them.

Roman Tesano clearly agreed with his wife's impression of Mick. Several times during the course of the conversation, he used the edge of his napkin to dab tears of laughter from his dark eyes. The group had enjoyed a delicious lunch where Quest shared what he knew of the goings on in the family. Afterwards, Quest caught up with Imani while Mick continued to converse with Roman and Pike. Once Quest and Imani returned to the table, the main topic of discussion resumed.

"You have my word on this son; no harm will come to Sabra or Sabella because of anything going on in this family." Roman cast his son an assuring look as well.

"I appreciate that sir," Quest locked his fingers atop the table and leaned forward. "Others in my family may not agree. I'm not so sure I can agree especially following the deaths of my aunt and uncle."

Roman's jaw tightened into a grim line. "I am sorry for what happened to Houston and Daphne. I had every reason to believe my family was to blame for it."

Michaela stroked Quest's wrist when she noticed him clench a fist.

"You know better than anyone how deeply the unrest goes in our family Quest." Roman brushed the pad of this thumb across the face of his watch. "I promise you on the life of my children, that Daphne and Houston's deaths weren't sanctioned by the family. I threatened to go after them with all my resources when I suspected…they were terrified and rightly so. They gave up the party responsible- suffice it to say a small group of the family however has pretty much…gone *rogue*." Roman slanted a meaningful look at Pike who understood the hint.

"They were intent on obtaining the card keys," Roman continued. "I understand they're no longer in your possession."

"That's right."

Roman nodded. "Just know that I *am* sorry. That doesn't mean much now, I know and I can't say any more at this time but I guarantee that those responsible, will pay."

"I won't tolerate another attack on my family, sir." Quest's promise was delivered softly but just as powerfully.

"They have no interest in harming those girls." Roman's bronzed features took on a more sincere tint. "They want my sons. Always have."

Quest nodded. He knew Pike and his brothers had struggled all their lives to remain on the honorable side of the Tesano clan. There was one brother however who hadn't struggled because the *other side* of the Tesano clan didn't want him.

There in lie the seeds of unrest amidst one of the most powerful families on the East Coast. The group talked a little longer and then reluctantly parted ways as the elder Tesanos had a trip to prepare for, while Quest and Mick had yet to visit their room.

"It's wonderful that they visit your mother's homeland once a year." Mick was saying in reference to the trip Roman and Imani were taking to Mozambique.

Pike leaned back in the chair he'd occupied and smiled in the direction his parent's had exited. "It's important to my dad. He always felt my mother missed out on so much being so far from her home. "'Course, she visits whenever she wants, but it's always concerned him, so she humors him."

"Well I think it's wonderful. I can tell they love you a lot." She caught Quest's eye and knew he was trying to figure if she was regretting her own family or lack thereof. Offering a refreshing smile, she pushed back from the table and both men rose to their feet when she stood.

"It was great meeting you Pike." She said, laughing when Quest leaned close to judge the kiss his friend planted on her cheek. "I'll see you upstairs." She patted Quest's stomach and left the table.

"She's incredible Q. You're a lucky man."

Quest's hazy gaze was unwavering. "I am. Are they safe, P?" He asked in the same breath.

"I promise you yes."

Quest's expression didn't soften. "Your father promised and because I respect him as much as my own father, I accepted that. So this is for you. One hair- *one* hair on their heads harmed or even threatened and the Tesanos won't have to worry about destroying themselves because I'll take a personal interest in seeing to it myself."

"Understood," Pike nodded coolly enough though his features were drawn into a dangerous mask. "And because you're one of my best friends, I'll keep my temper out of it. Hell, do you think I'd ever let anyone touch her Q?" He clutched the hand Quest offered as a sudden grin flashed. "See you and Mick tonight for dinner?"

Quest reciprocated with an easy grin of his own and hugged Pike before they parted company.

CHAPTER NINE

"Stop that."

Mick looked up at Quest and fixed him with a playful frown. "I'm only breathing."

"Stop. It's arousing me."

"Well I'm sorry," Mick burst into laughter that brought tears to her eyes. "But *you* were the one who wanted to slow dance and if we're gonna do that to this incredible quartet *you* are gonna have to feel me breathing."

"Then I'm afraid we're gonna miss dinner with P," Quest was already fiddling with the skinny shoulder straps of Mick's butter rum dress.

She slapped his hands away from the loose straps that draped her shoulders. "Not on your life. I plan to hear more about what kind of playa you were."

"Nice try." He tugged on one of her spiral curls. "You just want to moon over him some more."

Her mouth formed a perfect O as she laughed and thumped his forehead. Mick propped her chin on his chest and looked up. "I was only admiring. The *only* man I see is you."

"Really?" He sounded every bit the adorable boy as his darkening eyes searched her exotic amber ones.

"Really," Michaela couldn't help but feel fascinated that the visually stunning man who held her close could be so absorbed by how much he appealed to her.

It was quite a heady feeling Mick decided as she leaned closer to inhale the scent of the cologne clinging to the charcoal brown jacket he wore over a crew shirt of the same color. She molded her palms to the chiseled outline of his torso and felt her own arousal begin a subtle simmer. The man would've had to have been blind not to see all the looks of unmasked…heat directed his way from almost every woman who saw him. Yet there he was Mick thought, concerned by her and by the 'heat' he saw in *her* look.

"I love you," she whispered standing on her toes to meet the kiss he leaned down to give.

The kiss intensified immediately and Mick whimpered as if tortured. All she wanted was to wrap herself around him and rub against the overwhelming hardness of his body. Quest maintained the cooler head and broke the kiss as the quartet announced a five minute break.

Arm in arm, Quest and Mick strolled back to the table they'd secured in the *Greenhouse* restaurant. With its elaborate design of lush foliage and man-made ponds, every guest had the sensation of dining in an indoor garden.

"He seems sad; I could see it behind all that laughter this afternoon." Mick said once they'd taken their seats.

"I doubt he can even tell anyone notices." Quest thought of his friend while downing a bit of the cognac he'd ordered. "Those of us who know and love him let him think he's got us fooled with that look of his."

"It's like total elation and the depths of sadness mixed into one and that *one* is impossible to describe." Mick took time to sip from her club soda.

"What?" Quest noticed her eyes narrowing further.

"Just thinking of *looks* that are impossible to describe, that's all…Nile," She said when Quest continued to stare. As her thoughts were then focused on Taurus' new wife, she didn't notice how sharp Quest's expression had become.

"At the wedding she…she just looked at me so strangely. I don't know." She took another sip of her drink. "Like a mix of surprise, recognition… Fear maybe?" She inquired but didn't really want an answer. She shook her head. "I'm probably just imagining it."

"Did you talk with her?" Quest focused on the impression his cognac glass made on the napkin beneath it.

Mick grimaced and shook her head again. "It was her wedding day and there was so much going on. Besides, you seemed pretty anxious to leave."

Quest smiled in spite of himself. He guessed he hadn't disguised his *anxiety* as well as he thought. "Guess I must've been preoccupied about taking this trip."

Mick's sunny expression returned. "Well, I'll thank you just the same for bringing me along. Even though I miss Quinn like crazy, I really needed this time with you." She bit her lip and reached out to take the hand he extended. Her heart thudded in her throat when his beautiful stare filled with intense emotion.

Before Quest leaned close to ply her with another kiss, Michaela tilted her head toward one of the entrances. "Your boy's here." She waved at Pike who had just entered.

"Well that does it for me. I'm gonna turn in." Mick was announcing after the delicious feast of authentic French onion soup, braised salmon and bay scallops with almonds and chocolate profiteroles for dessert.

"Come on Mick, stay. I haven't told you half the dirt I've got on this fool." Pike slanted a wicked look at Quest who pretended to shush him.

"Nooo I think I've got enough ammunition." Mick pressed a kiss to Quest's temple. "I'm gonna give you guys time to catch up."

Quest and Pike moved their conversation to one of the hotel's bars once Mick left them. They had a great time talking and laughing over old times. Quest was nicely surprised to see the conversation steered clear of his cousin Sabella. It was just as well, for other serious matters did revisit the discussion.

Pike was floored when Quest went into full detail about Cufi Muhammad and how what happened tied into the Tesano family.

"Look P, I know how you and your brothers always worked to be what your dad wanted, but I need to know if you're sure you guys are still on the same page."

Pike drained the rest of his bourbon and signaled the waiter for another. "You're talkin' about Caiphus and Hill?" He referred to his younger and older brothers respectively.

Quest shrugged.

Pike reciprocated the gesture. “As far as I know.”

“As far as *you* know…you talk to Hill lately?”

“I try to talk to Hill as little as possible.” Pike reached for his fresh drink.

“Maybe you should. Just to be certain.”

“Last I heard he put down his pirate’s cap, Q.”

“Maybe he’d be willing to pick it up again for the right cargo.”

“What are you thinking?”

Quest shook his head reaching for his drink. “It’s probably nothing. Only with my dismantling Ramsey’s weapons division- a division that’s been catering to certain interested parties in your family- that leaves a lot of equipment a lot of product that’ll have to be sold, *shipped* and with this *research material* biological and otherwise…”

“Delicate stuff,” Pike noted.

“Mmm…” Quest smirked. “Something you’d want to entrust to family for instance.” He shrugged again. “Like I said P, I’m probably way off here with a bunch of nothin’. Just a feeling.”

“Just a feelin’ huh?” Pike grinned. “A lot of men I know base their business dealings on *feelings* from Q Ramsey. I’ll look into it.” He promised and clicked glasses with Quest.

Quest wasn’t surprised to find Mick already asleep when he returned to their suite. He leaned against the bedroom doorjamb; hands hidden in his trouser pockets, and watched her a long while. They’d return to the States tomorrow and would arrive in Chicago by dinner time.

He'd tell her then when they were back in Chicago- back inside her home. The home she'd shared with Driggers- a place she'd always felt safe. She would be devastated just the same but she'd be *there*. He finally accepted the fact that this news would have to come from him and not out of the clear blue. He thought of Pike then and recalled what being stunned out of the clear blue could do to a person. He didn't want that for Mick. He would tell her tomorrow.

Pushing off from the doorjamb, Quest took a seat on the edge of the bed and toyed with her hair. Eventually, she stirred and whispered his name in the dark.

"Shh…go back to sleep," he kissed her cheek and tucked the covers around her.

"Mmm…thanks," she turned on her side. "I got no strength left for sexual favors tonight."

Quest chuckled at the slurred statement. "That's fine, but just for tonight." He warned playfully and leaned close to nuzzle her hair. He waited until she'd fallen into another deep slumber then, fully clothed, he stretched out next to her and drifted off to sleep.

***

Taurus tried to keep the scowl from his face as he watched his wife descending the courthouse steps. She'd asked him to let her go alone to see her mother and he refused her request without hesitation. Unfortunately, he'd gotten tied up with an issue at Ramsey and she'd gone ahead without him.

Nile caught sight of her husband. She knew he wasn't happy that she'd left to handle the visit alone. She was so bless to have him, she thought loving the cool appealing image he cast while leaning against the passenger side of a dark Navigator that pretty much dwarfed the champagne Jag she'd driven into town. Taking the last step, she walked right into his arms and hid her face in the crook of his neck.

"It's alright," he soothed feeling her shudder and sob against him. "I guess I don't have to ask how it went."

"When I said Mick's name, I thought she'd die- she was so stiff." Nile smoothed her hand across Taurus' tanned suede jacket in long rhythmic strokes that seemed to calm her.

"Did she try to deny it?"

Nile shook her head against his shoulder. "At first she was confused but then she wasn't expecting Michaela Sellars to be the first words out of my mouth." She squeezed her eyes tight to ward off the dread filling her. "When everything began to register, she sat down and told me in the simplest calmest way how she shattered the life of her own child. It wasn't an involved heart wrenching story like I'd expected-hoped. Instead… instead it was like hearing the story of a child- a young girl who'd become a mother way too fast and who one day decided she didn't want the responsibility any more." She braced her forehead against Taurus' shoulder and took several deep breaths. "Cufi Muhammad could offer her the life she'd left Compton to find. But aside from her, he wasn't trying to take along any other baggage." Nile pulled back to fix her husband with a defeated look. "She had to go, you see? She may never have gotten another once in a lifetime offer like that."

"Jesus," Taurus massaged the bridge of his nose as tears for Mick suddenly pressured his eyes. "Did she say anything about just leaving her there like that?"

Nile almost laughed at the absurd response Yvonne had given. "She said Mick was usually running across the hall to play with a neighbor's child. She would've carried Mick over there but she was still eating dinner and my…father arrived early and was ready to go." Nile did laugh then though the gesture held no trace of humor. "She said she told Mick to go on over when she was done- figuring everything would fall into place for the neighbors when she didn't come to collect her and that they'd just look over her out of the kindness of their hearts."

"Bitch," Taurus growled and then dropped his forehead to Nile's shoulder. "Sorry."

"Don't be. It was the last thing I said to her after she told me how Mick sensed she was going for good and begged-*begged* her mother not to leave her…I left the room after that."

Despite the strength of his wife's words, Taurus knew she was shredding inside. "So that's how you left things?"

Nile sniffed and nodded. "I just want to forget I ever went there."

"You do know that once Quest tells Mick about Yvonne, you'll have to tell Mick's this story."

Nile was shaking her head even as Taurus spoke the words. "Never. I won't do it. No one should have to hear that. No one should have to learn how little their own mother cared for them."

"I agree." Taurus kissed her cheek and stayed close to nuzzle her ear. "But this has eaten away at Mick her entire life. She deserves to know Yvonne Wilson- Evette Sellars or whoever- isn't worth the energy it takes to bring her to mind. She deserves to be able to put that in her past in order to live her future."

Nile knew her husband was right. Without further discussion, she began to nod her agreement while Taurus pulled her into his secure embrace.

***

Michaela was like an eager child as she gazed upon the sight of her Chicago home. Like a wondrous wave, all the memories she'd created there came flooding back and she realized how much she missed the place.

Quest leaned across the gear console once he'd shut down the Denali's engine. "Sure you want to sell it?" He asked propping his chin on her shoulder.

Mick nodded, her curls bobbing wildly. "It's time for someone else to give the place new memories- it deserves that."

Dusk was approaching when the couple pulled into the brick horseshoe drive. They made quick work of bringing in the bags. Michaela had already put in a call to the realtor before they left for Switzerland. As the woman was scheduled to stop by sometime before lunch the next day, the Ramseys decided to make it a simple evening. Quest ordered out for Pizza while Mick made a quick visit to the market for a few other things they'd need.

***

A dark scowl was beginning to mar Quest's gorgeous features as his clicks to the remote's down arrow grew increasingly harsh.

Mick sat curled on the opposite end of the sofa and bit down on her thumbnail while attempting to stifle a grin. "Sorry," she muttered innocently when he uttered a frustrated curse.

"We've got almost fifty movie channels here- over ten that feature all action- all the time and you've seen every single one."

Michaela's shrug was a gesture of both contentment and pride. "What can I say? I love action movies."

"So do I and some of these even *I've* never heard of."

Mick snuggled down on the sofa. "And therein lies your real frustration- how could anyone know more than Quest Ramsey?"

"Stow it." He ordered, his brows drawing closer. He was determined to find something neither of them had seen.

Mick stretched out her legs and curled her toes into the soft fleece of his sweatpants. "We've also got a ton of stations that feature all porn- all the time." She sent him a naughty wink when he looked her way and she wiggled her toes against his thigh. "Let's find somethin' there and forget action."

Quest shook his head, tossed aside the remote and grabbed her ankle to tug her close. "I'll show you action."

His face was hidden deep in a wealth of cleavage when the doorbell chimed. Mick was torn between stripping off her top and seeing to the door when her stomach growled.

"Hopefully it's the pizza." She said when he grinned up at her.

"Forget it." His head dipped again. A hand curved about her thigh and his thumb skirted the edge of the cutoffs she wore. His fingers were mere inches from the lacy middle of her panties when she clutched his wrist. "We'll eat later," he growled into her bosom while maneuvering out of her wrist- clutch.

"I'm hungry now." She added a bit of whine to her voice for emphasis.

"Then, it's *your* dime." Quest eased back with playful challenge filling his hazy gaze.

Mick brows rose. "Shameful." She chastised watching as he shrugged and returned his attention to her chest.

The doorbell rang again.

"So you'll only pay if I put out?"

"Course. What do you think this is?" His tongue outlined the swell of one breast. "I'd even planned to spring for soda and those cinnamon sticks for dessert."

Mick's laughter filled the living room then. "Well since the pizza guy's here already and probably getting more pissed off by the second, how about I promise to fulfill your every sexual desire by night's end no later?"

"I'll take what I can get." He decided, supplying her with the money for their dinner just as the bell sounded a third time.

Mick kissed his cheek and was prepared to scoot off the sofa when his hand wound into her curls and he kissed her hand.

"You'll have to make up for this with interest, you know?"

Her lashes almost fluttered over sheer anticipation at his words. "I've got no doubt."

"Coming!" Mick sang as she sprinted through the foyer once ring number four had silenced. She pulled open the door while counting the money Quest had given her. "Sorry about that, we-"

The explanation quelled on her tongue. The hand holding the money now dangled at her side. The man on the other side of the door had definitely not come bearing pizza and drinks. He was almost as black as the night surrounding him with the exception of the bronzed face and gleaming grin that appeared as dangerous as the rest of him.

Instinct kicked in, making the fine hair along Mick's neck stand up and take notice. She wouldn't step back and openly admit to her unease but was ready to bolt at the slightest move the visitor made. She'd met with enough of the dangerous and unsavory in her lifetime to recognize one in her presence regardless of how much his looks overshadowed the fact.

She did at last manage to locate her voice. "Yes?"

"Quest Ramsey."

"And you are?" She tried to match the level of steel in her voice with that of the man who requested her husband.

Quest rounded the corner of the foyer before either Michaela or the mystery guest could speak. Immediately, his gaze narrowed in recognition and obvious suspicion. Without sparing Mick a glance, he headed for the door and tugged her behind him with he got there.

The man's grin broadened, adding an increased danger to his expression. "Jesus, Q," he breathed then and tilted his head to scan Mick's face and body with a look of unmasked appreciation.

Quest smiled then but his pitch stare remained focused and probing. "Mick, this is Hilliam Tesano. Hill, my wife Michaela."

Hill nodded his smile and expression taking on a less intimidating current. "Pleasure Michaela," he extended a hand.

She accepted. "Call me Mick."

"And I insist you call me Hill." He waited for her nod, then released her hand and waved his own behind him toward the night. "Q? Can we talk?"

Quest nodded and watched Hill move off into the shadows. His expression softened and he turned back to Mick who held the hem of his T-shirt in a death grip.

"It's alright."

"Like hell." She spat, her instincts on full alert as she frowned out into the blackness beyond her door.

"I'll scream if I need you to come save me," he promised and brushed his mouth across her forehead.

"Quest-"

"Shh…go on inside. I'll be there in minute. Go on." He tapped her bottom to send her on her way and followed the gesture with a sly wink.

Mick allowed herself to be bustled off like a good little wife but refused to leave the foyer when the door closed at her husband's back. She took a seat on the stairway and waited.

"Runnin' late, aren't you? I scrapped weapons a few weeks ago." Quest noted when he and Hill were leaning against opposing tree trunks in the front yard.

"Weapons, Q?" Hill stroked his jaw; his tone of voice bordered on laughter. "Such talk for old friends. Could it be I came to congratulate you on your marriage since I was unable to come to the wedding?" He reached into a back pocket on his sagging denims and extracted a pack of Black and Milds. "To this day, I still can't figure how my invite got lost in the mail."

"Cut the bullshit. What the fuck are you doin' here-come to talk me into changin' my mind?" Quest tacked on when he glimpsed Hill's smile in the firelight as he struck a match for his cigarette.

After a few deep drags, Hill rested his head back against the trunk. "Not at all. If anything, I came to talk you into *not* changing your mind."

Quest's silence was instruction enough for Hill to continue his explanation.

"Your rep for being a goody two shoes in business has finally pushed quite a few folk over the teetering edge into full blown dislike of you."

Quest pushed off the trunk. "I got enough friends."

"And your new enemies are aware of that." Hill took another drag from the long brown stick of nicotine. "That doesn't mean they won't seek ways to…encourage you to reconsider your decision."

Quest had strolled a ways off from the trees but turned at Hill's last words.

"What I'm saying is that you got a lot of folks scramblin' to find a new home for weapons manufacture, storage, research…folks in my family especially might get sloppy." There was a lengthier drag from the Black and Mild. "We're actually counting on it."

"We?"

"This could be just the in we need to start bringin' down the whole fuckin' mess."

"We, Hill?"

He cast a look across his shoulder toward the house and then stepped closer to Quest. "No one knows Caiphus and I are trying to do this."

"Caiphus?" Quest recognized the name of the youngest son of Roman and Imani Tesano."

Hill walked to the curb and tossed the cigarette butt to the street. "Pike and Smoak think we're scum and they need to keep on thinkin' that." He flattened the butt beneath the heel of his Timberland. "They need to think we're in league with them up to our damn foreheads, Q."

"Why?" Quest breathed, now standing on the curb as well.

"They just do."

"Why'd you come here to tell me this, Hill? House calls aren't your style."

"I think you know." A sliver of moonlight illuminated the grin that crinkled the corner of Hill's very deep gaze. "Everyone looks to you to get things gone. Everyone aspires to be like Q Ramsey. Hell if I weren't so content on bein' a scoundrel I'd try it myself." He took a moment to chuckle then turned serious again. "Listen, I don't know what Pike knows but I know Smoak has somethin' brewin. I can't have my brothers' good deeds getting in the way here. They wouldn't exactly approve of the way Caiphus and I…handle things."

Quest's expression sharpened with a dangerous intensity. "You expect me to report to you?"

"I expect you to do what has to be done to shut down Ramsey Weapons and quickly. I also expect-*hope*-you'll trust me as it may eventually pertain to certain… treasures."

Crystal clarity hit Quest then and he tilted his head back. This time, it was him who cast a quick glance across his shoulder at the house in the distance. "I'll tell you what I told your brother- one hair- *one* harmed on their heads and I go after all four of you. To hell with any Tesano family revenge plots y'all got goin'."

Hill's nod was solemn. "They're safe, Q."

"Hmph, you'll forgive me if the word of a Tesano means less than shit to me where my cousins are concerned. One hair, Hill. I mean if a bird so much as swoops down and swipes a fuckin' lock, it's your ass."

As his word meant less than shit, Hill offered no verbal response. Instead, he extended his hand and offered a grim smile when Quest accepted the shake.

***

At last, they were enjoying a delicious pizza feast (with soda and cinnamon bread sticks) as well as a six pack of Red Stripe between them. They ate in the den and finally decided to watch a political thriller on one of the movie channels. They were relaxed, full and drowsy on the sofa by the time the movie credits began to roll.

Mick wiggled her toes and tried to stretch as best she could with Quest smothering her by his weight.

"Ready for bed?"

Mick could only grunt her confirmation.

Quest eased up over her and began to nibble her lower lip. Mick's lashes fluttered open in time to spot something serious flash across his face.

"What?" She tried to stifle a yawn.

"You look worn out."

A lazy smile curved her mouth. "Not as young as I used to be- that fantastic trip of yours wore me *completely* out."

Quest dipped his head. "You sound happy about it." His nose trailed a gauzy strap of the black and white Babydoll tee she wore.

"It was good. I could sleep for a week but I know that's foolish talk."

Quest smiled and brushed his thumb across the mole above her mouth. "I miss her too," he said in reference to their daughter.

Mick smoothed her hands over his bare chest and linked them behind his neck. "So now it's my turn to ask what's wrong with you?" She asked and spotted the guilt flash in his eyes before he could mask it. "Hey?" She caught his face in her palms before he could turn away. "What is it? You look almost terrified." She laughed at how little sense that made. "Is this about Hill Tesano's visit?" She had to ask anyway.

"Not a bit. Hill Tesano doesn't visit, so his dropping by caught me off guard is all."

Mick lowered her gaze. "Wanna discuss it?"

"Not at all. Not ever."

Mick knew that was the end of things. She'd have to do some pretty nifty prying to get anything out of him about what they'd talked about in her front yard. Worthy of pursuit, Mick admitted she was just too dog tired to focus on it now. Still, her husband's mood- which she'd noticed long before the Tesano house call- was mounting her concern. She said so to her husband and watched as he tried to shrug it off and move away. Mick was having none of that.

"I've watched you like this for a while now. When we started the trip you seemed to snap out of it but now it's back."

Finally Quest allowed her to see the full intensity of his emotions. "There's something I need to tell you." Frustrated, he rubbed his fingers across the rich waves of his close cut hair. "I can see you need to rest though and we can talk in the morning."

"I'm fine to talk now." She spoke amidst another yawn.

"In the morning, alright?" He smoothed back a curl that hugged her ear.

It was Michaela's turn to look uneasy then. "You know um…there was something you said the night before we left for the trip. When we were…on the patio."

Quest nodded lowering his head to gnaw her shoulder while memories of the erotic scene replayed in his mind.

"You said everything you do is for me- that you'd never hurt me."

"You're my life." Quest raised his head. "I'd give mine for yours-no question- no hesitation."

Mick pressed her lips together and prayed her eyes weren't shimmering with tears. "I guess that means you're not going to tell me you're having an affair, huh?"

The somberness left Quest's soulful hazy stare and was replaced by humor. Laughter soon followed resonating from the depths of his chest. Propping his elbow on the sofa cushion, he braced his forehead against his fingers while his eyes traced every inch of her face.

"Don't you know by now that I'm no good for anyone else?"

Before Michaela could answer, she moaned feeling the stiff extent of his sex against the heart of her.

"That doesn't happen for anyone but you whether you're right in front of me or an image in my head. You're everything to me."

Mick's lashes fluttered again. "I'm sorry." She shuddered.

"It's okay," Quest dropped a kiss to her temple. "You're entitled to say something stupid every other week or so. Now shut up so I can have my way with you."

"I thought I needed rest."

"Later."

Her mouth was captured then in a swift deep kiss. His tongue mimicked the thrusting motions of his hips. Mick wrapped her legs around his lean waist ready to take all he wanted to give.

"No please…" she moaned her disappointment when he broke the kiss and pulled her from the sofa. "Quest-"

"Shh…"

"What are you doing?" She braced against his hold upon her wrist. She wasn't at all certain she could wait until they travelled upstairs to her bedroom.

Muttering a low curse, Quest picked her up and deposited her on the futon some twenty feet from the sofa.

Realization rushed forth. Memories of the first time she saw Quest Ramsey standing in her den- memories of needing him to take her anyway he wanted on the very futon she sat upon.

"Since you're selling the place, I guess we better go on and break this thing in, right?"

She nodded obediently. "Right."

Quest's left dimple sparked in response to her giggling once he'd angled his bare foot beneath the front of the futon and pulled in into the flat position.

Eagerly, Mick moved to loosen the ties at the bodice of the black and white floral print Babydoll. Quest stopped her, preferring to remove the naughty piece of lingerie himself. Removing it however, seemed to be the last thing on his mind. His kisses seared her body through the satiny material. She arched fiercely when his lips grazed past the flyaway cut of the garment to touch her skin.

Quest wound his fingers around the waistband of her matching bikinis but chose to leave them in place at her hips. Mick was practically out of her mind with desire and sobbed when she felt his tongue invade her sex through the crotch-less underwear. Every part of her trembled and only served to stroke his ego. Several times, he raised his head to savor the display of emotion on her lovely dark face. She could barely gasp his name when he held her bottom snug in his palms and fed upon her as though he were starved.

He pleasured her to a devastating orgasm and continued to drive his tongue deep inside her even as she quivered beneath him and begged him to wait. Mick didn't even realize he'd stripped her of her things until her eyes fluttered open and she caught sight of the lingerie tossed carelessly on the floor.

He gave her no time to recover from the exquisite climax. He flipped her to her stomach to lavish her back and bottom with the same erotic attention from his tongue. She was thoroughly limp with desire and pliable to his hands. He pulled her up and back next to his chest then. He didn't bother with fully removing his loose black cotton sweats and only took time to free himself and plunge his shaft into the part of her that he; and he alone, commanded.

Burying his face in her fragrant curls, Quest took her from behind. Mick squeezed his hands as his fingers manipulated her firm nipples. The entire lower level of the house was alive with the sounds of their pleasure.

Much later, in the midst of a smattering of clothes, the lovers dozed content and completely satisfied.

CHAPTER TEN

Michaela took a moment to get her bearings when she woke the next morning. She lay on her stomach raking her fingers through her curls and smiling as the memories replayed from the previous evening spent breaking in the futon she rested on.

"Quest?" She called, knowing he couldn't be far and wanting to interest him in one more romp before getting up for the day.

"Quest?" She groaned when she finally decided to try and track him down.

It didn't take long for her to determine he wasn't downstairs after she'd left the den and peeked in a few rooms on the lower level. When her search of the second floor proved to be just as futile however, her curiosity began to mount.

Mick pulled open the front door and surveyed the yard, but the Denali was there parked in the driveway right where they'd left it the day before. As she was only attired in the Afghan taken from across the back of the sofa, a more thorough search of the grounds wasn't possible just then.

Forcing her curiosity not to mesh into concern, she closed the door and leaned against it for a while. She noticed the message light flashing on the phone and couldn't be sure if it'd been blinking when they'd arrive the previous day. It could've been a new message from Quest.

"One way to find out," She sighed and headed over to check what turned out to be over ten messages.

There was one from Shelly Manders, the real estate agent coming by later that morning. Next, was the first of what turned out to be twelve messages from Contessa. The messages only consisted of County uttering a quick 'call me Mick.' But with each passing message, those three words gained intensity.

"Probably calling to bitch about the wedding," Mick rolled her eyes and simply deleted her friend's urgent requests. She checked the clock on the phone and figured she'd better hit the shower if she was going to be ready to meet the realtor.

Casting one last look at the front door, she figured Quest probably went for a run or something. For the life of her, she couldn't imagine the man needing more of a workout than the one he'd put in the night before. Smiling naughtily at the thought, she sprinted up the stairs.

Quest had indeed put in a workout and one his wife would witness soon enough when she saw the state of her gazebo. He woke that morning, intending to make breakfast for them and then dive into the heavy conversation they needed to have. He decided to let her sleep in until breakfast and then recalled the realtor coming and chose to push back the talk until the afternoon. He was about to scramble eggs, when he opted to grab the paper first. He found *The Times* on the hood of the Denali and grabbed the mail that had followed him unopened halfway around the world.

Quest barely made it back inside the house. His legs were as weak as twigs when he tore through the box and found his own personal copy of "Royal Ramsey" by Michaela Sellars. Though part of him was impressed by her nerve, it was unfortunately, a very small part. It was too small of a part to override the rage that began a slow rumble in his gut before it churned up to ramming speed.

As if in a daze, he took the book and headed around the side of the house and towards the backyard. His handsome dark face harbored an element that overshadowed the allure of his appearance with something more menacing. Being defied wasn't a thing he was familiar with. The fact that it was Michaela who had defied him, was almost incomprehensible. There was no premise for this and he had absolutely no idea what to do with the frustration welling up inside him.

Well…he'd known what to do with *some* of it. The massacred gazebo was proof of that. Sadly, the relish he'd taken in tearing apart the elegant structure only served to stimulate the rage. Afterwards, he sat amidst the shredded planks of wood and turned the book over in his hands. He traced Mick's photo on the back cover and closed his eyes as if meditating- trying to will the anger to cool. It didn't help. Instead, he tore the jacket from the hardback and watched it land amongst the debris around what was left of the gazebo. Rising to his feet, he stormed off with the book in hand.

***

Michaela felt she'd done a professional and gracious job during her meeting time with the realtor which was approaching the hour mark. This was quite commendable especially since her mind was almost totally centered on Quest who she hadn't seen yet that day. He hadn't returned when she'd come downstairs after her shower. The Denali was gone, so she tried to call his cell phone but received no answer. The message light wasn't blinking, so he hadn't tried to call her. For a split second she wondered if his vanishing act could've been about the strange visit from the mysterious and dangerous-looking Hill Tesano. She shook off the thought, instinctively knowing it was about far more than that. Unfortunately she had no clue about what *that* was.

Thankfully, Shelly Manders arrived promptly at eleven a.m. eager to view a house in the development she'd often admired.

"This area could even be used as an upper level lounge." Shelly remarked on the attic while jotting possible selling points in her notebook.

"Mmm…I thought of using it for a library once," Mick idly agreed while looking up and around the spacious dim area. "I've only gotten around to using it for storage." She said, spotting two small boxes in a corner near the stairway.

"Left behind from the move?" Shelly asked, having spotted the boxes as well.

Mick brushed away cobwebs and gasped when she noticed Driggers' name on both. "No," her voice was soft in a reverent sort of way as she traced Driggers' familiar scrawl upon the boxes. "They um…they belonged to a dear friend who passed away a-a few years ago." Her fingers lingered over the boxes- one labeled *letters*, the other *photos*.

"Well I do believe I've gathered enough info for my prelim portfolio." Shelly could tell the boxes and the person they belonged to were bringing round a wave of heavy emotion for her new client. "I may want to take another look around again soon, but for now I think I'll be saying good day to you."

Mick stood with the boxes in hand. "I'll arrange to have duplicate keys sent to your office. That way you can come and go as you please."

"Oh that'd be great," Shelly's tanned face beamed with excitement. She was thrilled by the opportunity to show such a lovely home and continued to chat on it while she and Mick made their way out of the attic.

"I don't even think it'll take a month to sell the place." Shelly was predicting as they walked into the kitchen. "It's charming inside and out."

Mick blew a curl from her forehead while setting Driggers' boxes to the marble counter top. "Thanks Shelly. I feel good about putting the place in your hands."

"Oh goodness…" Shelly was tugging a lock of her shoulder length red hair behind her ear. "What happened there?"

The hushed surprise in Shelly's voice sent Mick to frowning. She turned to look in the direction the realtor stared past the sliding glass doors leading to the backyard.

"A gazebo, isn't it?" Shelly noted the feature in her book. "Prime selling point, but it'll need to be repaired before-"

Mick was already out the doors and racing toward the damaged structure. Her mouth was a perfect O and as wide as her eyes as she stared in wonder. Heavy planks of wood seemed to have been peeled right off the once beautiful shelter.

"Should we call the police?" Shelly was slightly out of breath, having raced out after Michaela.

Mick couldn't answer, still in shock as she continued to survey the damage. She caught sight of what looked to be a crumpled paper and realized it was the jacket for "Royal Ramsey".

"God," her heart somersaulted clear to her throat as her legs lost their strength.

"Michaela what-"

Unable to tend to Shelly's concern then, Mick only raised her hand to plea for more silence.

"We're gonna have to um…finish this another time Shelly." Mick calmly and finally told the woman.

"You don't look so good Michaela."

That's an understatement lady. At last Mick was able to brace her hands to her knees and push herself to stand. It took some doing, but she was finally able to assure Shelly that everything was fine and that she'd take care of it. Alone then, Mick decided to return County's calls.

Hearing Michaela's voice on the other end of the line had County thanking God in one voice and cursing her friend in the other.

"Do you know how crazy I've been? Where the hell do you get off not returning my calls for damn near a month?!"

"Would you just cool it? I'm returning them now. What the devil is going on?" Mick practically groaned the question as she already knew the answers. She could hear County on the line softly urging herself to calm before going into the full story.

"Somehow Quest's name was left on the manifest for a preview copy of "*Royal Ramsey*".

Mick closed her eyes and slid down the wall with the phone clutched in her hand.

"He could get the book anytime girl."

"He already has." Mick sounded as though she were talking to herself. "Shit County how'd this happen? What the hell were you thinking?"

"Now just hold on a damn minute. This was an error that would've never been made if you hadn't tried to be Billie Bad-Ass and publish the thing after bein' told not to!"

"And don't *you* go forgetting you were right there to publish it for me. It didn't take much persuasion to get you to go along with it."

Silence covered the line for several heavy moments.

"This isn't helping." County muttered a curse.

Mick did the same. "You're right."

"You just said Quest already knows. What happened?"

"I um, I haven't seen him." Mick fidgeted with the scoop collar of her black Henley sweater. "He was gone when I woke up this morning."

"God Mick what are you gonna do?"

Mick's shuddery breathing was the only response she could provide.

"Will you be alright?"

"I'll be fine. It'll be fine- everything'll be fine." Mick knew she was trying to convince herself as much as

County. "I'll just talk to him when he gets here. It'll be fine once we talk."

"But what if-"

"County *please*, please alright?" Mick rose to her feet with resolve on her face and in her voice. "We'll talk and that'll be that. He'll understand why I needed to do this and that his word isn't law- not when it comes to me."

"Brave words," County let the phrase hang on the air for a time. "Will you be able to say them to Quest?"

"We'll see. I gotta go."

***

After talking with Contessa, Mick settled herself in the den and went through the box of Driggers' old photos. She hoped they'd ease her mind and her nerves. Her hopes were fulfilled- at least for the first two hours. Mick delved into the chore of cleaning the house- a task that worked off her frustration and calmed her for another hour at least.

Following a second shower, she shaved off another two hours watching a movie in her bedroom. Around six thirty, she decided to stop fooling herself and took up residence on the front stairway. She watched the door for her husband and the confrontation he was sure to bring with him. Her skin was riddled with gooseflesh but she dared not move to grab a sweater to cover the coral tankini she wore with fading jeans. She'd never relished confrontation- least of all with her husband.

She heard his key scratch the lock just before seven. The words she'd rehearsed all afternoon fled her mind at the sight of him. Haggard; was a mild observation. The olive green Adidas sweatshirt and pants were heavily wrinkled and looked to be sprinkled with dirt and brush. The shadow of a beard darkened the lower half of his face. No surprise there as he hadn't shaved the previous two days either. Mick recalled telling him it was sexy, now it just made him look dangerous.

The setting sun streamed through the windows along the foyer ceiling and gave the area an ethereal allure that was anything but soothing. Mick stood and watched him cross the foyer. Quest's expression was closed, dark…unreadable. Never had she seen him appear so cold. She smoothed clammy hands across the seat of her jeans. No, confrontation had never been something she'd relished and that fact was amplified when she whispered his name and saw despise in his pitch stare.

"Remind me to have you sign this for me." His voice was soft and cool yet carried the distinct undercurrent of rage.

Mick retreated a step when he waved the book before her face on his way up the staircase.

"Quest? Quest please let me talk to you."

"Not now."

"I need to tell you why."

He continued on up the stairway. "I don't want to hear it Michaela."

"Quest please-"

"I don't want to hear it!"

The sheer force of his roar caused her legs to water and she dropped to the stairway trembling violently.

Quest's entire body shook as well. He stopped on the first floor landing and slammed the book against the wall nearest him.

"Pack up. We leave in the morning." He said and then he was gone.

Somewhere in the distance, Mick heard him slam a door. The tiny muffled sound of her crying filled the lower level soon after.

***

The flight to Las Vegas was thankfully void of conversation but the tension stirring between Quest and Michaela filled the void nicely. Even the flight crew seemed to sense that all was not kosher between the couple. As a result, they kept their visits to the passengers few and brief.

Mick kept her eyes on the passing clouds outside the small windows in the main cabin. Her skin tingled as if pricked by a thousand needles and she knew without a doubt that he watched her. She didn't need to make eye contact to know his gaze raked her face and body with a mixture of simmering rage and…something she couldn't quite finger. Disappointment, maybe? She let her lashes flutter and clenched her hands to resist smoothing them along the cotton sleeves of her navy flare leg jumpsuit.

Whatever lay in Quest's look, it was just as powerful and more unsettling than words could ever be. Three times, she tried to drink the bottled water she'd requested. Each time, her hand shook so badly she had to set the bottle aside.

Finally, she dug up the courage she knew she had stashed somewhere and met his narrowed onyx stare with defiance shimmering in her brilliant amber one.

"How long are you gonna try to rattle me Quest?"

His eyes narrowed further while a smirk began to curve his mouth. Mick saw no humor fueling the gesture. When he stood, she willed herself not to react when he curved his hands over the arms of her chair.

For a time, he only leaned across her- head bowed eyes closed. Michaela almost whimpered she was so hungry for his attention- his gentleness. She allowed herself to believe he was softening and courageously nuzzled her cheek into his.

"Quest please…" she inhaled the crisp scent of soap and cologne on his skin and curved her fingers at the collar of the sandstone shirt that hung outside his dark trousers. "I need to tell you why, please…" her mouth brushed the corner of his.

She was seconds from kissing him when he jerked her hand from his shirt and set her back against the seat.

No hint of the beckoning gray showed in his eyes. Any trace of softness was gone. "You don't want to talk to me about this now." He said. "Trust me. Trust me."

Mick waited until he moved away. Then she allowed tears to pool her eyes.

***

Sabra Ramsey was accustomed to having all eyes on her. Tall and curvaceous; with a mane of wavy black falling to her waist, the stunning thirty one year old had the no nonsense aura of a woman far older. Sabra would be the first to tell anyone she'd learned her lessons young, but she'd learned them well.

Coolly, she both acknowledged and dismissed the interested and downright blatantly lustful stares she drew. Her wide light brown gaze sparkled when she saw the two people she wanted to greet in the lobby of her hotel/casino.

Squealing, she ran towards Quest and Michaela and enfolded them in a double hug. She was so elated; she didn't notice how loose the couples' return embraces were.

"Oh I've missed you guys so much! We're gonna have such a good time, I've got it all set. Mama's away on one of her spa weeks so we won't have to worry about her being in our hair either. Oh I can't wait to show off all the changes I've made since y'all visited a few years ago."

"Any of these changes include new employees?" Quest asked his voice low and monotone.

"Damn right." Sabra confirmed and leaned close to press a happy kiss to her cousin's cheek.

"I want to see paperwork on all your new hires."

Sabra rolled her eyes. "I really don't think my new people have anything to do with those calls, Q."

"But you don't know for sure?"

"Well I can't be-"

"I'm gonna check in and I'll see you in your office. One hour."

"Well hello to you too," Sabra called to Quest's back as he walked off without a backward glance. "Who planted a stick inside *his* ass?"

"That would be me," Mick groaned and scrubbed her face in her palms.

Concern replaced Sabra's curious expression and she clamped a hand on Mick's shoulder. "What's goin' on? What happened?"

"He's furious with me."

"Bullshit." Again, Sabra rolled her eyes. "You guys are perfect. Beyond perfect."

Mick could only sigh as she blinked and looked up at the elaborate maze of escalators that crossed the lobby's high ceilings. Clearly, she was trying to keep more tears from sliding to her cheeks.

"Hey?" Sabra drew Mick close. "Come on with me."

"Okay just let me-" Instinctively, Mick turned with intentions of waving goodbye to her husband but he'd already left the front desk. The simple, cold feeling of being dismissed killed her a little more inside.

Sabra shared her twin cousins' love of extensive work space. She occupied the entire top floors of dual scrapers that bore her name. One was for business- the other for living. Both were spectacular.

"Hold my calls!" She yelled to her flustered assistants and ushered Michaela inside her private office. "Now what the hell is going on? He looks murderous." She demanded once the doors were closed on her assistant's inquisitive stares.

Mick slouched back on a burgundy suede sofa and groaned. "I need a drink."

"You got it." Sabra headed for the juice bar.

"Anything alcoholic."

Sabra halted. "Mick alcohol won't solve-"

"Dammit Sabra!"

"Alright, alright!" She cried and raced to the office door. "I don't keep it in here." She explained. "Lee Lee, bring me a vodka-straight." She sent an assistant to handle the order.

Now Mick was slumped forward on the sofa. Her elbows rested on her knees and her hands were hidden in the unruly blue black curls covering her head.

"Do you know why I came to Seattle back when I first met Quest?"

"Yeah," Sabra folded her arms over the obscenely snug capped-sleeve top she wore. "You were doing a book on the family or something."

"Mmm hmm- a book he didn't want me to write."

"*And*?" Sabra prodded when Mick's gaze slid off into the distance.

"*And*, it's written, it's out, your cousin has a copy and he's furious."

"I see…" A rare moment of speechlessness ensued for Sabra. A soft knock on the door helped her regain her composure. It was the assistant with the Vodka.

"So what now?" Sabra passed Mick the tall drink. "Did you guys have a fight?"

The clear liquid practically burned a hole in Mick's chest but she braved the fire and downed a healthy bit. "Hmph-fighting's not your cousin's style."

"Don't I know it?" Sabra closed her eyes as if realization were setting in. "He can be one scary mutha. Everybody in the family practically jumps when he speaks-like he's Gandhi or somebody."

In spite of her upset state, Mick couldn't help but laugh. Sabra not only had the gift of gab, but an intensely wicked comedic streak. Mick couldn't put into words how much she treasured it just them. Sadly, the humor faded much too soon.

"He won't even let me talk to him- explain…he just watched me in that angry, quiet way of his. I hate it." She swallowed another bit of Vodka. "And I hate not having the guts to stand up to him."

"Hell girl, join the club." Sabra slid into a chair and threw a leg across one of the arms. "In Q's defense though, me and my cousins practically put the crown on the boy's head. He's lived all his life cleaning up our messes. Lotta responsibility with no time-no *one* to really talk to about his *own* messes. He just puts that quiet guard in place and deals with it."

"Until he just explodes?" Mick finished, taking a longer swig of her drink then.

Sabra simply shrugged.

"To hell with that," Mick coughed on the Vodka still burning her chest and stood. "I'm not one of his screwed up family members." She winced. "Sorry."

Sabra stood as well. "Forget it. But you're family sista and in Quest's opinion that makes you just as *screwed up* and in need of guidance as the rest of us."

"Damn that." Bravely, Mick drained the contents of the glass cooler. "How'd y'all let him get away with that all these years?"

Sabra's dark face harbored a somber expression then. After a while, she strolled toward the windows and stared out over the hectic beauty of Las Vegas. "Person comes to pull you out of the ugliest times in your life, you don't ask for details on how he's gonna do it. You just let him and you're thankful he was there."

"Well no one was there for me." Mick had come to stare out the windows as well. "And Quest Ramsey can forget it if he thinks I fought my way through hell to give up who I became when I landed on the other side."

CHAPTER ELEVEN

Sabra refused Michaela a second drink once she discovered Mick had nothing to eat since the day before. She took Mick to her suite and arranged for a hearty meal to follow. When Sabra returned to her office, she found Quest there. He looked quite at home seated behind her desk. Sabra could only stand a few moments of watching her assistants trotting to and fro doing her cousin's bidding. The bitches never moved that eagerly for her, Sabra coldly acknowledged.

"Make yourself at home." She slammed her office door.

"Thanks." Quest never took his eyes from the papers he studied.

Sabra decided to help with that. She stalked over to her desk, reached across and snatched the pages from his hand.

"Why don't you go upstairs and talk to your wife instead of snooping into my business?"

But for leaning back in the chair and massaging the bridge of his nose, Quest appeared completely unfazed. "Didn't you call Seattle upset because you had Tesanos on your phone?"

"I called Ty."

"Wanting her to ask us what was going on."

"Yes. So?"

"So that's what I'm trying to find out." He gave a flip wave toward the papers cluttering her desk. "How thoroughly have you checked out all these new people you've brought on board?"

"*Very* thoroughly," Sabra spoke through clenched teeth, her wide gaze impatience-filled. "Now why don't you go upstairs and handle Mick?"

Quest stood. "I handle her just fine."

Sabra was unfettered. "Mmm hmm and the way you're going, you're gonna *handle* yourself right out of a wife."

"Don't worry." Quest stroked his jaw and moved closer to his cousin. "This isn't you and Smoak we're talkin' about here."

The words were as hard as a blow and the impact was reflected in Sabra's devastated expression. She stiffened and looked up at the ceiling while Quest bowed his head in regret.

"I'm sorry."

She shook off his apology. "S'okay."

"No it's not. This has nothing to do with you." Quest pushed a lock of hair across her shoulder. "I really am here to help and you're right- this is probably unnecessary. According to Pike and his dad that call had nothing to do with you."

Sabra blinked. "They were looking for Smoak?" her voice caught a bit on the name. "Is he alright?"

Quest was already nodding. "He's fine-talked to Quay just recently." He watched her bracing as though she were absorbing the news and squeezed her arm. "I'm gonna get out of your way here, but we'll talk later alright?"

"Mmm hmm…Quest? Please talk to Mick."

"Don't worry." He kissed her forehead and walked out.

Sabra found no reason to put much stock in the way he delivered the phrase.

***

That evening, Quest and Mick joined Sabra for dinner in one of her hotel restaurants. Talk revisited the Tesano situation and whatever calm Sabra had been enjoying vanished like mist.

"He can't come here. He just can't." Sabra's voluminous mahogany gaze was wide with apprehension as she bumped her chin against the hands clasped tight before it.

"If he does, you'll deal with it. He'll be gone soon, I'm sure. You'll survive."

Michaela and Sabra looked over in unison toward the man calmly browsing the menu. If stares could kill, Quest would have been on the floor.

Mick turned back to Sabra and reached over to squeeze her wrist. "Though I wouldn't have said it in a way that made me sound like such an asshole, he does have a point, Hon."

Despite her worry, Sabra actually smiled over the quick flash of surprise and- was it, hurt? That stirred in her cousin's dark eyes. "Thanks Mick, but…you don't know how it went down between us. If he shows up here, it wouldn't be pretty." She straightened then and tossed her heavy tresses. "I've brought this place too far to let some old drama put a shadow over it."

Quest set aside his menu. "Sabra, like I said-"

"Would you just shut the hell up?" Michaela's voice was little more than a hiss.

Sabra felt her earlier amusement give way to a feeling of distinct unease. She'd seen the expression Quest now wore enough times to know that things were about to become undeniably ugly between her cousin and his wife.

Mick was already pushing away from the table. "Good night Sabra, we'll talk in the morning."

"Oh Mick don't-" Sabra replaced her word with a sigh as she watched her storm off. Before she could turn to blast Quest, he was out of his chair and storming off as well.

Mick had already detoured into a casino bar located a short distance from the restaurant where they'd dined with Sabra. She could scarcely believe those were her words at the dining table- but they were. She wouldn't deny how good it made her feel to say them.

Quest took up residence leaning against one of the columns that lined the entryway to the tiny pub. He chose to be patient and allow her one drink- all her tolerance level could handle. Muscles flexed noticeably along his jaw when more than a few men strolled up to offer her more drinks at their expense.

Mick refused their proposals, choosing to pay for her own spirits. When she requested her third refill, Quest left his post.

Folding a hand on either side of her along the bar rim, he dipped his head close to hers. "What the hell are you doin'?"

"Drinking," Mick offered the bartender a dazzling smile and reached for her glass.

Quest intercepted it. "You don't drink."

"Hmph, and you just know so very much about me, don't you?"

Quest slammed the drink to the bar unmindful of the contents sloshing over his hand and silver wristwatch. Grabbing the back of the barstool, he whirled her around to face him.

"Damn straight, I do."

Exotic amber clashed with bottomless obsidian as their gazes held. The emotion there quickly mellowed from anger into something more basic. Mick blinked watching his stare drop to her bosom which threatened to heave right beyond the confines of the square bodice of her knit top.

The warmth between them unfortunately iced over and quickly.

"Let's go." He said and moved away from the barstool to allow her up.

Setting her head at a stubborn angle, Mick leaned back against the bar rim and silently refused.

Quest moved in closer than he'd been before. "Get up or I get you up."

Try it was on the very tip of her tongue. She was almost mad with the need to have it all out right there and be rid of what felt like a year's worth of tension. Across Quest's shoulder though, she noticed a few men looking curiously upon them. She remembered what he'd done to her gazebo and knew he'd tear into any well meaning rescuers like fire into paper.

Of course, she intended to hold onto some shred of badness and wrenched her arm from his hand when he meant to help her from the stool.

***

If Michaela had ever wondered whether Quest's chivalry was genuine or a put on to get her into bed, then she had her answer when they returned to the suite. In spite of his mood; which even his cool demeanor couldn't hide, he remained the gentleman.

Michaela bristled when he pressed a guiding hand to the small of her back as she preceded him through the door. Mick wanted to kick herself for feeling even the slightest tingle at his touch. No surprise she couldn't help it. She missed him in every way.

They passed through the elaborate quarters in silence. There were still a few things Mick wanted to unpack and she set off to do just that. When Quest walked into the bedroom twice only to leave each time without so much as a grunt in her direction, Mick felt her temper rise. When he grabbed the blanket and extra pillow from a closet; with clear intentions of sleeping on one of the sofas in the other room, she'd had enough. She was sick of being looked through-ignored. Wicked juices flowing rampant, she was intent on stirring an emotion from him other than the quiet passive anger he'd perfected. As her stunt in the bar hadn't elicited quite the reaction she'd wanted, Mick decided to resume their dinner conversation when he returned to the bedroom to find sleepwear to replace the clothes he'd worn that evening.

"Gosh Sabra's so worried," Mick sighed without looking her husband's way. She pulled a few frilly pieces of lingerie from an overnight bag and laid them across the armchair nearest the bed. "In spite of what happened to

Houston and Daphne, I honestly don't think she's in any mortal danger but it's easy to see she's most preoccupied by Smoak Tesano. Their relationship must've been quite…explosive." Idly removing the toiletries that lay in the bottom of the case, Mick noted Quest watching her and smiled. "I don't think she's got anything to fear from Smoak- least of all Smoak." Her heart lurched when his voice filled the room.

"As usual my cousin isn't thinking straight." He tossed his sleep clothes into the open suitcase nearby. "All she sees is the surface appeal of handling things her own way without taking into consideration all the side effects."

"That a subtle dig at me Quest?"

"I don't know," he slammed down the top of the suitcase then. "Maybe I should give subtle a try since my telling you outright to forget that damn book didn't seem to work."

"*Told me outright*?" Mick spat, whirling around to face him. Her exotic ambers glazed over with anger and disbelief combined. "You're my husband Quest. Not my father. Don't ever forget that. I'm your *wife*, not your brother or your cousins who need the benefit of your exquisite wisdom."

"So what you're telling me is that my concerns over you publishing this thing are unfounded?" The maddening cool of his voice was undeniable.

Mick was too angry to care. "Dammit do you need me to beat you over the head with it? Yes! That's exactly what I'm telling you!"

"Yet you decided to go behind my back to get this done- even though my concerns were unfounded?"

"Because you stifled my handling it any other way! Jesus, why are you being so obtuse about this?"

Quest squeezed his darkened eyes shut then and forbid himself to massage his arm. He *was* being obtuse- frustration over so much…not to mention the fact that he was practically blind with need for her. God, he had to get out of there…

Michaela didn't realize she was holding her breath until she heard him slam the suite's front door on his way out.

The room was quiet when Quest returned an hour later. It was either go back and face his wife or drown his sorrows (and guilt) in drink- a ton of it. His nostrils flared when her perfume led him toward the bedroom. Leaning on the doorjamb, he watched her sleep for a couple minutes before trudging over. He eased down on the bed and toyed with the hair framing her face in midnight ringlets.

Michaela shifted, murmuring something incoherent as she turned to her side. Deftly, Quest trailed the back of his hand along her bare arm which rivaled the satin sheets upon the bed for softness. The room was practically dark, lit only by the shallow light spilling in from the hallway. He didn't need light to guide the trail of his hand which strolled the bend of her elbow before venturing off to outline the curve of her breasts beneath the T-shirt she'd worn to bed.

Mick's incoherent murmurings took on the sound of moaning and she reached for him in her sleep. Her brow furrowed seconds before her lashes stirred and she gasped at the sight of him there above.

"Quest," her voice was low, flavored with uncertainty.

He snapped to and made a move to pull back but her grip on his wrist then was surprisingly strong.

"Mick…" Quest tried to tug his hand free, halting when she scooted close to trail her mouth across his wrist, forearm and higher still. Soon she was inhaling the scent of cologne against his neck.

"Quest please…please I miss you." She nibbled his earlobe amidst the confession. "Don't go," she straddled his lap and cried out when he suddenly clutched her waist and locked his hand around her neck to keep her still for a plundering kiss.

Mick whispered her approval and began to grind on the power swelling below his waist. Her tongue stroked his, along the ridge of his teeth and the roof of his mouth. Her heart beat double time when he weighed and squeezed a breast while gripping her bottom to control her movements on his erection. She could have climaxed from the sheer pleasure of his arousal nudging her aching sex.

She wanted more of course. Hell yes, she wanted more- much more and that was the problem. The communication they shared had been terribly damaged and she wanted back every bit of what they held dear before things had gone so wrong. Dismayed by the fact that her wants might be impossible to attain, she did the unthinkable and pulled his hand from her neck.

The resulting silence spoke for itself. Quest was too stunned to stop her and could only watch as she left the bed and ran from the room.

***

The next morning found Mick standing in speechless wonder as she surveyed the space before her eyes. The studio was grand to say the least with a never ending line of mirrors encasing the walls in glass wonderland.

"Thank you," she breathed.

Sabra stood leaning against the door. A knowing smile curved her full mouth. "I figured you could use a break and the time to let off some steam." She pushed off the door and somehow eased both hands into the back pockets of her very snug-fitting jeans.

Mick gave a slight twirl when she reached the middle of the dance studio. "This is incredible…" her voice sounded awe-filled.

"I guess it'll do." Sabra began to eye the room skeptically. "But I'm willing to bet a kickboxing class would serve you better. You'd probably get a greater workout by pasting my cousin's face to a punching back and beating the shit out of it."

"No Sabra, this is what I need. What I've been missing." Mick confessed even as she slid the woman a wickedly amused look.

"Well then, I'll leave you to it." Sabra clapped her hands once and headed for the doors. "Out of all the practice areas here, my dancers swear by this one, so the place is all yours for the morning." She called cross her shoulder.

Alone, Mick basked in the silence and solitude the sound proofed space provided. In spite of the room's promised serenity, she couldn't stop her thoughts from shifting to Quest. For what had to be the fiftieth time, she cursed herself for turning him away the night before. What was she thinking? Her skin still tingled from the glide of his fingertips against it. She was hoping to make a statement. In the harsh light of day however, she admitted that she couldn't have picked a worse time to make it.

Shaking off her regrets, she ran her hands along the front of the blueberry colored leotard she'd chosen for her workout. Strolling across the quiet room, she went to browse the almost never-ending supply of CDs framing a sound system which boasted the latest technology. She selected a few CDs and set them to the changer- once she'd figured out where the changer was amongst all the gadgets on the elaborate piece of equipment.

Music soon filled the room and Mick took several moments to absorb the unfamiliar swirl of jazz that colored the studio. After a while, she began to move in sync to the music allowing the rhythms to calm her mind and speak to her body. An original routine followed, with Mick using every bit of the considerable space available to her. The performance consisted of jumps, twirls and kicks sure to work off all the frustration that had mounted to overflowing.

Michaela had gone through two CDs and taken three breaks by the time thoughts of a full breakfast began to call to her mind and tummy. She pushed those thoughts away and ordered herself to focus. There was still a ton of tension she needed to work off. She was beginning to consider Sabra's suggestion of a kickboxing class, when the first track off a vintage collection of Luke merged in. Mick gave a silent prayer of thanks as all those distracting thoughts merged…out. In moments, she was in the throes of a strenuous yet sultry routine fueled by the pounding bass and suggestive lyrics.

Quest had left the suite that morning long before Mick woke. Returning to find her gone, struck something inside him whether he wanted to dwell on it or not. It didn't matter. He set off to find his cousin and; after yet another lecture regarding his treatment of his wife, Sabra told him where she was.

The floor that housed the rehearsal studios was quiet thanks to the soundproofing installed throughout the area. Only the soothing hum of air conditioning filled the dim wing. Quest's steps slowed the closer he ventured to the room Sabra had noted. He knocked once, silently acknowledging that she couldn't have possibly heard the pathetic excuse for a knock. Without realizing how on edge he was, Quest breathed deeply and twisted the knob.

A sense of déjà vu washed over him when he peeked inside and found his wife. Memories surged of a long ago afternoon when he'd been treated to a performance that she'd had no idea he was looking in on. Slowly, Quest pushed the door shut behind him and simply watched. Like before, he was entranced and aroused. Like before, he tilted his head this way and that trying to capture every nuance- every movement of her lovely body. *Not* like before however, this time he had intimate knowledge of the pleasure her body was capable of evoking. *Not* like before, he wasn't watching her from a window in a room overlooking her yard. *Not* like before, *this* time, he intended to do something about it.

Michaela's gasp went unheard when she bumped into something warm and unyielding. The Luke CD had ended and the seductive crooning of John Legend chimed in to begin the cool down of the exhilarating work out. When she found Quest standing there, any thoughts of *cooling down…*grew distant.

His mouth came crashing down on hers and the resulting moans were muffled against the volume of the music. He lifted her against him and her legs immediately locked about his waist. Mick shivered on the feel of his denim jeans and the shirt that hung open to reveal the white jersey-T beneath. Desperately her fingers stroked his neck where silky hair tapered off at his nape.

Holding her high against him, Quest carried her to the nearest mirrored wall. Their kissing was passionate madness personified. Quest molded his hands to every part of her encased in the suite she'd danced around in.

Mick's brain was so fuzzy; it took some time to realize that his roaming hands were seeking a way to get the leotard off her body. She assisted, never breaking the kiss while reaching behind her neck to undo the fastening clasps.

Quest took over from there, pulling the material from her body. His brows drew close as he kissed his way down every inch of her that was exposed.

Somewhere in a deep recess of her mind, Mick accepted that this was physical need at its best. Nothing would change because of it, but God how she wanted him. She wouldn't allow the issues resting between them to rob her of this chance.

Quest didn't bother to undress- he didn't think his need would wait long enough. Instead, he freed what hungered for her.

"Quest-" she seemed to hiccup his name as he took her with a beautiful savagery that had both of them wincing from the sheer bliss of feeling.

Mick wanted to rest her head on his shoulder and just take the seeking plunges of his length, but she also wanted more. She met his fire with her own, her legs squeezed his back like a vice. She arched into a bow and allowed her powerful desire for him to numb her mind and beckon her body to take over. Quest's grunts were breathless at times while he chanted her name frequently…helpless to stop.

Somehow they climaxed as one. Quest felt his strength give beneath the potency of it. His hands splayed alongside Mick on the mirrors when the shudders that wracked his body began to ebb.

But for the long breaths between them, there were no other sounds. When Quest withdrew, Mick didn't bother to look his way. She knew the guarded sheen had returned to his haunting stare. They disentangled with an eerie ease and fixed their clothing. Quest left the studio as quietly as he'd entered. When the door closed behind him, Mick eased down to the floor, huddled into a ball and rested her forehead on her knees.

***

Mick felt rested in body if not mind when she met Sabra for brunch. She'd been foolish enough to hope she and Quest could use the purely physical act which had occurred earlier that morning to pave the path toward communication. Those hopes gave way to cowardice when she returned to the suite to change from that morning's workout and found him there- still cold, still distant. They moved around one another in that ridiculously huge room like there were boulders all around that kept them from touching.

"Sorry I'm late girl. I swear this place never stops!" Sabra was breathless when she took her place across from Mick at a table in one of the restaurants inside her hotel.

"You handle it very easily." Mick complimented, draping an oversized linen napkin across the mushroom gauchos she sported.

Sabra propped a fist beneath her chin and narrowed her eyes. "Maybe I should've let *you* handle things on my overnight shift. You look like you hardly got a minute of sleep."

"I won't argue there. The workout in the studio helped, but I'll be much better when I'm back home."

Sabra took Mick's hand once she'd finished raking it through her curls. "Why not stay on here for a while? Let Q go back on his own."

"That's tempting." Mick closed her eyes and smiled. "*Very* tempting."

"Guess y'all didn't talk last night or when he stopped by the studio, huh?" Sabra pretended to be interested in the peek-a-boo ties of her cement colored Henley top.

Mick braced her elbows on the table. "We didn't talk a bit. All these years I've fooled myself into believing I had so much courage…this shows me how little I really have."

"Now you need to stop this." Sabra slapped one of Mick's arms. "Your husband worships you and now he's acting like a damn fool. Any woman would be turned around by this."

"Thanks."

"So? Why don't you stay a while? Put some distance between you."

Mick almost laughed. "We don't need to be in different states to have distance.

"I really just need to see my little girl." Mick said once Sabra had given their orders to the waiter who stopped by the table.

"That'd do you a world of good." Sabra predicted with a refreshing look on her dark face. "Hey! Why don't you bring her out when she's old enough to travel and we can have a girl's weekend- the three of us?"

Mick did laugh then. "You'll be waiting a while for *that* trip. I'm afraid Quinn's not quite ready to play the slots yet."

"Forget the slots. We can sit around and talk shit about all the men we've loved before."

"Mmm…" Mick's lashes fluttered. "That would be interesting. Thanks." She told the waiter who'd arrived with coffee.

"Damn right." Sabra raised her large mug in toast. "We can male bash and eat baby food right out of the jar."

"Ha! Now I know you've gone crazy."

"What? Strained peaches are da bomb!"

Laughter continued well into the delicious brunch. Mick was chewing bacon and laughing over Sabra's comments regarding a men's health conference when her glee was brought to a screeching halt.

"Don't tell me. The fun police just arrived." Sabra dropped her napkin to the knee of her white cargo pants.

As Quest crossed the dining room, Mick thought it was perhaps the first time since she'd known him that she actually dreaded his approach.

"Time to go," Were his words once he stood near the table, hands hidden in the pockets of his charcoal carpenter's pants.

"She needs to eat first."

"We'll be ready to take off in a couple of hours." Quest continued as though Sabra hadn't spoken.

"Well I'm sure they'll wait." Sabra added more volume to her words that time.

Mick kept her head bowed suddenly chilled in the apple blossom capped sleeved tee she wore. Quest allowed softness to touch his expression as he watched her. When at last she looked up, he'd put the coldness back in place.

"I'll be waiting in her office." He cocked his head in his cousin's direction.

Sabra stuck out her tongue as Quest walked off. "I really wish you'd reconsider staying. A few days alone might make him see what a big idiot he's being."

"Thanks Sabra but I really just want to go home." Mick wiped her hands on the napkin and dropped it to her plate. "There're some papers I had sent to Seattle from my place in Chicago. I should go through 'em before I get too lazy." She thought of the two boxes of Driggers' belongings.

"Alright I'll stop pressing." Sabra finished the rest of her coffee. "Just promise you'll come spend a few days if things get too tense at home? 'Your room's always ready at Sabra Ram's'", she quoted her slogan and added a wink.

It felt good to laugh. "I'll remember." Mick promised.

***

Georgetown, VA

Lamont Pevsner sat with his squared chin propped in his palm and an unreadable glint in his eyes. Still, he could do nothing about the small yet humorous smile which played about his mouth.

Inappropriate or not, Lamont always considered it a privilege- a pleasurable privilege to watch one of his loveliest agents when she was unaware that she was being observed. The scant smile he wore twitched just slightly as he imagined the tongue lashing he'd be in for if she ever heard him call her lovely.

"So are we just gonna sit on these or are we gonna generate some mileage from them?"

Lamont's sky blue stare rose from the sensibly shod feet that dangled a few inches above the floor. "What sort of mileage did you have in mind?"

Sybilla Ramsey shuffled through the unassuming tin locked box while scanning the all-important key cards. "Possibilities are endless," her childlike voice was whisper soft as always but with an added tinge of awe.

"Endless… Such as?" Lamont returned to the simple black leather chair behind his desk. He felt the jolt when her stunning slate gray gaze flickered to his face.

Suspicion ignited a furrow in her brow. "Lamont, surely your…brain trust has more ideas than I could ever dream up."

He chuckled while stroking that square jaw of his. "Your confidence in us is overwhelming. We've been tossing around some things." He added when she only glared. "Our best ideas would actually require *your* participation."

"Please," Sybilla rolled her eyes toward the office's low ceiling. "You know I've been dying to get involved with this." Her face took on harshness then. "My devil uncles darkened my family's name for decades. Best vindication would be for a Ramsey to clean up the whole mess." She grimaced at her feet dangling above the short unappealing carpeting and leaned in to plant them firmly on the floor.

Lamont leaned forward as well. "The Ramsey part in all this is pretty much done. Everyone knows who the real culprits were- there's nothing for your to prove Bill."

Hissing a curse; and dragging a hand through the haphazard of clipped waves upon her head, Sybilla stood.

"Thank God Marc and Houston are no longer an issue, but that still leaves the people who gave them power, doesn't it? Until they're finished a Ramsey needs to stay involved." Slender shoulders rose beneath a time worn blazer. "That Ramsey should be me."

Obviously pleased, Lamont nodded. "I'm glad to hear you say that Bill." He waved a hand toward the chair she occupied, urging her to sit. "I hope you'll feel the same once you've got all the details."

Sybilla crossed trouser clad legs and shrugged. "So long as my undercover package is flawless, I'm really to be briefed."

Lamont scratched through his shaggy brown hair then bridged his fingers atop his cluttered desk. "It's the uh…undercover part that might change your mind about coming in on this." He passed her the folder.

Sybilla's unruly boyish cut, framed a face that became a picture of disbelief when she scanned the folder's contents. Somehow, she managed a grin. "You're joking, right?"

***

Going home was the right move, Mick thought when she saw Quincee. Her heart soared and happy tears pressured her eyes when Quinn wiggled in Sonja's embrace.

"My girl…there's my girl." Michaela whispered carefully taking her daughter into her arms. Eyes closed, Mick held Quinn close and inhaled her soothing baby smell.

Sonja was going on about everything she felt the returning parents needed to know regarding how well their daughter slept, ate, played…

Mick only half listened. All that mattered then was holding Quincee close and hearing the baby's delighted cooing in her ear.

"Thank you so much Sonja." Quest was saying and pressed a thick envelope into the girl's hand.

Sonja gasped, spotting the cash inside the envelope. "Mr. Ramsey the- the service already sent the payment for the job."

Quest only squeezed her hand. "As long as you're with the company we want no one else looking after our child. This is just a small bonus for giving us peace of mind while we were away."

Flustered as much by the gesture as she was by the man himself, Sonja nodded and uttered a soft, shaky 'thank you'.

Mick leaned in to kiss Sonja's cheek and squeeze her forearm before heading into the sitting room with Quincee.

Sonja returned upstairs to finish packing her things. Meanwhile, Michaela spent her time playing with Quinn and talking about all the things she saw on the trip. Quest gave mother and daughter their time together. He only paused briefly to kiss Quincee's forehead and tiny mouth, before going to sit on the other side of the room and make calls.

"I've um, I've got a meeting at Ramsey."

Michaela's fingers clenched minutely about Quincee. Her heart lurched at hearing Quest's voice directed her way. Slowly, she moved to put the baby in the bassinette.

"I'll just give you some time with your daughter before you go."

Quest kept his gaze hooded as he watched Mick leave the room. Alone with Quinn, he let the phone drop from his weak hand and massaged the bridge of his nose.

This situation was killing him. All he wanted was to go upstairs, forget everything that happened and talk to his wife. Leaving the arm chair, he went to Quincee and drew her from the bassinette.

"Daddy's made Mommy very sad and he should apologize, but he doesn't quite know how and the longer he takes the worse things get."

Quinn only squealed and cooed, her gray eyes sparkling up into her father's.

As Michaela had done earlier, Quest pressed his nose against Quincee's shoulder and breathed in drawing strength from her soothing smell. He helped himself to more than a dozen kisses before taking Quinn upstairs to the nursery where he helped himself to a dozen more.

Afterwards, Quest ventured into the master bedroom looking for Mick. Instead he found two boxes on the bed and took a moment to inspect them. The box of photos held his attention for several moments. Snapshots of Driggers and Mick- or just Mick alone brought a smile to his face and a rush of warmth and need to the rest of his body. He rubbed a hand across the taupe long sleeved crew shirt that hung outside his pants. A ball of frustration was swelling inside his abdomen and only served to intensify the warm rush of need for his wife.

He moved on toward the bathroom when the sound of running water caught his ears. The smell of her shower gel teased his nostrils the second he looked past the cracked door. Strolling inside, he reached for the robe she had lying across the back of the armchair facing the shower. Taking a seat in the chair, he rubbed the material between his fingers and pressed the garment to his nose. Torturing himself a bit longer, he studied her silhouette against the glass doors of the shower.

Helplessly he watched transfixed by her movements. His dark gorgeous features tightened as the waves of arousal grew more defined. He started to knead the material of the robe as though it were Michaela he held. He was so lost in thought that he didn't realize she'd shut off the shower.

Mick squeezed a few remnants of water from her hair while stepping from the stall. She took a moment to observe her body in the floor length three way mirror near the tub. She was on her way out of the bathroom and using a small dark towel to dry her curls when she saw Quest seated and watching her.

The tiny shriek Mick uttered seemed amplified in the bathroom. Reflexively, she folded her arms over her chest and realized it left the rest of her enticingly bare. Quest made no secret of the fact that he was enjoying the view. Still kneading the robe he held, he shifted in the chair and raked his pitch stare across her body.

For Michaela, maintaining eye contact was impossible. Especially once Quest stood and walked toward her.

"I um…I put Quinn in the nursery. I got this meeting at Ramsey." He stood impossibly close, his expression lost and apologetic as he towered over her. "I'll be there if…if you need me."

Mick barely nodded and kept her eyes on everything except her husband. Quest left the robe on the counter and brushed his fingers across the small of her back in his way out.

Mick spent a little more time playing with Quincee and feeding her before the baby drifted off to sleep. Alone with her thoughts- they were totally centered on Quest's behavior before he left for his meeting.

Was he softening? Was he ready to listen to her? Was he ready to hear her tell him she published that book to remind herself what it felt like to not be smothered by protection or *over* protection as it were? Would he listen to her tell him that she needed to do as she saw fit when she saw fit to do it?

"Stupid…" Michaela hissed silently and called herself a fool.

There was desire in his eyes but no remorse. After all, Quest Ramsey apologized to no one. Why should he when he was always right? Mick left the nursery shaking her head to clear her mind as she returned to the bedroom where Driggers' boxes waited.

She was pleased she'd had the forethought to send them on ahead when they left Chicago. The smile on her face mirrored the one reflected in her eyes when they settled on the box of photos. The snapshots brought back so many wonderful memories. Amidst the wonder however, was the bittersweet aftertaste of regret.

Driggers…if only he were there. He would know how to help her handle this. He'd tell her how to approach Quest. Driggers always knew what to do. Unfortunately, he wasn't there, she acknowledged and set the photos back in the box. Smoothing her arms along the sleeves of her robe, she made a mental note to purchase albums to preserve the pictures.

Next, she moved closer to the center of the bed and turned her attention to the box of papers there. A good lock box would be perfect to keep them protected until she had a better idea of what to do with them. For a while, she shuffled through old news clippings, reviews of her work that he'd saved and other miscellaneous items. Her curiosity peaked just a bit higher when she glimpsed the edge of a page peeking out of an envelope. The words '*Mr. Morgan I wanted to apologize...*' prompted her to pull the sheet from its time-worn packaging and read further.

Mr. Morgan,

I wanted to apologize for the confusion I caused you on last week. It was purely on impulse that I even dared to come there. You were right of course. The time has long passed for me to make any sort of attempts to form a bond or even a communication with someone I treated so horribly.

As I said, it was an impulse as so many things in my life have been. I called myself a fool many times- to believe the name Michaela Sellars on the cover of that book could be the same Michaela- my Michaela...the child I discarded as if she were nothing more than an afterthought. In truth, I never thought to meet her when I visited- only to see her. Only to prove to myself that it was her and that she was fine- doing well. That what I'd done- what Evette Sellars had done hadn't ruined her.

As an older, wiser Yvonne Wilson, I now realize that she's far better off never knowing about any of that. She's far better off thinking I no longer exist. She's so very blessed to have you in her life and I appreciate the time we took to speak. Thank you.

Sincerely,
Yvonne Wilson

But for the slow rise and fall of her chest, Mick didn't move. After a moment, the letter drifted from her loose fingers to settle on the surface of the satin bed comforter. Her hand remained extended as if she still held the brittle page.

Needles began to prickle the soles of her feet as she'd sat kneeling in the middle of the bed for quite some time. Mick registered none of that. At last, she blinked and her eyes fell right to the paper that rested atop all the others.

Time passed slowed for Michaela as she scanned the words again and again. Her body turned cold from devastation.

CHAPTER TWELVE

Quincee woke needing to be changed which was the only thing that jerked Mick from her daze and forced her to leave the bedroom. She performed her motherly duties with the usual love and tenderness. Cozy and content, Quincee drifted back into an innocent slumber while her mother drifted back into a daze.

Instead of returning to the bedroom, Mick went downstairs. Her mind seemed blank yet at the same time it teemed with a collage of thoughts that bumped against one another in a crazed dance. For a time, she sat in the living room looking out over the front lawn but not really seeing anything. She went into the kitchen, opening her refrigerator but taking out nothing. She held open the chrome door and stood, looking in for at least five minutes.

The slow shuffling of her feet led her into the den where she studied the room in an absent manner. Newspapers from the past few weeks cluttered the area around the matching reading chairs and Mick knelt to put them in some type of order. The headline: *Alleged Child Prostitution Leader Gunned Down At Gallery* drew her brows close but for a moment. Faintly, she recalled having heard something about the matter but the lost glint returned to her amber stare and she lost interest in the story.

Finished with the task of straightening the newspapers, Mick sat on the edge of one of the reading chairs and looked around the room. The flashing of the answering machine drew her to her feet. She checked the messages which were few as Quest had handled the chore before he left the house for his meeting at Ramsey.

One message was from County who wanted to talk. Another was from Catrina saying how much she and Damon enjoyed having Quincee and saying how much they'd like to have her again. *You and Quest should get away more,* she'd said.

The shameless request for more time with their granddaughter actually brought a smile to Mick's face. The last message was from Taurus, saying how much he and Nile would like to get together with her and Quest for dinner.

Suddenly, Michaela blinked and her head whipped round to the stack of newspapers. In seconds, the papers were in their former state of disarray. Mick found what she was looking for and began to read feverishly.

"Alleged child prostitution leader Cufi Muhammad was gunned down Thursday at Charm Galleries. Muhammad; wanted for questioning regarding his suspected role in various abductions spanning at least two decades, was shot and killed by his wife Yvonne Wilson as the couple's daughter- renowned artist Nile Becquois- looked on."

Mick pressed the paper to the carpet and hunched over to re-read the write up.

"Jesus," she breathed and then raced from the den.

***

Quaysar Ramsey never thought he'd see the day when his twin could be accused of procrastination. The man had never wasted time getting things done- from homework when they were in school to paperwork when they began the land development division at Ramsey. This uneasy, displaced side of Quest's demeanor was quite surprising indeed. Of course, how Mick took the news, was the first thing Quay wanted to hear of his brother's trip. He could tell Quest was struggling and tried to be understanding as he listened to the excuses.

"...and then I opened up that damned book..."

Quay rolled his eyes toward the copy of "Royal Ramsey" that Quest brought to show him. "And?" He prompted when his brother's explanation drew to a halt. "What Q? Your anger justified you to keep this thing from her a little longer?"

In spite of his unease, Quest was able to spare his twin a deadly glance.

Quay dismissed it like an annoying gnat. "I hope you didn't come down on her for this?" He waved the book in the air.

Quest shrugged. "I didn't *come down* on her at all...that much," he massaged the back of his neck and paced the conference room in the office. "I barely said anything at all to her." He winced and sat on the end of the long pine table. "I hurt her just the same as if I'd spent a week roaring after her over it."

Quay bumped the book against the thigh of his chestnut trousers. He felt his own temper boil over the need to knock some sense into his brother's usually sensible head. Thankfully, the elevator doors opened in the penthouse office and the sound of their meeting attendant's voices stayed his hand. Tossing aside the book, he stepped close to Quest.

"Fix this Q, fix it quick."

***

Nile checked the posts on the backs of her dangling gold earrings as she descended the stairway. The ringing doorbell had her checking the time. Her meeting with Claire Boyer wasn't for another three hours and she hoped there hadn't been a mix-up. Smoothing her hands across the seat of her casual black drawstring pants, she headed to the doors prepared to meet with Yvonne's attorney. Still, she was careful to peek out the secure window to check. Gasping at the sight of her visitor, Nile wasted no time opening the door.

"Michaela."

Barely crossing the threshold, Mick caught Nile's arm in a firm grip. "You knew who I was. You knew when we met at your wedding."

Nile blinked. "Yes." She began to nod as if entranced.

"God," Michaela leaned against the doorjamb. She felt faint.

"Michaela…please- please come in." Nile was already tugging her hand.

Instead, Mick chose to take a seat on one of the cushioned benches in the corridor outside the penthouse entrance. Her dazed expression had returned full-fold. Her amber stare was wide yet blank while focused toward the wall.

Nile left the doorway to join Mick on the bench. Tentatively, she reached for Michaela's hand and smiled when Mick clutched it and squeezed back.

"Mon Dieu, I'm so glad that's over." Nile rested her head back against the wall and smiled up at the ceiling. "I'm so glad you know everything."

"I feel…" Mick smoothed a clammy hand across a jean-clad thigh. "I don't know what I feel."

"Well I know you've got lots of questions." Nile gave Mick's hand a couple of quick squeezes. "There's so much to talk about. I'm so glad Quest finally told you."

A silent moment passed and then Mick; still leaning against the wall, rolled her head over and frowned at Nile. "Quest?"

"We all wanted him to tell you right away but he didn't want to say anything at first and then…" Nile sighed completely thrilled by the turn of events. "I'm just glad he didn't wait too long."

Mick gave Nile's hand one last squeeze before pulling her own free. Drawing keys from the breast pocket on her worn denim jacket, she weighed the jangling mass of keys in her palm and then stood.

"Michaela? Mick?" Confusion registered in Nile's midnight stare as she watched Mick walk back to the elevator and disappear inside.

***

Quest was more than grateful for his brother's handling of the meeting that afternoon. He silently appraised Quay watching as the man addressed concerns during the Q&A portion of the conference. Quay had assumed the role as primary head of their land development division with the same aggressive charm he did everything else. Quest admitted had he known this, he'd have let Quay run the place single handedly long ago.

Of course, Quest realized his twin hadn't just been magically ready for the role. Many factors played a part- the greatest being his wife and sons. Tykira brought the importance- the meaning to his world and Quest could practically see the transformation Quay made to become a man worthy of such love. The twins Dinari and Dakari were the added blessings that continued to nourish Quay's soul with everything good.

Quest thought of his own family then. Michaela and Quincee had brought as much meaning to his life. He'd come alive when he found Mick and he couldn't function without her. Now, there he was treating the one he couldn't function without like she was less than nothing.

What the hell am I thinking? He hissed silently and admitted he had no interest in sitting in a meeting when he should be home begging his wife to forgive his coldness. He was moving to stand from his chair and excuse himself when he saw Mick walk into the room, grab a vase from the credenza behind her and hurl it at his head.

Someone screamed. The decorative porcelain piece missed Quest by mere inches and shattered against the glass encased map on the wall behind him.

"Mick! What the hell?" Quay had recovered before anyone else.

Mick only saw her husband through the rage in her exotic stare. "Hypocritical jackass," she seethed, preparing to accomplish what the vase hadn't.

Quay's reflexes kicked in and he pulled Mick back against him before she charged for his brother. She struggled like a wild cat, her curls flaying wildly about her face and partially shielding her furious glare.

"Get off me!" Her elbow connected with Quay's muscled abs to emphasize her order.

Quay grunted but kept his hold firm on her arms.

"Get off me dammit!"

"Mick what-"

"Get the hell off me Quay!"

Folding an arm about her waist, Quay lifted his sister-in-law clear off the floor and turned to the fourteen people who stood stunned around the conference table.

"Everyone, I'm afraid we're gonna have to adjourn the meeting a little early." He addressed the speechless onlookers as though there were nothing extraordinary about him restraining the infuriated woman in his arms. "You'll all receive an email about rescheduling. We'll talk soon. Good night."

The group wasted no time setting out. Quaysar Ramsey's temper could make a grown man wet his pants but it was nothing next to his twin's. Quest had yet to move or speak.

Quay waited for the room to clear of the execs before he carried Mick to the conference table and perched her on the edge. He patted her knee in a reassuring gesture.

"Now baby just calm down and tell-"

Mick simply slammed her fists into Quay's chest. Wild and still fully enraged, she scrambled down the long table intent on reaching her husband. She got there before Quay could stop her. Her hands curled into the collar of Quest's shirt and she slapped him full and hard.

"Lying bastard! How could you do that?! How could you?!"

"Jesus Mick! Q, what the hell?!" Quay cried once

again pulling Michaela back against him and frowning over the way his brother just sat there looking uncertain and well…terrified.

As Quay held onto her denim jacket, Mick shrugged herself out of the garment and took advantage of her momentary freedom. She'd scrambled halfway back down the table before Quay caught her again.

"Mick dammit now! Calm down, calm down, come on…come on…that's it." Quay pressed a kiss to the top of her head as her struggles ceased. "Now please tell us what's wrong?"

"Why don't you ask your jackass of a brother?" Mick stopped straining but her chest heaved rapidly beneath the red wash worn T-shirt she sported.

"Q?!" Quay fixed his brother with a bewildered look. It unsettled him more than he realized to see an equally bewildered look reflected on his brother's face. Squeezing Mick closer, he nudged his cheek against hers. "Sweetie is this about the book?" Quay prepared to receive another blow to his gut. Surprise registered on his dark face when the sound of her laughter filled the room.

This laugh however held a wicked intensity that matched the glazed fury in the stare turned on Quest.

"The book…" she purred and settled back into her brother-in-law's embrace. "I really don't know about *the book* Quay. This horse's ass hasn't said a damn thing to me since he found out." She shrugged, her mouth curving into a scathing smirk. "But then I guess writing a book you were ordered not to write is so much worse than hiding the truth about someone's mother."

Quay looked at Quest whose expression sharpened with understanding.

"Hmph," Mick grunted.

"Q?" Quay whispered.

"*Q*?" Mick parroted.

Quest's gray stare raked his wife's tiny frame in disbelief. "Let her go." He told Quay and finally left the chair he'd been glued to. There was no movement and he nodded toward his twin. "Let go of her." His voice held a bit more steel then.

Mick left Quay's side when he released her but she didn't race over to inflict more pain on her husband.

"You can go Quay." Quest said.

Unnerved more than he could ever remember being, Quay hesitated. Mick turned with freshly stoked fire in her eyes and propped fists to her hips while waiting on him to obey.

Quay hooked a thumb across his shoulder. "I'll just um…" he began a slow retreat toward the conference room door. He spotted the copy of *Royal Ramsey* and carried it with him on his way to the elevators.

In the conference area, Quest and Mick circled one another like caged animals. Actually, it was Michaela who circled. Quest stood there on edge and waited to be attacked again.

"You know?" He asked.

Mick folded her arms over her chest. "Damn straight."

"How?"

"Oh don't worry; no one disobeyed your orders not to tell me." With a sneer marring her lovely dark face, she strolled closer. "So who exactly were the members of your inner circle? Moses most likely. I never could get him to call me back on Charlton Browning a.k.a. Cufi Muhammad, right? I'm sure." She confirmed her own suspicions and sent Quest a saucy wink before turning her back on him. "Nile knew which probably means Taurus does too. Who else?"

"Mick-"

"Who else?!"

"Fernando."

Mick's eyes were narrowed to thin amber slits when she looked at him. "And County?"

When Quest's gaze faltered, she closed the distance.

"And *County*?" She grabbed a wad of his shirt.

He nodded. "Fern had to tell her."

"And she couldn't tell me?" Mick didn't really expect a response and let her hand fall from his clothes.

"I asked them not to."

The rage funneled back up in a wave and Mick slapped him hard.

"Liar! You *told* them not to! Quest Ramsey who *tells* and orders and expects his will to be done. Who the hell gave you the right? Don't answer that." She raised her hands and smiled. "I already know- your family. Everyone always running to you to handle things." Feeling her palm ache with the need to strike him again, she moved away. "Let me clarify a few things *Q*, I was cleaning up my own shitty life long before I ever knew you were gracing the world with your presence. You had no right!" Her chest felt as though it were filled with too much air. "No right," she began to cry and her breathing increased at a frantic pace. Tears pressured her eyes and soon spilled to her cheeks. "You had no right," she whispered then.

His heart broke at the sight of her weeping. He reached out to console her, but she moved away. On the verge of tears himself, his fist clenched and fell loosely to his side.

"Mick this thing has eaten away at you for years. How the hell was I supposed to tell you that bitch left you to go raise a monster's child?"

"Nile isn't a monster." Mick wiped tears with the back of her hand.

Quest smiled amidst his grief. "No, she's an incredible woman in spite of the parents she had. You're an incredible woman in spite of the fact that you didn't have any." He shook his head. "All I could think of was telling you and watching it destroy you. I couldn't live with that."

"*You* couldn't live with it?" Mick looked as though she wanted to laugh and scream at once. "What about what *I've* lived with Quest? Did you even stop to think of that? 'Course you didn't." She answered before he could response. "You didn't because it's always about Quest Ramsey and what *he* deems necessary."

Quest felt his chest tightening. His pulse churned with fear and uncertainty at what he saw in her eyes.

"I told you…I told you that you would lose me if you couldn't see what this *way* of yours was doing to me-that it was smothering me."

"Mick-" Quest stopped himself as he could only watch her just then with terrified expectancy lurking in his gray eyes. "Mick," He tried again, reaching out that time for what he felt was slipping away.

She stepped back, evading his grasp. "I can't. I can't do this." She whispered, suddenly unable to breathe as she continued to back out of the room.

"Mick?" Urgency now mingled with the uncertainty in his rich voice. He moved to block the conference room entrance and only shook his head when she tried to brush past. He stepped forward, forcing her back until he'd crowded her between the credenza and the wall.

"No Quest." She read the determination in his haunting stare. "Stop," she tried again more firmly feeling the power of his lean frame when he eased closer.

Again, he only shook his head even when she began to pit her fists against him. Quest captured her wrists in one deft move and imprisoned them against his chest. His other hand caught her neck and held her still for his kiss.

Michaela couldn't stifle her moan and the sweet intensity of the kiss made her want to slide down the length of the wall and take him with her. The act quickly became a heated testament to all the hurt and frustration they'd endured amidst the consuming love that pulsed between them like a live being.

Mick stood on her toes and kissed him desperately. Her tongue thrust shamelessly against the bold lunges of his. She drank him in, whimpering needy sounds that were mirrored in the force of her kiss.

Quest groaned into her mouth, brows drawn close as he absorbed all that she offered. He released her wrists and pressed his fists to either side of her head against the wall. The kiss took a slow, delicious turn and Mick curled her fingers weakly into his shirt while becoming lost in what she most wanted. Tears streamed from the corners of her eyes as she summoned strength to do the last thing she wanted.

Quest stumbled a bit when she suddenly pressed against his chest and maneuvered out of his embrace.

"Michaela please," His breath had almost completely deserted him.

"Quincee's with your parents." She grabbed her jacket from the floor.

"Michaela please."

"I dropped her off before I…" she trailed off, her heart shredding at the desperation in his eyes. But she needed just a little time to put her thoughts together and wrap her head around all that she'd learned- all there was still to learn.

Quest didn't know that. All he saw was her leaving and all he felt was powerless to stop it.

"Mick," he barely whispered, clutching the doorjamb as his strength abandoned him. When she disappeared into the elevator, he blinked at the realization that she was gone. He wiped at the moisture outlining his eyes. His chest ached, taking his mind from the ache in his arm. Massaging the area only increased the pain; yet in the midst of hurt, anger eased in cold and heavy.

Yvonne Wilson was at the front of his thoughts. She'd discarded the woman he loved like she was garbage- left Mick to fend for herself amongst the slime of the world. Now she was there once more to pull Mick into despair and pain. Damn her.

The solid ache in his chest grew more pronounced until the rage fueling it became just as unbearable.

CHAPTER THIRTEEN

Quest pushed off the doorjamb and returned to the conference room. The chair he brushed past proved to be his undoing. Seconds later, that chair joined the broken vase and shattered glass frame against the wall. Other chairs followed in rapid succession as he heaved one after another across the room. Next, he went to work on the table- turning the massive piece of furniture on its side and trying to break off the legs with punishing blows from his boots.

The room was quickly and efficiently demolished but Quest wasn't done. Furious over what he couldn't control, he moved on in search of other targets to wreck. The living room of the penthouse office was next. In seconds, the stuffing inside sofa cushions filled the air with looming puffs.

Mick was halfway to her car before she realized she had to go back to him. She *wanted* to go back to him.

God, what a mess, she thought pressing a hand to her face and feeling it moist with the tears that streamed it. There was no way she'd make it through this without Quest to lean on. In spite of it all, he was her rock. He was the man who'd made her believe love was something real and not just a word spoken in moments of desperation and fear.

Hissing a curse, she turned on her heel and raced back toward the building.

Broken glass, wood and other debris crunched under Quest's shoes as he savaged the office. The elegant dwelling now resembled a war zone with nothing but destruction left. Nothing was spared- not even the elaborate models of various Ramsey projects. The large mounted booths that showcased the recreations were overturned and destroyed.

During the vicious spree, Quest's emotions moved from anger to despair and back again. The demolishing of the office was a poor substitute for the pain he wanted to inflict on Yvonne Wilson for the hurt she'd cause- the pain he wanted to inflict on himself for helping her do it.

"Damn her," he muttered reaching for a heavy plaque and doing his best to break it in two.

Michaela stepped off the elevator and immediately spotted the wreckage. Heart racing double time, she went to find Quest. A thunderous crash sent her whirling round and she moved toward the sound whispering his name as she ran. Finding him in the middle of the destructive scene, sent her hand to her mouth and stretched her eyes wide.

On silent steps, she ventured just a wee bit further into the living room area. She was riveted on the set, menacing line of his profile. His eyes were surely black as crude oil by then and anger kept his broad shoulders captive in a rigid line. Mick's stunned, defeated expression had little to do with the horrific state of the office or the fact that her husband was responsible for its appearance.

Instead, it was the words '*damn her*' that he uttered as though they were some part of a sadistic chant while he slammed one heavy plank of wood across another. Mick felt as if every part of her were trembling. But she managed to back out of the room without ever making a sound that would alert him to her presence. When the elevator doors closed before her once again, she slid to the floor of the car and hugged herself to ward off the shivers that froze her body.

***

Quay couldn't remember the last time he'd settled down to read a book. Since he was fairly certain that the stories he read to the twins didn't count, he figured the answer was probably-years.

Just then however, reading was the only thing that kept him from going back up to the penthouse office. He thought there had to be some sort of irony in the fact that he was reading the book his sister-in-law and brother were fighting over. Still…*Royal Ramsey* was an engrossing read and Quay finally understood what Quest meant when he'd once said Mick's work was nonfiction that read like a novel. He was hooked. Moreover, he was impressed. In almost 1½ hours he'd gotten almost halfway through the story.

A quick knock rapped the door of the executive lounge just before Jasmine stuck her head inside.

"Hey? Ty's on the phone. You wanna take it in here?"

"Thanks Jazz." Quay set down the book and reached for the phone. "Tyke," His voice was a lazy rumble that matched the relaxed picture he made reclining on the leather sofa.

"Hey um…is everything okay? I got your message."

Quay grinned and massaged his jaw. "I don't know if everything's okay since Mick just came here to kill Q."

"What?"

"Mmm…He told me to leave so…as mad as she was, I'm betting she succeeded."

"Mick…" Tykira's sigh was a mix of relief and unease. "So that's where she is."

Quay shifted a bit higher on the sofa. "What's up?"

"Nile called looking for her- said she tried to get through to you guys in the office."

"We were in conference-always send any calls directly to voice mail during those meetings. I doubt Q thought about unlocking the phones."

"Well Nile said Mick left her place in a daze and she was worried. Quay what's going on?"

"What isn't?" He slanted a gaze toward the book. "Royal Ramsey's about to hit the shelves, but all this is about a damn bit more than this book being published."

"So he knows about the book…"

It was no surprise that Ty's words piqued her husband's curiosity.

"County told me, Mel and Johari that Quest was sent a preview copy of the book by mistake. She tried to call Mick while they were away but…"

"Jesus…"

"You said they were fighting over more than the book? What'd you mean?"

Quay leaned forward, tapping his fingers to the coffee table as he spoke. "Mick knows about her mother."

"Her mother?"

"Long story."

"Well what's happening now?"

"I don't know." Quay cast his dark stare toward the lounge's tiled ceiling. "I haven't been up there since they started."

"And how long ago was that?"

"Too long."

"Quay…"

"Yeah, I know." He pushed off the comforting sofa. "Talk to you later. I love you."

Quay seriously considered staying safely inside the elevator once the doors opened on the top floor. Having been on the receiving end of his brother's anger more times than he could count, Quay wasn't too sure he wanted to check in on Quest and Mick once he glimpsed the state of the office. He couldn't help but wonder if it was his twin or his sister-in-law who was responsible for the damage.

Rolling the cuffs of his shirt above his forearms, he took his courage by the throat and moved off the elevator. Carefully, he took the corridor to the left, wincing at the wreckage he observed. He stopped in Quest's office and found him sitting on the edge of his desk. Quay watched him there-arms folded while he massaged the aching brand and looked out over the view of the city they had helped to build.

Quay pressed his lips together and continued onward to take a seat next to his twin. "You survived." He clapped a hand to Quest's shoulder.

"She left me. She-she's gone."

"She didn't leave you, Q." Quay shook his head and gave his brother's shoulder a quick squeeze. "She wouldn't. She couldn't. For some reason the girl's in love with you."

It was Quest's turn to shake his head then. "You didn't hear what she said. You didn't see her." He looked out over the Seattle view but only saw his wife's face. "I knew it was wrong to keep what I knew about Yvonne Wilson from her and when I was finally ready to tell her, I saw that." He glanced toward the book Quay held.

"Go find her, man. Talk to her."

Quest smirked off his brother's advice. "She doesn't want to hear what I have to say."

"And since when has that stopped you from tellin' anyone *anything*?"

Quest's withering look only earned him a grin from Quay.

"Why don't you check out this infamous book while you're making up your mind?" Quay squeezed Quest's neck and stood. "It's damn good." He left the hardback on the desk and walked out of the room.

***

Quay felt it was grossly unfair to have worked at soothing Quest's temper only to arrive at his own home later that evening and have *his* temper unexpectedly rattled.

"It's Vegas," he complained, twisting at the edge of the pillow he's snatched from the headboard when he'd flopped down to the bed. He arrived home from the office to find his wife packing for a trip to *Sin City*. His temper was *unexpectedly rattled* over the fact that he wasn't being invited along.

Tykira was unfazed. "It's for Mick." She spoke in a cool matter-of-fact way as she changed her mind about one frock and chose another. She selected another outfit and was carrying the items to the bed when she noticed her husband's fixed stare. "Baby please, Sabra says Mick got there an hour ago barely holding it together so…we'll just go and see what's up."

"And no men allowed?"

"That's right and you'll have the place to yourself since your folks decided to take the twins. They're gonna have their hands full with them *and* Quincee but they say they're looking forward to it."

Quay bristled over the way she coolly went about her packing. "It's Vegas." He reiterated and moved off the bed.

Ty finished with the suitcase she'd packed and sauntered across the room to link her arms about Quay's neck. "What is this? Are you uneasy?" She murmured into his skin.

Quay leaned against the doorjamb and kept her close.

"I promise to be a good girl," she cooed and nibbled his earlobe. "I promise to be a very good girl." She trailed her nose along his jaw.

The promise did nothing to soothe Quay. "Plenty of ways to be a *good* girl."

"Mmm…but those ways are all for you."

"They better be," Yohan finished. He'd given his wife a speech similar to his cousin's and received a similar response.

Melina savored the feel of his hard frame against her for just a moment longer. She looked way up and brushed the back of her hand across the flawless dark of his beautiful face then went to resume her packing.

Yohan's pitch stare took on a more probing intensity as he watched her. In spite of the cool she exuded, he sensed her mood as easily as he ever had.

"There's more to this."

Mel only hesitated a second at the sound of his voice, but it was a telling hesitation. She didn't bother to deny it and turned to fix him with a resigned smile. "Yeah…yeah there is and you'll find out soon enough."

"That doesn't make me feel any better." Moses said to Johari as he watched her select toiletries for her trip. "Besides, it doesn't look good for you to leave me so soon after we got married. People will talk." He added when Jo turned to gawk at him.

Those words coming from someone who cared little-if anything, about the opinions of others-roused heavy laughter from Johari.

"Would you feel better if I told you it was for Mick?" She stopped with an arm full of shower gels, lotions and shampoo to press a quick kiss to his jaw.

Moses leaned against the bathroom doorway. His gaze was alive with curiosity. "He told her, didn't he?"

"I don't know." County was telling Fernando. "Your cousin Sabra told Ty that Mick was hysterical, saying Quest hated her. I don't know if it's about Yvonne Wilson or-"

"That damned book." Fernando moved to block the suitcase before she could add more items. "We asked you to leave it alone."

"You didn't exactly *ask*, Ramsey." County tugged at his FUBU sweatshirt in an attempt to move him aside. He wouldn't budge. Nonplussed, she stepped around him and tugged the case to the other side of the bed. "Look, it's too late to do anything to change it now." She slammed the case shut and propped fists to her hips. "So kiss me, will you? I got a plane to catch."

***

"I got steak and eggs, hash browns, biscuits…Having breakfast for dinner is sooo comforting. Let's give it a try, huh?"

Mick only turned her face into the pillow when Sabra came closer to the bed.

"Honey, please?" Sabra sighed smoothing the flaring violet rose material of her dress beneath her as she sat on the edge of the bed. "You need to eat something and it'll help you think more clearly."

"I am thinking clearly." Mick's voice was muffled beneath the pillow.

Sabra's smile was a mix of humor and distress. "Honey, Quest doesn't hate you. I know what it looks like when a man hates a woman. Quest doesn't have that look."

Slowly, Mick raised her head and studied Sabra. "You're talking about Smoak?" She watched her nod. "What happened there?"

"Ohhh…" Sabra tried to act as if the memory of it all had lost its power to shred her heart. Trailing all ten fingers through her lengthy tresses was simply an act to appear strong instead of sad. "What *didn't* happen? Lots of ugliness. Lots of misunderstandings. He thought I betrayed him…I didn't try to correct his thinking. Pride and all…" she winked but the gesture held no amusement. "When I tried to make it right, he wouldn't listen."

Mick turned onto her back. "So you…you just let him go?"

Nodding, Sabra finally acknowledged the tear clinging to her lashes and smoothed it away. "I'd already lost him. I could see it in his eyes. Maybe if I had faced all the lies right off…" She shrugged. "I don't know. Just…Mick please don't let this go on too long, alright?"

Mick kept a promising smile in place until Sabra left the room. It faded once she was alone with her thoughts.

***

Yohan leaned against the passenger side of his Jeep and watched his brothers and cousins turning into the driveway of Quest and Michaela's home. "It's been two days, maybe he left town." He noted when Quay left his Hummer.

"Nah, Quincee's with my parents and with Mick gone, he wouldn't just leave without tellin' 'em somethin'." *At least I hope he wouldn't.* Quay shook the thought from his mind.

The group headed for the front door. Quay used his key to let them inside. He called out to his brother but expected no answer. The guys fanned out into the house all calling Quest's name.

It was Quay who emerged the victor when he found the man in the nursery. He came and sat next to Quest against Quincee's crib. Quay grimaced when he noticed Quest with the copy of "Royal Ramsey" in one hand and a bottle of Hennessey in the other.

"She sat right there." Quest looked at the rocking chair three feet away. "She sat there and told me I'd lose her if I didn't stop tryin' to run rough shod over everything- if I didn't learn to stop being so… 'my word is law' with her." He rolled his eyes away from the chair and took a healthy swig from the bottle. "I looked right at her and said I'd try. She was right to call me a liar."

Quay noticed Yohan, Fernando and Moses at the nursery door and raised a hand to urge them to keep their distance. When they were gone, he gently eased the liquor bottle from his brother's hand and replaced it with his own. "You tried, man. You tried."

"I didn't." He jerked his hand from Quay's and began to rub it methodically across a jean clad thigh. "It took me no time and no remorse at all to tell Moses and the others to bury what they knew."

"Hell, Q you were trying to-"

"Protect her. Yeah, that's the problem. She doesn't want or need me to."

"She does but…" Quay rubbed his fingers across the dark waves covering his head and tried to choose the best words. "It's…the *way* you do it. That ask no questions, I'll take care of it crap that worked so well for *us* doesn't play with her. She's used to knowing the worst of it- no need to sugar coat shit for her. She's gotta have that control. Without it, she's lost."

Quest smiled and looked down at the book. "Probably why she wrote this."

"Good, huh?"

"Damn good." Quest was unaware of the love and pride evident in his voice. "I gotta admit I'm surprised you read to the first chapter." The beginnings of humor lurked in his words and eyes when he turned to his twin.

"Try chapter eight." Quay boasted with unmasked haughtiness in his voice. "And I've got my page marked, so don't mess with it."

"I didn't." He weighed the book in his hand silently lamenting the fact that he'd allowed it to cause so much trouble. "It's yours to take. I'm done with it."

"And Mick? You done with her?"

"Never. But I'm not ashamed to admit that I haven't got a fucking clue what to say to her. The way she looked at me…probably won't believe a word that comes out of my mouth."

"Forget about that. You've been strong and pro-active your whole life. Now is definitely not the time to punk out."

Quest ran both hands across his face and groaned. "I don't even know where she is."

Quay grinned "Vegas baby and we're on our way."

CHAPTER FOURTEEN

When Michaela woke that morning, she thought she was still dreaming. Slowly, she inched up beneath the covers and frowned at the women and conversation filling the bedroom of her spacious corner suite at Sabra Ram's.

Contessa was first to spot her friend awake and trying to sit up. "Well it's about damn time." The fabric of her plum wrap skirt swished softly as she came to perch on the bed. "Get your ass in the shower so we can get out of here and have breakfast."

Mick was massaging the heel of her hand into her eye. "What are you doing here?" Still in the midst of waking, she was more than a little stunned.

Country shrugged. "Since you're not answering your cell, I had to come in person to tell you." A deep breath was required first. "I'm sorry. So sorry," her brown eyes filled with the tears she'd tried to stave off for the past few weeks.

"Oh Honey, don't," Mick soothed and pulled her friend into the tightest hug.

Contessa only squeezed back and cried harder when she felt Mick kiss her cheek.

"What are you guys doing here?" Mick scolded the other women in the room as she watched them across County's shoulder. "Don't you have a new husband to take care of?"

Johari waved off the question. "He'll be alright." She chose her spot on the massive bed.

Melina was next to take a seat and reclined a little on the satiny black comforter. "You really need to get dressed because we've got a full day planned."

"And Sabra already reserved our places at the spa." Tykira shared, leaning next to Mick against the headboard and pressing a kiss to her cheek.

"Can't believe y'all came all this way to see about me," Though she abhorred crying, Mick didn't begrudge the tears in her eyes.

Johari found Mick's foot beneath the covers and squeezed. "You're our girl," she drawled.

"And we've all been through our share of…issues with the Ramsey men," Ty added.

Mel raised her hand. "The Ramsey *gods* as the society pages and a great many of their female employees call them."

County laughed. "If they only knew!"

Everyone's laughter filled the room then.

***

"You're all telling me to *talk* to him. What you don't seem to get is that I don't know how. He's so angry-he looked so fierce in that office he tore apart, all the while damning me…" Mick closed her eyes on the memory while she absorbed the relaxing steam in the heat of the sauna. It was a welcomed treat following a full day of sight seeing and shopping.

"I think it all finally got to him Mick." County spoke from her prone position on the wooden slab in a far corner of the foggy area. "I think he was carrying so much inside, so much he wouldn't or felt he *couldn't* tell you. I think he just lost it."

Mick pulled away a wet curl clinging to her cheek. "I'm sure my surprise visit didn't help much either."

A round of outrageous laughter mingled with the sauna's steam.

"I would've paid good money to see you throw that vase across the room." Johari could barely talk amidst her giggles.

Ty was thinking of her husband. "I'd have paid good money to see Quay trying to hold you back."

"When all is said and done Mick, you just have to ask yourself if letting this thing continue to cause you pain is more important than forgiving Quest and moving on."

Mick smiled at Contessa's words. "It is County. It is."

***

Later that evening, Sabra secured the best tables in her highly publicized gambling/nightclub *Ace of Sabra*. Everyone chuckled over the woman's weakness to vanity for having everything she owned bearing her name. Sabra accepted the digs good naturedly and assured them the trend would continue.

The table of beauties drew massive amounts of attention. A varied array of men visited more than once in hopes of sharing a drink, dance or something more pleasurable. They were turned away with a soft 'no thanks' followed by voluminous laughter when the gentleman left defeated.

Melina and Johari ventured off to try their luck at the slots while Mick, County and Ty stayed talking at the table. They were laughing over one of County's bawdy comments when a man stepped up behind Michaela and covered her eyes.

County smiled and slanted Ty a reassuring wink.

Michaela pulled away the hands before her face and looked up to find Raegan Crawford smiling down at her. A squeal eeked past her lips seconds before she jumped from her chair.

"What are you doing here?" Mick pulled back to search his handsome face before leaning in to hug him again.

Rae scanned the crowded club and grinned. "Scouting for a possible move. I can't take many more Chicago winters. What's up Count?"

"Rae…" County stood to hug him when he rounded the table. She kept her arm linked through his and gestured toward Ty. "Raegan Crawford, Tykira Ramsey Mick's sister-in-law."

"It's a pleasure." Raegan moved over to take one of Tykira's hands in both of his.

"So have you decided where you'd like to set up shop in this town?" Ty asked in a teasing fashion.

Rae grinned. "No where near this place, that's for sure. More business here than anywhere I've seen yet."

The women laughed.

"Sabra'll be pleased to hear that." County predicted.

Rae brushed a hand along Mick's bare arm. "How 'bout a dance?" He took her hand when she nodded.

Tykira and Contessa continued their conversation, but it wasn't long before they were interrupted by another wave of gentleman callers. The second round however seemed a bit more persistent than the first.

"That's very nice of you to offer to pay for my room, but I still can't accept." Ty swallowed the ball of laughter as she sweetly but firmly dismissed the very interested gentleman who tried to turn her on by leaning in close every few seconds as though he were inhaling her perfume.

"I like a woman who enjoys paying her own way."

Smoothly, she extracted her hand from his. "Actually I know the owner."

"Ah convenient…do you suppose we could arrange for adjoining suites?"

Ty put a phony apologetic look in place. "I doubt she'd go for it, her being my husband's cousin and all."

"Ah…married."

"Mmm… Very."

"Vegas is no place for such a beauty on her own." The man had to be all but blind not to see the tired, unimpressed glare Ty focused his way. "Tell me, where is your husband?"

"Funny you should ask." Ty had glanced towards the club's entrance and did a double take. Amused shock tap danced along her spine when she found herself looking right at her husband. "You're really gonna have to excuse us now," she snapped her fingers to gain County's attention. "Looks like our dates finally got here."

County waved to urge silence from the man trying to talk her into bed. It was hard not to spot Fernando entering the club with his brothers and cousins. The smile curving her mouth enhanced the sparkle in her warm brown eyes.

"Tough break guys," Laughter hugged County's words when her interested suitor cast a yearning last look at her bosom alluringly encased beneath the lace-up bodice of her aqua blue jumpsuit.

"Just in the nick of time, I see." Fernando was already pulling his fiancée back against his chest as the disappointed *suitors* hurried from the table.

"We were just letting them down easy." County exchanged an amused look with Ty and then shrieked when Fernando pinched her bottom.

"Likely story," Quay hooked a finger inside the push-up bodice of Ty's stunning emerald green wrap dress and pulled her close.

"It's true," Ty deliberately heaved her breasts to envelope more of his finger. "I told you I'd be a good girl."

"Right. Shut up and kiss me."

While Tykira followed her husband's orders, County told Yohan and Moses where they could find their wives. When they strolled off, she saw Quest. He was clearly pensive and obviously in no mood to be part of the glitzy energy surrounding him.

"Hey Quest," County spoke in a hushed tone and heard his soft absent reply in turn. She was about to explain Michaela's absence but there was no need.

His gray stare had already strayed across the room toward the dance floor. Mick dancing slow in another man's arms rendered him weak- from rage or despair he couldn't be sure. He appeared as lost as a little boy whose favorite toy was in another child's possession. Still, he couldn't look away even though the familiar manner in which they held each other threatened to stop his breath.

"We've known him for years, Quest." County shared from her snug position in Fernando's embrace. "Mick's known him since she was a kid."

"Name's Raegan Crawford and he's only a friend." Sabra was adding as she waltzed over to hug Quest. "Why don't you go cut in?"

He shook his head easing one hand into the deep pocket of his midnight blue trousers while the other flexed methodically against his thigh. "I don't want to upset her."

"She won't-" Sabra ceased her argument when she caught Quay's meaningful eye. "Listen, how 'bout somethin' to eat?"

Appreciating her concern, Quest brushed a soft albeit dismissive kiss to Sabra's forehead. "I'm just gonna head up to my room. I'll just catch her later." He cast another wilting glance across the club and blinked away from the sight of Mick's fingers curled trustingly around the lapels of *her friend's* sport coat while the man stroked her bare skin through the dress straps crossing her back.

Sabra wasn't giving up. "Well before you head up we'll just make a pit stop by the front desk and get you a key to your wife's suite." She nodded when Quest absently acquiesced and let her escort him from the lively establishment.

"I knew something was wrong when you looked up at me. Why'd you have to go digging around in this, dammit?"

Mick had shared the dramatic events that had transpired since their phone conversation. Raegan scolded her promptly and she absorbed it as they danced.

"I just felt like I *had* to know." The pitiful argument made her grimace at her own stupidity.

Raegan took pity and kissed her forehead. "How long you gonna torture your husband before you forgive him?"

Mick fidgeted with a button on Rae's dark shirt. "I've already forgiven him, but I'm terrified that it's too late to tell him so."

"I don't believe that."

"No one does, but me."

"Is she that important, Kayla? Is finding Evette *that* important?"

Mick's amber gaze glistened with certainty. "Not near as important as fixing things with Quest."

Rae gave her a tiny shake. "That a girl."

Mick tugged on his jacket lapel again and sighed. "I think I'm gonna call it a night."

"Want me to take you back to the table?" Rae's heavy browns drew close as he scanned the club. "Although it looks empty over there. I think maybe your girls deserted you."

"S'okay. I'm gonna take the long way back to my room-need to think alone for a while." She graced Rae's cheek with a playful slap. "I'll see you before I leave?"

"Count on it."

***

A girl's *day* out was the plan for the following morning through late afternoon. Everyone had successfully hidden from Michaela the fact that her husband along with his twin and cousins were in Vegas and sharing the same hotel.

Catrina had given a call shortly after breakfast to tell Mick they'd have Quincee for a few days. Mick ordered herself not to ask about Quest and simply thanked her mother-in-law for letting her know the plan.

From there, the day was filled with strolling the strip, shopping and taking in shows-a few of them quite lurid thanks to County. Mick sent up more than a few prayers of gratitude for the friends who filled her days with laughter and excitement. They refused to allow her to wallow in anything heavy and solemn which resulted in a much needed spiritual lift for Mick.

The exciting day ended on an even greater high when the ladies returned to the hotel and received a dinner invite from Raegan Crawford.

***

That evening, the piano bar *Sabra's Keys* seemed to be the preferred Ramsey hangout. The guys had chosen to dine their as well. The crowd was light that evening, making it easy for Quest to spot his wife arriving in the dining room on Raegan Crawford's arm.

"Son of a bitch."

Quay heard his brother's muttering and drew his dark gaze in the direction Quest glared. Seeing Michaela with her childhood friend brought a wicked tilt to the sculpted curve of his mouth. "Ty told me he seems like a pretty good guy." The look Quay received in turn told him his remark wasn't appreciated. Sliding down a bit in his chair, he re-focused on the menu in hand.

"Man, why don't you just go talk to her?" Fernando whispered, having heard Quay's words.

"She'll realize we're all here sooner or later." Moses added.

Quest blinked and lowered his eyes to the table as though he seemed to be considering his cousin's words. He took another look at his wife. It had been so long since he'd seen her that way-the animated look as she laughed and chatted with Raegan Crawford…He knew the second she saw *him*, that look would fade- unease and sadness would set in.

"You're bein' a fool, man." Yohan's unhurried baritone slipped in and he rolled his eyes when Quest shook his head.

"She won't want to hear anything I've got to say. Not now."

"Man, don't assume that shit." Moses leaned forward to hiss the words.

Dejectedly, Quest shook his head again. He brushed his fingers across the silverware lying before him. He'd never felt so stifled. What's more, he'd never felt so unable to do anything about it.

Dinner passed happily along with several rounds of drinks. Once Contessa and the others arrived, the evening was full of old stories from days in Chicago. County's own knack for storytelling had tears of laughter filling everyone's eyes. Michaela laughed loudest of all, until she caught sight of her husband across the room.

Certain she had to be imagining things, or that it was the affect of too much wine, she squeezed her eyes shut tight. Then, she looked again. Nope, it was Quest Ramsey alright. As if she could ever truly mistake seeing him anywhere.

Johari was reaching for her ginger ale when she noticed Mick's expression. She glanced across her shoulder. "Oh…yeah," Jo's verbal skills deserted her when Mick's gaze snapped to her face.

"The guys got here last night," Melina chimed in for her cousin.

"Last night?" Mick's voice was a whisper.

"Calm down, girl," County ordered, "you weren't in any mood to hear about Quest last night."

Mick flopped back in her chair. "Oh, you mean like I'm in a mood to suddenly see him sitting across from me in a Las Vegas dining room when he's supposed to be in Seattle?"

County's eyes glinted toward her best friend. "Don't start, Mick."

"We were surprised to see them too, Mick." Ty intervened before Mick could speak. "They just took it upon themselves to show up."

"Quest had nothing to do with it," Johari finally found her tongue. "They made him come along. He'd been holed up in your house for two days tryin' to drink himself to death."

Mick swallowed her gasp, yet her expression was still lost and she tried to focus everywhere except the table where her husband sat. Unable to make it work, she pressed a hand to her mouth.

"'Scuse me," she murmured, pushing back her chair.

Across the room, Quest watched her leave. He was pushing his own chair back from the table a split second later.

Mick left the piano bar through a rear exit and strolled around for a while. Her thoughts were deep and wholly centered on the man she loved. Part of her toyed with just saying 'to hell with it' and doing whatever she had to do; begging included, to get him to forgive her. Quest was all she wanted. She was almost weak with wanting him- wanting to feel him against her, inside her…

Eventually, her steps carried her back to her suite. She didn't bother turning on lights preferring the dark with illumination only from the moon, stars and glitter that signified the elaborate nightlife of Las Vegas.

Stopping in the middle of the living room, she kicked off the chic peek a boo pumps that were beginning to ache her toes. Massaging her neck, she then applied the same pressure to her scalp while padding through the plush suite and into the bed room.

On the adjoining balcony, she chose a cushioned chair and leaned forward to brace her elbows to her knees while observing the busy view. The scene was surprisingly soothing and for a time, she felt at peace.

Mick turned away from the view, sensing his presence before she ever saw him. Quest stood there in the balcony entrance, a picture of humble uncertainty. If he'd had a hat it would have been in his hand.

She didn't hesitate and neither did he.

"I'm sorry."

They spoke in unison. Both blinked and cast their gazes elsewhere before looking back at one another.

Mick had but a moment to come to her feet before Quest had bounded over and dragged her against him. Their mouths met in a collision of want and regret. Smothered cries jumbled in Michaela's throat as his kiss practically stifled her breathing. She welcomed the force of it all and thrust her tongue just as eagerly- just as powerfully.

Quest's legs gave beneath him them and he took her down as he went to the floor of the balcony. Deftly, he removed everything she wore. He didn't bother with the straps and clasps on the gold frock that accentuated her delicious curves. He simply tugged to bare more of her to his darkening stare.

Mick tried to help, but those chic dress straps proved to be effective restraints once Quest had tugged at them long enough. Her head arched back into the stone flooring and she almost cried amidst the exquisite and missed sensation of his mouth on her body.

He cupped both her breasts and alternated suckling the firming nipples. He soothed the taut flesh and with wet languid tongue strokes.

"Mmm…Quest…mmm…" she wanted so much to touch him. Sadly, her hands were not only trapped in the straps of her dress but they were too weakened from the pleasure he subjected her to.

His darkly beautiful face was a picture of intensity as his hungry mouth continued its descent. His lips grazed the satiny undersides of her breasts. His nose followed, outlining their shape, reacquainting itself with their scent. Then onward, he tickled her mercilessly when his tongue explored her navel.

At last, he discarded her dress and Mick felt the extent of the cool stone slabs against her heated flesh. Her only attire was the sheer stockings her husband hadn't seen fit to remove.

Quest smiled when he lifted her from the floor and heard the moan of disappointment. "I'm not done," he promised and cradled her against him silently giving thanks for the chance to hold her again.

Mick felt the soft decadence of the bed beneath her then. Instantly, her hands went to the dark jacket he wore over a black crew shirt. She was obsessed with having him out of his clothes and tugged the material from his shoulders-elated when the coat was a distant memory.

Quest helped her tug the shirt over his head. An instant later, Mick's French tips were grazing the carved perfection of his torso. Needing to feel her next to him, Quest stripped away what remained of his clothing and covered her with the length of his body.

"Christ, Mick," He shuddered when they touched flesh to flesh. For a time he rested his head against the crook of her neck and cherished the reality of having her in his arms.

"Don't leave me again. Don't ever leave me again," he squeezed his eyes shut as if to compel her to obey.

She needed no urging. "Never. I'll never go again Quest."

He gathered her close as she wrapped her legs around his back and began to mimic tiny thrusting movements with her hips. Feverishly, she reached down and attempted to direct him inside her. She cursed her frustration when he brushed away her hands.

"Please Quest…"

"Count on it." He dropped ragged open-mouthed kisses along her dark chocolate form.

"But I want *you*," she insisted when he cupped her bottom in his hands and prepared to take her with his tongue. "I want *you*." Her voice was a mixture of elation and torture when his nose grazed the silken petals of her sex.

"Count on that too," he reiterated seconds before he began to make love to her with his mouth.

Michaela buried her fingers in her curls, arching and rotating on his wicked tongue until a potent orgasm hit her hard and fast.

He was inside her before she came down off the addictive high. "Wait…Quest, please wait." The overload of sensation threatened to burst her heart.

"I thought you wanted this?" He teased while deepening the strokes inside her.

"Too much…" She was caught between a dizzying world somewhere between the last orgasm and the next one rapidly approaching. She curved into a perfect bow beneath him and cried out.

He chanted her name fierce and passion-filled when a warm stream of her need oozed and drenched his manhood. His need erupted then and; gripping each other desperately, they relished the desire and love that engulfed them.

CHAPTER FIFTEEN

"I thought you hated me." Mick shared much later when they lay exhausted in the tangled bed.

Quest raised his head from her chest. "What?" His incredulous expression was visible only by the sparse lighting streaming in through the balcony. The disbelief however was vividly clear in his voice.

Mick smoothed the back of her hand against the sleek molasses dark of his chest. "I came back after we…fought. I saw you tearing down your office, saying 'damn her', 'damn her'…it wasn't hard to figure who-"

"Yvonne," Quest said, bowing his head as he recalled the scene. "I meant Yvonne Wilson and I *do* hate her, Michaela. I hate her for what she did to you. I hate myself because I let her…resurfacing in your life cause me to hurt you."

"Shh..." Mick arched up to brush her mouth across his. "You were only looking out for me- protecting me...I can accept that now."

He dipped his head again and a splice of light captured the harsh grimace he'd set in place. "I've spent my life protecting my family- *working things out* for them...and they never questioned how I did it." Smiling then, he toyed with the curls framing her face. "I'm not used to having a partner bold enough to tell me that my protective nature is bordering on power-tripping obsession. I've got no idea when I'm doing it so I'll need you to help- to show me."

Mick smoothed the back of her hand across his face. "You know I'm always available to slap some sense into you."

Quest caught the dig and laughed, sparking his left dimple. "Just please don't hit me as hard as you did that day in my office."

"I promise." She kissed his cheek but the playfulness in her eyes dimmed with regret. "I'm sorry. I really am."

"I felt proud when I first saw the book. The fact that you *defied* me- didn't let my passive bullying persuade you." He kissed the mole above her heart shaped mouth. "This is why I love you."

Mick laughed. "Because I can whip your ass."

"Because you've got the nerve to try."

"Ah..." her sigh merged into a giggle as another kiss ensued.

"I thought you hated me too." He confessed once the kiss had ended. "For keeping what I knew about your- your mother."

"How could I ever hate you?" She reached over to turn on the stout bedside lamp. "That could never happen." Soft gold light illuminated her face and the love radiating there. Turning the tables, she pushed Quest to his back and draped herself across him.

"I could no more hate you than I could Driggers. Those boxes I had sent home from Chicago?" She prompted when he watched her in confusion. "I found a letter in one of them. It was from- from her to Driggers." Mick sat up over Quest as she remembered. "She came to my place, met Drig, and wanted to see me. I must've been at a homecoming game- Wiley State." She gave a perky toss of her curls. "I started going up there more frequently once I began choreographing the girls' routines…" She rubbed her hands across her bare arms to ward off a sudden chill. "He never told me she'd come there. I never suspected a thing and I don't know what would've happened to me had I known then."

Absently, she raked her nails across the rigid array of muscle in Quest's abdomen. "Guess I'd have gone off on some wild goose chase to hunt her down. Hmph, might've gotten myself killed in light of what she was involved in."

"And I would've never met you." Quest acknowledged and drew her down into a hug.

"He always protected me." Mick snuggled deeper into her husband's embrace. "He looked out for me even when I didn't know it and I love him more now than I ever did."

A muscle flexed in Quest's jaw. "And Raegan Crawford?" His gray eyes shimmered with the hint of uncertainty. "He protected you too, right?"

Mick eased up, propping her fist to her cheek and nodded. "I used to play with Rae when we were kids." Her expression was tender as she smiled on the memories. "His mom was a teacher- she was the teacher who found me. She'd come by that first day when I wasn't in school but I hid in the closet- too scared to answer the door."

A low sound grumbled deep in Quest's throat. He gathered her close, holding her tight and thanking God for watching over her and bringing her to him.

"You know I saw her?" Mick shared after they'd embraced for a while.

Quest pulled her up to search her face.

"The day Houston and Daphne were killed. She was talking to Johnelle and Josephine. I thought maybe it could've been her. Anyway, next thing I knew, shots were ringing out and you were pushing me to the floor."

"And what about now?" Quest made her sit up and straddle him again. "Do you want to see her?"

Mick pressed her lips together and considered the answer that came without hesitation. "If I said 'no' I'd be telling you the truth, I swear." She added when his gaze narrowed. "But how could that be? How could I *not* want to see her? I've waited a lifetime, haven't I?"

Quest tugged lightly on one of her curls and watched it spring back into a coil. "Maybe you realize there's nothing for her to say that would hold value for you, for what you've become."

Mick responded with a saucy wink. "Wife, mother, girlfriend, author…"

"And my very *best* friend." Quest emphasized as much with his words as he did with the look in his eyes.

Mick cupped his face in her hands and drew him into the sweetest kiss.

***

Nights in Las Vegas had a tendency to be brisk, but the guests soon to arrive on the rooftop would be quite pleased. Sabra had arranged for her club there, aptly named *Sabra's Rooftop* to be closed for a private party for her family.

The *party* was a celebration of all being right in the world again. As far as Quay, Tykira, Contessa, Fernando, Yohan, Melina, Johari and Moses were concerned Michaela and Quest's return to stability set all their hearts and minds a little easier. While they were all happy and content in their respective relationships, seeing Quest and Mick back on track was further verification-no matter how corny- that love conquers all.

The group begged Sabra to join them for the evening. After all, having the couple holed up in the same area and being thrown together had proven to be the greatest weapon in forcing them to face each other.

Alas, Sabra had had enough of *couples*- happy or otherwise. She left instructions with her wait staff to inform the group of her absence and asked them to tell her cousins and the women they loved to enjoy themselves.

Enjoyment was certainly the order for the evening. As the arrival in Vegas was rather unorthodox, everyone was in separate rooms. Therefore, guests arrived at the party in a singular fashion. Ty was first on the rooftop and spent the first five or ten minutes swaying to the sounds of Kool and The Gang's "*Summer Madness*" while she enjoyed the stunning view of Vegas at night. Her serene smile merged into one more sensual when the dress straps crossing her back were smoothed aside to make way for gliding lips.

"Mmm…" Ty leaned back into the caress. "My husband's around and he's got a pretty bad temper."

"Screw him," Quay growled into her neck.

Turning with a wicked glint in her mahogany brown gaze, Ty walked her fingers up his chest. "I'd love to," she purred.

Quay chuckled but soon his expression grew solemn and he leaned in for a hug.

Through their embrace, Ty could sense what felt like the weight of a burden being lifted. He squeezed her tight and held on for a long moment.

"You were afraid for them?" She asked, already knowing while smoothing her hands across the fabric of the wine colored shirt which hung outside his navy trousers.

"Terrified," Quay admitted in a voice muffled against his wife's shoulder.

"Because they're the stable ones of our group?" She felt him nod in response.

"Everything's always been right with them…no ugly pasts…hurt feelings to move beyond…" He cleared his throat and pulled away. "Seeing something like that come out of nowhere and rock them like that was pretty scary."

"But they survived it." Ty's gaze lowered. "Are you wondering if we could?"

The muscle along his jaw danced when he looked down at her hands clasped tight within his. "All I know is that I don't want you to keep anything from me. No matter how much you think I may not want to hear it. You tell me." He gave her a little jerk. "You tell me, Tyke."

She nodded immediately. "Does the same go for you?" Her voice sounded small, but she continued. "No more hiding things or doing outrageous acts in the name of protection."

The heart-melting right dimpled grin appeared. "Right. Protection…the word we use to justify all our idiot moves." He laughed softly. "No, no more of that. No more of that." He shook his head and turned serious again. "I swear it, Tykira. I swear it."

Quay drew Ty into a branding kiss that she returned with her own branding power.

Melina was busy checking her thick, bouncy hair in the elevator's shimmering gold siding when the car stopped and her husband stepped in. She couldn't get past how; in all the years she'd known him, he could still make her heart somersault clear to her throat.

Yohan didn't bother with a greeting, but moved straight in for a kiss. Mel savored the feeling of being taken down by overwhelming arousal. She engaged his tongue eagerly with her own while raking her nails across the flawless pitch black of the taut skin stretched over the dark loveliness of his face.

A sound of guttural need rumbled someplace deep within the massive expanse of his chest. Mel knew instinctively that the wispy coffee toned wrap dress she wore was about to meet its demise.

"I'm not gonna be presentable for the party," she moaned when he freed her mouth to drag his down her throat.

"You're plenty presentable for what I've got in mind." The words seemed to vibrate through him.

"Mr. Ramsey, the things you say to women you find in elevators."

"You have no idea."

Within seconds, the vampy act got the better of them and laughter filled the gleaming confines of the elevator. Tears filled their eyes and were soon streaming their cheeks. They each leaned on opposite sides of the car, clutching their stomachs and trying to catch their breaths.

"Whew," Mel blinked away the tears still clinging to her lashes. "I pity the person who walks on this elevator now."

"Tell me about it," Yohan tugged at the cuffs of his gray shirt and chuckled. "They'll be pretty stunned to find a married couple laughing."

"With each other," Mel qualified. "Did you ever think *we'd* be laughing like this? And on an elevator car?" She raved when silence had settled between them.

"No." Yohan rested his head against the wall and studied the mirrored top of the car. "But then again, I never thought we'd see Q and Mick at each other's throats."

"And now all is well."

Yohan nodded his agreement and pushed off the wall. "Now, all is well." He agreed, closing the distance between them to plant a sweet kiss to his wife's lips.

The doors opened and Yohan offered an arm to Melina which she happily accepted.

Johari bit her lip on the moan that was threatening to escape. She and Moses had been dancing to some slow, unfamiliar erotic tune that drifted on the air. His arms were locked neatly around her waist but his hands roamed her back in a coaxing massage before they moved to cup her bottom.

"We're in public, Ram."

Moses didn't bother to look round or move his hands for that matter. "I don't think we're fazing Quay and Ty."

Jo stood slightly on her toes. "You're right." She said after peering across her husband's shoulder and spotting the couple locked in a kiss. Weariness crept into her silver stare despite the easy mood swirling about them. "I feel like we've been through the obstacle course from hell and that's really selfish since it was Quest and Mick who went through the trial."

"It's accurate enough." Moses smirked. "Considering how much all of us craved the kind of bond they had when ours were traveling their own obstacle courses."

Johari's smile was both serene and rueful. "Our own obstacle course would've been welcome-at least in an obstacle course you're rewarded with another obstacle that gets you closer to the prize." She brushed her thumb across the pulse point at the base of his throat. "There was no prize with us- no reward. All that time was just hell."

"Amen," Moses breathed and brushed his forehead across hers. "I was never more terrified in my life than on the day you walked out my door." He leaned in to inhale her delicious scent. "I put my life on the line countless times to top that feeling, wipe it out…nothing ever came close." He let her see the anguish in his dark gaze. "Then Zara died and I believed I'd lost you for good."

The sound of her sister's name brought tears to Johari's eyes. They weren't tears of sadness however. "There came a time when all hell was breaking loose and I…I just knew that no matter what I wasn't going to lose you again." She looked upon him with awe tingeing her expression while trailing her fingers across his shaved head. "When Zara died…I still knew that- nothing had changed. I'm never losing you, Ram."

He toyed with a lock of her bright hair. "We're never losing each other." He corrected and they sealed it with a kiss.

County was rushing to the door of her suite while tying the tassels of the teal frock she'd chosen for the evening. Her hands stilled when she heard the door locks click. Fernando stepped into the room and her mouth fell open. "How? How'd you get in?"

Faking confusion, Fernando waved her key card in the air.

She rolled her eyes. "How'd you get it?"

"Last night," he stalked her until she was near the jamb of the doorway leading to the bedroom. "You told me to take it while I took you…"

"The hell I did!" County couldn't help but laugh.

Still, feigning confusion, Fernando tapped fingers to his temple. "I'm pretty sure you did but why not refresh my memory?"

He'd only kissed her lustily for a few seconds when she pushed him back as far as he'd allow. "Ramsey stop…I'm gonna ruin my underwear." Her cheeks burned as she made the admission.

"So take 'em off." His order was gruff against her ear before he suckled the lobe. Moments later his fingers were plundering her underwear and helping her take heed to his suggestion.

Contessa gave herself a figurative pat on the back when she found the strength to resist him. "We can't be late."

"I'm pretty sure we won't be the only ones."

She moved away to check her earrings in the mirror above the message desk and did a fine job of ignoring her fiancé. That is, until he strolled over to *inspect* the bodice of her form fitting dress. She slapped his hands without turning away from the mirror. "I can't wait to see if you're this horny after we're married. Ramsey!" She cried upon finding herself being whirled around to face him.

"Do you think I'm not serious?" His light gaze was narrowed with suspicion. "Or are you having second thoughts?"

"Don't do that…" her voice was soft yet strong. "I know you're serious- as serious as I am."

Fernando released her and slumped a bit as though his strength were leaving him. "That drama with Quest and Mick," he muttered something foul, "Hell County, I thought all the drama period- would have you second guessing…"

"Second guessing *us*?" She asked in disbelief, propping her hands to her hips when he only offered a weary nod. She pushed him to the desk and stepped between his legs. She cupped his face.

"Never. Never, you hear?" She gave his cheek a soft slap. "I love you and I never thought such a thing was meant for me." Her smile was sad then. "I watched my mother give herself to a man who shattered her- left her questioning her worth as a woman…" She blinked, stunned by the words leaving her mouth. She hadn't thought of her parent's doomed marriage in ages.

"I'm tired of expecting the worst." She focused on Fernando's translucent gaze then. "I'm ready to enjoy the best."

"Me." He guessed, his eyes twinkling adorably when he grinned.

County mimicked the action. "You," She purred and instigated the kiss between them. "You were right, Ramsey." She said after pulling back a few seconds later. "We're gonna be just a little late."

The suite that Quest and Mick now shared was alive with the sounds of needy cries and provocative teases as they loved each other. Mick however, could scarcely form intelligible words as every thrust Quest subjected her to, stifled her breathing and made speaking near impossible.

Wanting to experience some of the power he enjoyed, she caught him off guard and pushed him to his back. Quest winced as she settled down over him. When he shifted to control her movements by gripping her hips, she stopped him by placing his palms flat on her bare breasts instead. Slowing the rotation of her hips, she smiled at the pleasurable torture that seemed to shudder through him. The moans forced from his throat were a cross between exuberance and exhaustion.

Overwrought then, Quest took her wrists in one hand and held her hip with the other-moving her to his will. Mick climaxed swift and sharply but Quest wasn't done. She felt on the verge of fainting when he grew incredibly stiffer inside her before erupting deep within…

"I thought I'd feel different when, *if* I found them." Mick was saying later when she lay across Quest's stomach. "It's why I asked Moses and Rae to help me- I was desperate to know." Absently, she outlined a pack of carved muscle in his abdomen. "Even after I told Taurus how little it mattered…how it couldn't change the good in us- what we'd accomplished in spite of the ugliness we'd been subjected to." She smirked and rolled her eyes. "That was a load of bull. I guess part of you; no matter how small, always wants to know."

"What are you gonna do now?" Quest trailed the back of his hand across Mick's shoulders. "Are you sure about not wanting to see her?" He asked when silence met his first question.

She nodded. "At least, I *believe* I'm sure. I always told myself that people with families were different- *better* and that they weren't bogged down by all the thoughts of worthlessness." For a moment, she buried her face into Quest's stomach and sighed. "I told myself that people with families never had to wonder if they mattered-even a little- to the people they should matter most to. If *that* makes sense," she added with a weary smile.

Quest sat up a bit and pressed a hard kiss to the middle of her head. "On behalf of the Ramseys, I'd like to say that we've effectively helped you to prove that *that* is the biggest load of bull."

Laughter resumed, and then kissing.

"Quest?" Mick whispered during the kiss as it gained steam.

"Mmm?"

"Do we have time for just a little more before the party?"

Quest's low, seductive chuckling filled the bedroom.

CHAPTER SIXTEEN

Taurus met Claire Boyer on her way out of the courthouse. He and Nile had taken separate cars to the hearing which he'd missed due to some business at Ramsey Legal. The proceedings appeared to be ending just as he took the steps leading to the courthouse's side entrance.

"How'd it go?" He watched as the attorney puffed out her cheeks and sighed.

"They're extraditing her to France." Claire cast a quick, foreboding glance across her shoulder. "The authorities there have a mountain of evidence and charges waiting to pin on someone and as Muhammad's dead…"

"Right…" Taurus' light gaze softened when he saw his wife exiting the courthouse. Nile held back several feet watching morosely as two guards led Yvonne Wilson by each arm. "So what now?" He asked, hiding one hand in the pocket of his hunter green trousers.

Claire stroked her chin as she observed Yvonne. "Back to the correctional facility to await extradition. She'll also have to answer for Cufi's murder. I'm sorry Taurus."

He frowned, looking away from his wife and her mother. "There's absolutely nothing for you to be apologizing for. I thank you for everything you've done."

"I was able to use the Ramsey name to allow Nile to walk out with Yvonne and the guards…I only wish it could've been more." Claire's round shoulders rose beneath her navy blazer.

Taurus dipped his head to watch her more closely. "We both know that with what you had to work with it couldn't have gone down any other way." He saw Claire off and then went to meet his wife.

Nile's steps had slowed and then they halted all together. Taurus watched her expression go from surprise, to realization to horror. When she began to run, his heart lurched clear to his throat.

Yvonne was slumping against one of the guards when Nile raced over and pulled her mother into her arms. There along the side of Yvonne's pale blue pantsuit was the stain of blood.

"Nile!" Taurus' raspy tone raked out as he bolted toward his wife while the guards drew their weapons.

Tears pooled Nile's eyes and coated her dark face with a damp sheen as they spilled. "Maman…Maman…" Gently, she laid Yvonne flat on a wide concrete step.

"Shh…Shh…" Yvonne's face was a picture of calm. The slightest hint of a smile even played about the curve of her mouth. "I knew they'd never let me go back to France. I…I'm surprised they waited…this long."

"Please don't talk…please…" Nile leaned down to press a hard kiss to her mother's forehead. "Shh…they're coming to help." She glanced round vaguely noting that the guards were more involved with tracking down the shooters just then.

"I don't need help…I'm so proud of you my Nile, so proud…" With effort, Yvonne shifted her gaze. "A beautiful husband," she noted when Taurus had dropped down next to Nile and kissed her temple. "You've done so well and-and my Mickey…a married woman with a baby she'll love and protect. Tell her…" She winced as the pain burrowed deeper. "Tell her I'm sorry-so very very sorry. She-she deserved a better mother. So did you."

"No…" Nile moaned, pressing her head to Yvonne's shoulder and weeping as the woman's life left her.

***

Quest knelt before Mick's side of the bed and watched her sleep. Gently, he reached out to trace her brow and the curls that framed her face.

"Mick," he grimaced when she murmured incoherently and turned over on her side.

Part of him said to let her sleep- *don't lay this on her now*. But that was only for *his* benefit. God, would she blame him for this? He wondered. In the same instant, he shook his head and softly cursed himself for allowing the thought to enter his mind.

"Mick?" A bit more force colored the baritone of his voice. When she would have funneled deeper into the covers, he squeezed her shoulder and nudged her gently. "Mick…"

"Mmm…"

"Come on now…" He spoke against the top of her head. "Come on…"

The soft coaxing roused Mick and a lazy smile curved her lips when she stretched and turned toward her husband.

"Morning…" she purred lashes fluttering as she gave another decadent stretch. "This is what I want," the seductive tone of her words mirrored the look in her exotic stare. Leaning closer, she lavished wet, open-mouthed kisses across his chest.

"Mick wait," he moved to stand, but her grip was surprisingly powerful around his waist. "Wait a sec-"

"Mmm mmm, come back to bed."

"Mick wait there's something-"

"Back to bed," She outlined his mouth with the tip of her tongue.

"Stop. I'm serious, Mick." Unfortunately, her tugs at his waist and her tongue in his mouth quickly wore down his already weakened defenses.

"Why are you dressed?" She fumbled with the hem of his Supersonics jersey trying to get her hands on his bare skin.

"Mick," he tried again and closed his eyes in submission when she pushed him to his back and rained those wet kisses down his body. Her mouth journeyed across the ever stiffening ridge of his sex. The fact that his gray nylon sweats still covered what she craved, didn't diminish the enthusiastic attention she showered upon him.

"Jesus," Quest lost his hands in her hair and winced in the pleasure she brought. Her lips grew bolder and in seconds he was mimicking faint thrusting movements. He wanted her mouth on him, but drew on a powerful wave of willpower instead.

"Babe? Wait, wait…"

Mick frowned when she felt his vice grip on her arms. "What's wrong?" He'd pulled her up and over him. "What?" Her voice was hushed when she saw his gaze falter. Straddling his body, she cupped his face urging him to look her way.

"Taurus called me this morning." His dark eyes connected with her bright ones then. "Yvonne Wilson was killed yesterday. She was leaving the courthouse. They don't know who." He saw the question cut through the devastation in her gaze. "They were moving her after the hearing when she was hit. No one even heard the shot."

Michaela seemed to wilt, blinking as she looked away. Quest sat up, keeping his hands over her arms-keeping her close.

"Are you alright?"

"What should I do?" Her voice sounded lost-empty.

"We can do whatever you want." He spoke against her temple. "You wanna go home?"

She barely nodded. "I think so…I think I should."

Quest rubbed his arms along the goose-flesh riding Michaela's bare arms. His chest pounded forebodingly but he had to know. "Are we alright, Mick?" His mouth still pressed to her temple.

Pulling back, she cupped his beautiful dark face in both her hands. "We're alright. We're *very* alright."

Seated in the middle of the bed, they hugged for the longest time.

***

Instead of attending the understandably low-key funeral proceedings, Mick decided on holding a dinner at home. All the couples attended, having returned to Seattle from Las Vegas. No one really knew if condolences were appropriate for Mick under the circumstances. They decided to save them for Nile who arrived with Taurus about an hour before dinner was set to begin.

Michaela held back, waiting until everyone else was done with soft words and hugs for Nile. They all discretely cleared the sitting room and gave the two women time alone.

Nile accepted a kiss from Taurus who crossed the room to hug Mick on his way out of the dim, quiet room.

"I know you have questions." Nile wrung her hands and then brushed them across the pleated pin striped skirt of her suit. "I only want to begin first by saying that I'm sorry."

Curiosity flashed on Mick's face but she said nothing.

"I never meant to hurt you anymore than you'd already been." Nile couldn't help that she rambled. Her hands wouldn't remain still either and she alternated between smoothing them across her sleek onyx mane and squeezing her arms as she walked the room. "None of us agreed when Quest said he wanted to wait on telling you. But seeing your face that day when you came over…" She looked up at the skylight that revealed more of the overcast day. "Seeing you that day, I finally understood why he wanted to wait. I've got so much to apologize for, but I just wanted to start with that. Michaela…a part of me will never know if I'd…come forward sooner maybe you'd have had that time to talk with Maman-Yvonne. Find out for yourself why she…"

Mick moved further into the room once Nile's words faded. She smoothed the straight, chic midnight blue dress beneath her and took a seat on the sofa. Patting a cushion, she urged Nile to join her there.

"Taurus said you had a habit of taking the blame for things that you have absolutely no reason to."

The unexpected dig brought an unexpected smile to Nile's oval face. The ice had been effectively broken and laughter filled the room for many treasured moments.

"I once told your husband that there was nothing…Yvonne could tell me about anything at this point in my life- that I was done with needing to know…at the time I think what I said was more to console him about his parents." Mick shrugged, looking out beyond the floor to ceiling windows in the sitting room toward the rolling lawn. "Maybe I was trying to console myself but I don't think I believed it much then. I talked to Quest before I even knew what happened. He asked me if I wanted to see her…when I said no, I meant it. I was okay with it and I don't think that it was until *that* moment that I truly believed what I told Taurus that day."

Nile bowed her head. "There're things she told me. Things I don't want to tell you verbatim but things that I should try to say just the same."

"Okay," Mick gave a slow nod and folded her hands in her lap.

Nile looked past the floor to ceiling windows as well. "Suffice it to say that she was offered a chance to follow her dreams and due to selfishness, coldness or the immaturity of youth, she felt that her eight year old daughter had no place in that dream."

The words stung no matter how gently they were delivered. Still, the sting was brief and not nearly as painful as Mick had imagined it would be. "Simple as that," she breathed providing an honestly refreshing smile while shaking her head in wonder.

"If it helps, Mick, she said that she was sorry and that you deserved a better mother."

"How could I ever sell myself short enough to think I could be like her? That I could even fathom doing that to my own child?" Mick was thinking of Quincee and a deep shudder whipped through her at the idea of leaving her willingly.

Nile leaned forward and braced her elbows on her knees. "She may've come back." She angled her head to fix Mick with a steady look. "She was a good mother to me. I think…maybe she was trying to make up for what she did to you. If it weren't for me-"

"Hey," Mick scooted to the edge of the sofa and laid a hand over Nile's wrist. "If she'd left you then, there's a chance *you* wouldn't be here and I'd never be able to say I have my very own sister."

Nile released the tears that she'd fought to keep inside for the better part of the day. Mick soothed her, drawing her close into a hug. The two of them sat crying and hugging for what remained of the hour.

***

Quest left early the next morning and Michaela celebrated his departure and loved him more for it. This was something she needed to do on her own. Well…almost on her own. In spite of her all-fired determination to seek answers, find results, confront her past, she was terrified. To herself she could admit that if it weren't for Nile, she wouldn't have the courage to go through with it.

When the doorbell rang, Mick was on her way downstairs with Quincee. She halted her steps and closed her eyes momentarily. The baby cooed and Mick squeezed her tighter.

"Mommy's a little scared, honey."

Quincee uttered another delighted coo which caused Mick to smile. "Good advice, love. When terrified- laugh."

Renewed with a sense of curiosity and excitement, Mick kissed her daughter's temple and headed on down the stairs.

Nile's dark gaze sparkled when she saw Mick and Quincee at the door. She rubbed Mick's arm, taking note of the gooseflesh there and winked. Then, she cast an animated look toward Quincee and wiggled her fingers toward Mick to instruct her to let her hold the baby.

Michaela was already looking past Nile toward the stout dark woman with lovely expressive eyes and an easy, understanding smile.

"Thereesa Sellars, this is Michaela Ramsey. Mick…this is Aunt Reesy." Nile said.

Reesy's wide almond gaze suddenly glistened with tears when she stepped closer and saw her baby sister's features on the face of the young woman standing before her. "God, Child." She gasped raising her hands in a tentative manner towards Mick's cheek. She caught herself and would have tucked the hand into the side pocket of the flaring blue knit skirt she wore.

Mick caught the hand as if on an impulse. Disbelief flooded her then as though she couldn't believe she'd done it. She blinked, looking at the hand she held like it was some rare find. Her fingers tested the strength she felt there beneath the still youthful, yet work-worn cocoa skin.

Reesy let the tears pooling her eyes slide down her face. Then, she was sobbing amidst the laughter filling her throat.

Mick could barely see her own gaze was so blurred by tears. In minutes, she was crying like a child with her aunt's hand gripped tight against her cheek.

Nile swayed back and forth trying to keep her sobs quiet so as not to upset the baby. Quincee however, was still as delighted as ever. Her coos grew louder as if she could sense the emotion in the air was of the happiest variety.

"Vette was always dreaming....the most outrageous dreams and it didn't take the rest of us long to figure it best not to tell her when she was talking crazy." Reesy shared later once she'd played with Quincee and been taken on a tour of the house. The baby was down for a nap and Reesy confided stories of her sister to the niece she never knew she had.

"When she finally left like she always boasted she would, I think we were all relieved- even Mama and Dad may they rest in peace." She inhaled deeply and seemed to blink back tears over the memories. "She never came back- not even when they passed. I hadn't even spoken to her since she left. Then...she called one day just like that out of the blue to ask if I'd take Ny." Reesy leaned over to slap Nile's knee.

"We only spoke by phone," Reesy went on after sipping from her tea cup. "All the time Ny was with us...she never came to see- to see for herself how Nile was living." She shrugged her brows. "I figured it was because Ny was practically grown- being eighteen and all. Finding out about you," she held out her hand toward Mick, "it makes sense- so much of it all makes perfect sense now."

Overwhelming emotion hadn't dulled Mick's curiosity. "So much of it?" She queried.

Reesy appeared as though she were looking back upon an old memory. "She called often once Nile came to live with me. I think she knew we were taking good care of her." Reesy let go of Mick's hand and began to twirl a lock of hair around her finger while she reminisced. "The calls were numerous but they didn't last long. It was like she… I don't know like maybe she was asking for forgiveness or understanding for leaving Nile."

Slowly, Reesy's gaze met Michaela's. "After three or four calls, I got the feeling she wasn't seeking forgiveness about Nile but something else altogether. She- she'd say things like- 'this time I'm gonna do right', 'this time I won't turn my back', 'I'm going to make it right', 'no child should have to pay for the selfishness and stupidity of her parents'."

"Mon Dieu," *My God,* Nile breathed, bringing a hand to her mouth. Her aunt had never shared such things with her.

"I thought maybe something was going on there with her husband." Reesy shook her head. "She'd only say 'no, no Reese. This is *all* about me. I'm the monster. I'm the monster who ruined an angel- one who loved me in spite of what I was." Reesy hid her face in her hands and inhaled. "She told me that during one of our last conversations. The calls started dwindling after that. Eventually they stopped altogether- to me anyway. I knew she was keeping in touch with Ny, so…"

Mick's amber stare held the same far away expression as Reesy's. "I thought…it was me. That there was something wrong with me, that I did something to make her go. That she hated me."

"No Mick," Nile scooted close to the edge of the sofa. "She loved you. She was tortured by what she did. What she did for me…getting me out of that house I think she was looking for redemption and knew nothing would ever be enough to erase what she did to you."

"God," Mick's voice was a soft, helpless mew.

"Baby," Reesy extended her arms and enveloped her sister's child in a hug that radiated love and welcome.

Nile moved over to become part of the embrace. The emotion between the three women merged gently from pain and sadness to thankfulness and joy.

***

"Thanks Jazz," Quest stood to accept the bourbon on ice.

"Sorry about meeting in this conference room, guys," Quay told his cousins while sipping Courvoisier. "Looks like this is our new home 'til the office is…reconstructed," he winked when Quest sent him a deadly glance. "We should be back in there by…next Christmas? That right, Q?"

Quest enjoyed his drink while flipping off his twin. A rumble of male laughter followed the gesture.

"So what's this about, y'all?" Yohan's expression grew pained. "Q man, please don't tell me you and Mick are cancelling Thanksgiving dinner? Melina'll have me in the kitchen for sure."

"So what's up?" Moses asked when the second round of laughter quieted.

"I got a visit from Hill in Chicago."

Everyone's head turned in unison.

"He actually showed up there?" Taurus asked, watching his cousin nod.

"Right on Mick's front door step," Quest said.

"What the hell for?" Fernando asked, from his spot perched on the end of the table.

Quest took a long swallow of his drink. "Who knows, where Hill's concerned."

Quay leaned close to his brother. "Well what'd he say?"

"Not much. Lotta round about shit. Said he wanted to make sure I didn't change my mind about shutting down weapons."

"Well that's not in his family's best interest, is it?" Yohan asked.

"I got the feeling he wasn't speaking for them."

"Hmph, you know that could've been smoke and mirrors?" Moses pointed out.

Quest stroked his jaw and shrugged. "I picked up enough to know that he wants to keep Smoak and Pike out of whatever he and Caiphus have cookin' up."

Fernando was frowning. "Caiphus?"

"They're working together on something." Quest drained his glass. "Whatever it is, he doesn't want his brothers to know about it."

"What the hell are they up to?" Taurus breathed, his bright eyes grown narrow from suspicion.

"Did he say anything about Belle and Sabra?" Quay asked.

Quest pushed back from the table. "I asked, he said they were safe. He knows he and brothers are dead if anything happens to them."

"So what do we do now?"

Quest slid a grimace Yohan's way. "We wait. We wait and hope whatever shit storm's brewin' with the Tesanos doesn't have a damn thing to do with our cousins."

***

Thanksgiving with the Ramseys went off without a hitch which said quite a bit for the family. Mick teased her husband relentlessly about his onetime refusals to never organize any family get togethers. Once all the dinner guests had assembled and there was laughter and easy conversation in the air, she encouraged him to admit he'd underestimated his family. Quest would only tell his wife that the day was still young.

Of course, even Quest had to acknowledge his happy surprise when the holiday dinner turned into even more of a celebration. Though having Crane Cannon there along with his ex-wife and mistress gave the host and hostess some cause for concern, there was no need to panic. Johnelle Black and Josephine Ramsey behaved like old friends which; in fact, they were to an extent. Kindred spirits may have been a more accurate description as the two had worked together to take Marcus Ramsey out of the picture.

The event on hand that day however was nothing quite as sinister. Johnelle cheered loudest of all when Crane proposed to Josephine and she accepted. It was a truly incredible moment with the newly engaged couple laughing and hugging while their son Yohan cheered and clapped with the rest of the guests on hand.

"Can you believe all this?"

Damon Ramsey smiled at the childlike awe coloring his wife's voice. The two of them were swaying to the light music filling the air while they looked out over the room filled with smiling faces.

Damon kissed the top of Catrina's head. "If it were anyone other than this family, I suppose I wouldn't be having quite as hard a time."

"Mmm..." Catrina closed her eyes and inhaled the familiar and always provocative scent of the cologne clinging to Damon's neck. "And since it is *this* family?"

Damon chuckled. "I'm afraid you're gonna have to pinch me several times a day over the next several years."

"I'll say...Crane and Josephine engaged Daphne and Houston...dead, Marcus..." Catrina shivered at the thought.

"Gone and I hope he stays that way." Damon smoothed his hands across his wife's back through the tan cashmere sweater she wore.

Catrina looked up. "You really think it's over?"

Damon let her see his face. "God, I hope so."

"But you're concerned?" She probed, watching his expression change.

"I was, but there's a calm I can't explain. I don't think he can hurt any of us anymore."

"And you're not the least bit concerned about him being out there somewhere. Maybe...plotting?"

"I'll be concerned about that until I know he's dead." Damon's deep voice was blunt then. "But the Ramseys have never been this strong- never all been on the same page before. I think we'll do anything to hold onto that, so my big brother should think twice before he decides to tangle with *any* of us again."

Catrina shivered again, this time out of sheer contentment and love for her husband and family.

"Hey? You okay out here?"

Johnelle Black smiled and looked back at Michaela who'd found her out on a secluded end of the patio. "I'm good." She called.

Mick tugged the bulky gray sweater tighter about her body and looked up at the gray skies. "I think we'll have an early snow."

Johnelle smiled up at the sky. "And a white Christmas."

Smiling then too, Mick joined Johnelle on the cushioned wooden bench she occupied. "I wasn't sure how you'd take it- Crane proposing to Josephine."

"Oh, I'm happy for them." Johnelle's voice held strength tempered with honesty. "Crane and I were never meant to be. He was a good man but he wasn't meant for me."

Mick nodded believing the woman's soft spoken confession.

"I've got no regrets." Johnelle warmed her hands about the olive green ceramic mug she held. She smiled inwardly at the fact that the cup held only fragrant hot tea and none of the other…additions she once often needed to get through a day. "But I do wish my Sera could have lived to feel the peace that I've been blessed to find."

Michaela leaned close to squeeze Johnelle's wrist. Silently, they remembered the woman's slain daughter and all that had transpired since putting together the pieces of Sera Black's murder.

"I think she's at peace." Mick nudged Johnelle's shoulder with her own. "*My* only regret is that we couldn't get Marcus Ramsey in a cell."

"Are you so sure he's not in one?" Johnelle sipped from her mug and stared out at the back lawn.

Mick toyed with a curl and shrugged. "Never say never, right?"

"Right. That man had a lot of enemies and it does my heart good to think he may be livin' out the rest of his days in a cell too short for him to stand in."

Mick began to chuckle. "Jeez, you're one tough lady. Would you at least give him a toilet?"

Johnelle finished her tea. "Hell, let him stew in it."

Sounds of wicked yet delighted feminine laughter wafted out beyond the remote corner of the patio.

The house was blissfully quiet a few hours later. Dinner had been a lovely affair. There was an optimistic aura that seemed to settle- especially over six of the couples in attendance. Once grace was said over the food and everyone commenced to digging into the delicious feast, they each silently sent up their own prayers of thanks.

The love, desire and friendship that were alive among them hadn't come without the tearing down of pretenses, the shedding of masks or the triumph over regrets. It hadn't been easy to find ones worth or the beauty that lay at the core of the soul. Still, they had done it and now the dream was theirs to cherish.

EPILOGUE

Chicago, Ill~

Instead of returning unsuitable, non-fitting or just plain unwanted gifts on the day after Christmas, Quest and Mick set off for Chicago. This time however, they didn't travel alone. Quincee Mahalia Ramsey tagged along to keep her parents in check.

Following all the very real and frightening dramas of the last several weeks and months, Michaela discovered planning a wedding definitely had its benefits. Immersing herself in the love and happiness that had found its way into her best friend's world, filled Mick with an elation she couldn't describe.

Still, she was surprised by the fact that thankfully it didn't stop her from planning *the* event of the year with all the gusto she used to attack everything else.

Mick's decision to sell her home had been postponed in the wake of all that had occurred. Now, that time was passed yet the bride to be insisted that no selling would take place before the elaborate home was used as the venue for her wedding.

The house would be on the market the week following the ceremony. Mick came to meet with the wedding planners and to say her own private goodbyes.

Yes; she thought while taking a stroll through the quiet corridors, a wedding was a perfect conclusion for a home where…she'd known such joy and with a wonderful man who was the only father she'd ever known. The only father she'd ever need to know. And there were friends like Contessa and family- a family she loved more than anything.

Michaela returned to the sitting room once the guests had scattered to various parts of the house. She appeared serene while staring out at overcast skies and tree limbs bare of their leaves lost amidst the onset of autumn.

An excited shriek caught her ear and she saw Quest standing just inside the doorway with Quincee.

"What are you two doing back there?" She scolded playfully, holding her arms out to take Quinn when Quest walked over to the sofa.

Quest sat close and began to play in his wife's curls. "You okay?" He watched her smiling and rubbing noses with the baby. It didn't take much guessing to know the house might evoke memories of Driggers.

Mick's expression sobered. "After all this I honestly wasn't sure. I'd ever be *really* okay, but I am."

"I wasn't sure where *all this* would put us." He confessed, rubbing fingers across the hair that tapered at his neck. "If I'd told you sooner, you would've had time to talk to her and-"

Quest please, alright? Don't." She leaned in to brush a kiss to his mouth. "You know, my main question would've been 'How?' How do you walk away from your family? See…I had to know that because I'd always feared whatever was in Yvonne that made her leave well…it would've been inside me too." Her amber gaze was soft as she watched the baby fumbling with the lapel pin on her mauve pantsuit. "When I knew Quincee was coming, it was like an obsession- something I *had* to know." She kissed the riot of curls covering Quinn's head. "Then when she was born and I held her, I understood that Yvonne Wilson wasn't qualified to answer that question because she had no concept of family- of *real* family and unconditional love and devotion…sacrifice. That was a thing she wasn't willing to do for me if it meant giving up her dream. Still…I like to believe that what she did for Nile…maybe she wasn't a complete monster. Maybe she finally realized what family meant.

Turning to Quest then, Mick laid her hand across the cuff of the crisp gray shirt he'd worn outside his trousers. "I have all those things and they were things I'd always wanted but tried to convince myself I could do without. Now I can't imagine existing without them."

"I love you." His declaration came in the form of a fierce whisper and he massaged his fingers through her hair. "I was terrified that I'd lose you over this."

"Never," She swore, her eyes glistening with tears. "You guys are my life." She looked down at Quincee and laughed when a tear splashed onto her little girl's forehead. She looked back at Quest. "You're my life and I'm not ready to stop living just yet."

Quest brushed his cheek against Michaela's and captured her mouth in a kiss of devotion and love.

Secure on her mother's lap, Quincee Ramsey looked up at her parents and smiled.

To Everyone,

It's been a phenomenal trip- the crafting of this series. I could never have imagined my idea to create this scandalous Seattle family would receive such a welcome from the romance community.

Your love, support and patience when the road to completion seemed rocky, has meant the world to me.

To everyone who has followed the Ramsey saga please know that I love and appreciate you. You've made me see how high I could soar with a pen, an idea and a dream...an author's dream.

For those of you who love the family too much to see them fade off into the world of happily ever after, never fear for the group will be seen often throughout the next segments of the saga which features the Ramsey cousins and the Tesano family.

Also on tap for 2010 is Book of Scandal: The Ramsey Elders. Before those titles emerge however, checkout the following pages...

Peace, Love, Blessings and Thanks,
Al
www.lovealtonya.com
altonya@lovealtonya.com

Coming December 2009

An AlTonya Exclusive of
A Ramsey Novel

"Lover's Allure"

Featuring
Darby Ellis
And
Kraven DeBurgh

Return to Scotland where Darby Ellis and Kraven DeBurgh embark upon a fiery, erotic romance that sets the stage for the next level of mystery, drama and revenge.

Coming Winter 2010

An AlTonya Exclusive of
A Ramsey Novel

A Ramsey Wedding

Featuring
Contessa Warren
And
Fernando Ramsey

Chicago sets the scene for a week of
Love, romance and drama like only
The Ramseys can provide.
You're invited to the wedding of the year
As Fernando and Contessa tie the knot!

Available exclusively from
www.lovealtonya.com
Each copy personally signed by AlTonya

Available Now

The Debut Erotica Title
By
AlTonya Washington

Writing As
T. Onyx

Truth In Sensuality

Ryken Gabrielle and Lucilla Fairchild are stars of a popular adult series in the U.K. Friendship and a steamy on-camera sex life was all the couple shared. Then a new man in Lucilla's life becomes more than just another flavor of the month. Ryken realizes that it's time for the relationship with his lovely leading lady to become more than just scripted.

THE SAGA CONTINUES WITH THE INTRODUCTION OF THE TESANO CLAN IN BOOK ONE "A LOVER'S SHAME"

PROLOGUE

What felt like the tip of a boot connected with his side and Marcus Ramsey smothered a groan. God no more, he actually prayed. Had he ever called out for help? Most likely not. After all, it was he who made others call for help, right? That wasn't true now and would probably never be true again.

Had it been months? Years? He'd lost track of the time. He had lived in hell- a hell he'd often threatened to send others to but not one he actually believed existed.

It existed. This hell was real and he had been an unwilling guest for what seemed to be; and probably would be, an eternity. The boot struck his side again and this time Marc's groan would not be silenced. He wondered what new form of torture he'd be subjected to this time? A new form of beating? Another rape? He squeezed his eyes shut. His life passed like a blur in his mind as it often did these days. He cried out apologies, prayers and pleas for forgiveness in the dark cell where they kept him.

He didn't expect forgiveness of course. He had done so much-*too* much-things that would haunt him until his captors decided to be merciful and kill him.

"Up Ramsey!" A male voice ordered.

Seconds later, Marc felt two hands beneath his arms and he was dragged to his bare feet.

"Stand now or bend later." Another man whispered near Marc's ear.

He obeyed as every nerve ending cried out in agony. He struggled, yet managed to remain upright.

"You've got a visitor."

The announcement stirred the first glimpses of hope in Marc's bruised and blood-shot eyes. He knew there was no reason for it, but just the sparse possibility made his heart leap.

A door clanged open and then he blinked twice to assure himself that this was no mirage.

"Carmen?"

Carmen Ramsey's smile was as soft and adoring as a younger sister's should be when she reached out to smooth her hand across the back of her brother's cheek.

He bowed his head and began to cry. "Car...help me. Help me, please."

"Oh Marc...Honey why should I?" Her tone of voice practically mirrored the sweetness of her smile.

"You-you're my sister." He all but sputtered the words in an attempt to speak over the sobs.

Carmen's smile lost none of its graceful allure. Not even when she pulled her hand from her brother's cheek and returned it in a backhand slap that sent him to his knees.

She stooped close and without a care for the chic eggshell pantsuit she sported. "I'm your sister?" Something cold and amused filled her wide stare as she watched him gasp and cough. "If only that were true Marc... If only you'd allowed me to simply be your sister instead of forcing me to become your lover."

Marcus went deathly still and Carmen's smile took on a grave intensity. Rising in one fluid motion, she turned to the men in the room and nodded.

"Do it." She ordered.

AlTonya's Title List

Remember Love
Guarded Love
Finding Love Again
Love Scheme
Wild Ravens
A Lover's Dream- Ramsey I
A Lover's Pretense- Ramsey II
In The Midst of Passion
A Lover's Mask- Ramsey III
Pride and Consequence
A Lover's Regret- Ramsey IV
A Lover's Worth- Ramsey V
Soul's Desire
Rival's Desire
Passion's Furies
Hudsons Crossing
A Lover's Beauty- Ramsey VI
A Lover's Soul- Ramsey VII
Truth In Sensuality

Find AlTonya on the Web:

www.lovealtonya.com
www.myspace.com/altonyaw
www.facebook.com
www.shelfari.com/novelgurl
www.goodreads.com

Made in the USA
Lexington, KY
05 February 2010